A
WHIMPER
IN THE
AFRICAN
STORM

AKWASI O. OFORI

BrazePoint Press

Paperback ISBN: 979-8-9987964-0-1
Hardcover ISBN: 979-8-9904106-9-5
Ebook ISBN: 979-8-9987964-1-8

Book cover design by Jess LaGreca, Mayfly book design

Library of Congress Catalog Number: 2025908782

First Printing: 2025

THE AFRICAN STORM

Lo in the horizon
A storm is brewing
The African storm is raging
The storm, powerful and intense
The old lady is angry
Annoyed and fuming with her children
She will take captives along her way
She will sweep aside the gullible and faint-hearted.
When she disappears, everything will disappear with her.
Everything, and everyone except the strong and sane-minded.
Except those who have their feet firmly planted on solid ground.
They will not be assailed by her destructive forces
Nor be impacted by her guile.
They would stand on their own two feet and not fall.

Lo in the vista
A storm is fomenting
The African storm is rampant
The storm, controlling and forceful
The ancient one is livid
Exasperated and irate with her offspring
She will take hostages in her track
She will sweep the unwary in her trail.
When she fades, everything will fade with her.
Everything, and everyone except the incorruptible.
Those not easily dissuaded
They will not be raided by her disparaging armies
Nor be obstructed by her craftiness.
They will remain unfazed and unshakable

CONTENTS

FOREWORD

Akwasi Ofori, the prolific writer, has done it again. This time around, Akwasi has used what is known in literature as realistic fiction to weave a compelling story around a reality that faces many people who make the crucial decision to return home after their studies in the West to serve their home countries. These patriotic citizens do not just acquire knowledge and skills in the western world, but also imbibe a culture of checks and balances that enhances the freedom to act according to one's convictions in order to make positive contributions to society. Armed with their expertise and convictions, these patriots return home to face a culture that is impervious or even hostile to any attempts at changing the status quo. In the case of Kofi, he faces the problem head-on with an altruistic desire to make a difference in reforming the society, no matter the cost.

Akwasi demonstrates an unsurpassed creativity in painting a vivid picture of Kofi's crusade to bring sanity into the culture that makes the reader feel as if they are walking with Kofi every step in his life journey. The moral of this gripping story is that the reader can make some personal decisions if he or she were in Kofi's shoes that can go a long way to really transform a society long riddled with corruption. Once again, I applaud Akwasi for this literary masterpiece full of intrigue and suspense that captivates the attention of readers from the beginning to the very end of the story.

Dr. Charles Owusu
Atlanta Georgia USA

ACKNOWLEDGEMENTS

I have learnt in life that having a family that supports what one does is a recipe for success. That is exactly what I have in my wife Betty and children Benefaa and Abena. These three amazing women have been supportive in my writing journey. To them I take off my hat. I also take a moment to express my appreciation to Mr. Alastair Tucker of the UK who helped with editing of the manuscript. Beside my family and the editor, others have also been instrumental in getting this book into print. The first and foremost is Dr. Charles Owusu who is always supportive in my writing projects. Credit also goes to Miss Adrene Lewis of Toronto Canada, and Miss Brittany Jones of Denver Colorado for reading through the manuscript and offering their support. Also worthy of mention is Mr. Anthony Frimpong of Jeroyaf Services Aurora Colorado for his unflinching support. Last but in no way the least are the numerous others who might have offered help in different ways to help get my thoughts going.

Akwasi O Ofori
Denver, Colorado USA

CHAPTER 1

YEAR OF RETURN

When Kofi Hope stepped out of the train, the die was cast and there was no turning back. Though he harbored some anxiety undertaking this journey, he was confident that he would be vindicated in his actions later. Hence, no amount of persuasion could convince him to change course. His friend, Frank Odoi, stepped down behind him.

"You still have time to reconsider your plans," he said.

Kofi tilted his head in his direction as he raised his eyebrows at him, his nostrils flaring.

"What are you saying, Frank? I am more than ready."

"Let me remind you that your way forward is fraught with uncertainty," Frank responded.

"Hey Frank, my mind is made up so stop your negative talk."

Frank fell silent momentarily and seemed to weigh his words before speaking again.

"Do you remember all the guys who went back home and had to return?"

Kofi looked at him now his eyes about to pop out of his head. Then he turned abruptly and pointed his index finger at him.

"Frank, please just let me be. Remember, no person has ever been successful who did not embrace the odds."

"I'm not in your way Kofi," Frank blinked rapidly, "you are old enough to know what you want."

"Frank, you have known all along that I will return home when I finish my studies."

"Kofi, that was a no-brainer, but it is the way and manner of your return."

"Way and manner of my return? I have a job waiting for me, what else were you expecting me to do?"

"At least you should have built a house before going."

"I'm going to help the people, and I don't need a house to do that."

Frank shrugged his shoulders and gazed at him with mock intent. "Get over your hero complex, Kofi. Are you better than those of us who have decided to make America our home?"

Kofi knew that Frank and his other friends in Colorado wanted him to remain in America. However, he had no desire to acquiesce to their request. He knew his services would be put to better use working for his people. He would be one of many in Colorado, USA, but in *Abibiman*, his home country, he would be one of the few. It is the difference between a small fish in a large pond and a big fish in a small pond. Besides, when he left the land of his birth, five years ago, he had promised to return to help weed out corruption from the system so that the country could march forward.

There was an upwelling of desire mixed with aspiration, to be his very best for the sake of his people. He could achieve those ideals by seeking to work every day for their uttermost good, without reservation or hesitation—just a simple desire to be of service to humanity. A heavy-set woman on oxygen stepped in front of them. She was struggling to breathe, and her steps were slow and labored. She was gathering her belongings and did not appear to see them behind her. As Kofi waited patiently for her to gather herself and get out of the way, his friend whispered.

"You must find a way around her if you don't want to miss your flight."

She might have heard Frank because she glanced at him from the side of her eyes, leering scornfully simultaneously. She had contempt written all over her face. Kofi signaled to his friend to wait as he watched her struggle to put on her nasal cannula. The sight of the woman led him to picture the difficulty one experiences from being starved of oxygen, the breath of life; but he perceived that it might be even harder to be starved of the right to life, and a right to associate and be who a person was. Likewise, it evoked memories of the plight of the people of *Abibiman*; they were a people suffocated by the greed of their leaders and the complicity of its citizens in the wanton misuse of its numerous material and human resources.

When one person cannot breathe it is miserable but if a whole group of people cannot breathe, it is not just miserable, it is heartache. It is even more lamentable if they cannot breathe because of their own doing. The blame for the people's deplorable situation falls equally on the ignorant masses as well as the blind intelligentsia. In their insatiable chase for wealth, the ruling elite have abused the people's trust and made a mockery of the duty they took on their behalf. The masses have also been complicit by tacitly supporting them even when they know they are wrong. As his friend urged him to speed up, his mind turned to the short, overweight woman struggling in front of him, and he showed concern.

"Do you need assistance, ma'am?"

"No, I think I will do just fine."

She replied without lifting up her head to look at Kofi. She was struggling and would need some help, but she was probably upset by his friend's comment, so she didn't want to show any signs of weakness. Perhaps she was also probably disgruntled by the lack of support from her kith and kin who could not assist her in getting to the airport. He could picture his people in the frustrations of this woman. Leaving her in her plight, they pressed on, but the encounter had set his mind wandering. Like this vulnerable woman, the life of the people of *Abibiman* had easily become a mass of disgruntled rejoinders because others had ceased to care. In a land where communal life and care amongst the community members was the norm, people no longer lent a helping hand; life had become only "about me first" and not about "my neighbor next door".

People take the largest chunk of the national cake for themselves and do not leave any for their neighbors, let alone think about posterity. All this would change when the young people sit up and right the wrongs of the immediate past. He was so excited about this new possibility, but his excitement was tempered with apprehension about the challenges of participating in this daunting but laudable task. These thoughts were crowding his mind as he got off the train to the long escalator that would take him to the sixth level slated for departures. As they rode the escalator upstairs, he remarked to his friend,

"One of the things I will miss going back to *Abibiman* would be traveling through this beautiful airport in the heart of America."

His friend looked at him and smiled wryly.

"It is not too late to change your mind," he suggested.

People milled around like a sea of lush green plants blossoming in their season. Every one of them was involved in a rat race of a sort, to find their assigned airline to set their travels in motion. Kofi and Frank mingled with them as they headed towards the location of the airline that was going to fly the former home. When they found it, he went to the check-in desk to print his boarding pass. Next was to check in his luggage. There were two people ahead of him in the line at the check-in counter. They seemed to be together, probably a man and wife. They had a lot of luggage.

He waited and prayed that they would be quickly processed so he would not miss his flight. When it came to his turn, things were not going fast enough. He had already wasted a lot of time, and he could miss his flight. He was late, but he had excess luggage, and he was not going to leave it behind. He signaled to Frank, who was still waiting to see him off on his journey, to buy him an extra suitcase from an airport shop. In *Abibiman,* even someone else's discarded items were valuables to others. He would not abandon his excess gear, knowing it would come in handy at some point. So, he packed his extra luggage and was ready to leave. After all the waiting suddenly, he was ready to say the final goodbyes to his friend.

Now alone, Kofi went one level down, to the security screening line. Usually when travelling within the USA, he used the TSA pre-check clearance lines which were shorter. Today, he couldn't use that because he was traveling internationally. He joined the normal security line which was long and winding; winding around some retractable crowd-controlled stanchions. As he moved forward in line, a TSA official continued to shout instructions to travelers to empty their luggage of liquids and aerosols.

Another TSA official was also going around with a sniffer dog. The canine sniffing at him heightened his anxiety; he recoiled on impulse, but he was not so much afraid of what the dog could do, but of the incendiary anger of a deranged grouch who could allow his anger to go overboard and commit atrocious offenses against his fellow humans. The guard looked at him and smiled.

"You don't have any contraband, do you?" He asked as an afterthought, probably because of his reaction when the dog sniffed him.

"No sir," he replied.

The guard tapped him on the shoulders.

"You're alright buddy."

He lip-smiled at him and moved on to the next person in line. Like other passengers, he was willing to endure the inconvenience of taking off shoes or taking off belts, and even body searches. Soon he got to the TSA official who inspected his traveling documents and told him to "proceed" to the security screening machines and to the train. The train goes from the terminal to the different concourses where travelers could hurriedly find their departure gates without a long and wearisome walk. As the train stopped at the concourse that Kofi needed to get off, a bunch of people rushed out. A young man bumped into him and fell over.

"Excuse me," he yelled as he gave Kofi a nasty look. "I'm sorry man," he said.

The young man ignored the apology and pressed on. He, in turn, rushed on to his departure lounge. There were two smartly dressed ladies at his departure gate. He handed them his ticket and waited. One of the ladies looked at him and said,

"We are sorry Mr. Hope but we cannot get you on board because this flight has already been cleared for departure."

He put his fingers to his forehead and exhaled sharply.

"Isn't there anything you could do?" He frantically yelled out his question.

"No," the lady replied.

He paced up and down before finding a seat nearby to sit down. He sat with crossed legs, slightly swinging his right foot absentmindedly; at the same time, he was so deep in thought that he did not hear the airline official calling him. A middle-aged man tapped him on the shoulders.

"Are you Mr. Kofi Hope?" He jumped up when he heard his name. "The lady was calling you," he said.

He got up and went to the officials.

"Mr. Hope, we have another flight leaving in the next thirty minutes, would you like to get on board?"

"Please if you could." He beamed relief flooding his face.

"There is one problem though," she said.

Kofi braced himself for the next bombshell.

"What is it this time?" He asked.

"This flight is going to Amsterdam, so you would have to make a transit there," the lady explained.

"That will be no problem," he replied, "but what about my luggage?"

"It will be waiting for you in *Sikakrom* when you get there," they told him.

He collected his boarding pass from the airline official and ran to the new gate shown on his ticket. When he got there, the boarding process was almost over so they allowed him to head for the jetway to the plane. He had his two carry-ons with him.

"The overhead bins are full, so we will have to take your luggage into the cargo hold," a flight attendant told him.

He surrendered his luggage and went on to board the plane.

"They will transfer onto your next flight so look for them in *Sikakrom*," the flight attendant said.

It was exactly midnight when they boarded the plane. He knew it was going to be a long flight, so he braced himself for it. Aboard the plane, he began to think about *Abibiman* and the friends he had there; friends he played and had fun with. Were they still going to be there for him? Have they been bitten by the bug of growing up, when one's friendship sphere diminishes? When one no longer cared for his cycle of friends and relations except the immediate family? He consoled himself with the thought that even if all had gone away, his bosom friend Kisito, would never do. He had always been there for him. He would always answer the call of friendship. Unfortunately, he had been the bad one. He had not written to him during all his days in America. When Kisito had sought his address and written to him Kofi had not replied. He was continuously bogged down by coursework. However, was that a good enough excuse not to have answered the call of friendship? No, it was not, but he knew the old boy would understand.

He was enthralled by the flight though it was going to be long-haul and demanding. He was excited because he was heading home; a place he had missed and always recalled with nostalgia throughout his time in the USA. He was not in any way afraid of what lay ahead. A long-haul flight, divided into two with a stopover at Schiphol Airport in Amsterdam. It seemingly lessened the anxiety of a long-haul flight, but the lengthy stopover reduced the joy of travel. In flight, he spent most of his time watching movies. In the end, his only wish was to be on the ground where the action could begin, not in the air where life was full of inertia and instructions to be obeyed. Where others, not you, controlled your life.

"Please stow away your luggage;"

"Please turn off your electronic device;"

"Please sit down with seatbelts fastened."

There was always a long list of directives but not a long list of tangibles, a long list of demands but not a long list of freedoms. That was what long-haul air travel demanded, and travelers endured so they could reach their destination. Perhaps in life, it was also the same. There was no gain without toil. If you wanted to be free you could not sit down with folded hands. You had to participate. In the end, though, his fear of a long-haul flight was unfounded because the in-flight movies relieved the boredom and monotony. Moreover, the transit lessened the anxiety of being airborne for ages for in just six hours, after takeoff from Amsterdam, the flight was due in *Abibiman*. The voice of the captain came on the speakers:

"Ladies and gentlemen, we have begun our descent to *Sikakrom*."

"*Sikakrom*, of course, the place where the action begins," he whispered to himself.

"Thank you," the passengers chorused.

They were all beaming. For Kofi, his real journey would begin when he was on the ground in *Abibiman*. He would take the road less traveled and move against those who through their corrupt activities were raping and pillaging the country daily. Friends and family had always told him that in *Abibiman*, corruption could never be rooted out. Notwithstanding, that was the challenge he had taken on and he would not renege on his promise. He had not informed family and friends that he was coming home so he was not expecting any of them to show up. The only person he was expecting was John Adams from the Freedom Convention Party who he was told in his communication with the party would come and meet him.

His thoughts were interrupted when the plane landed abruptly. The pilot had warned over the intercom that there was a rainstorm so he would have to land sooner than planned. They landed and taxied over the entire runway length because of the nature of the landing. When the plane finally came to a stop, all the passengers clapped appreciatively. He was seated at the rear of the aircraft so he had to wait for everyone ahead to disembark. When it came to his turn, he opened the overhead carrier to get his carry-ons, but they were not there. As he stood there wondering, he remembered he had surrendered them to the flight attendant in Denver, which meant they transferred them to his next flight. Relieved, he joined the other passengers to go through the jetway to the arrival lounge and beyond immigration and customs. The custom officer he was directed to was a smart looking lady who was dressed in a neatly ironed green shirt and black skirt.

"Do you have any firearms, or drugs with you?" She enquired as she checked his luggage.

"No ma'am."

"How much money do you have on you in foreign currency?"

"Ten thousand of my own money and five thousand which other people gave me to give to their loved ones."

"You will have to pay tax on the five thousand since you are only allowed to bring freely into the country a limit of ten thousand dollars," she declared.

She directed him to a booth to pay the taxes on the five thousand dollars. At last, this country has woken up, he thought. There used to be a time when people came and went bringing abundant goods and money and paid nothing to help the country. After going through immigration, he made his way to baggage claims. The two luggage items that were on the flight he missed were already waiting in the airline's office. He collected those and went to baggage claim to wait for the two carry-ons the attendant took to the cargo hold. They had not yet come to the carousel, so he waited there with the other passengers from his plane. The wait was unusually long, and he anxiously wondered why the delay. Finally, his bags appeared on the slow-moving conveyor belt to his relief. It moved at a painstakingly slow pace, tumbling its load on the floor instead of retaining them on the carousel.

"Welcome to Africa, welcome to *Abibiman*," he murmured to himself.

He grabbed the two pieces of luggage, added the other two he was carrying, and put them on carts that the airport authorities had freely made available to travelers. By now, although weary, he was beaming happily. He was back home. He had one more hurdle to clear though, before he could go to the arrival lounge to wait for John Adams, his contact from the party. He had to clear customs to be able to take his baggage outside. Several customs officials were sitting in the lounge. Was this country suffering from overemployment with multiple people performing tasks that a few could undertake? One of the customs officials walked up to him.

"Do you have anything to declare?"

"No, I don't."

"Please open your luggage so I can see their contents."

"They are my personal items, sir," he explained.

"You still have to open them, sir," he insisted.

Reluctantly he opened his luggage one at a time. He had three packets of toothpaste in one of the suitcases. The officer took one pack without asking him if he could.

"You cannot take that, sir," he protested.

Another official took a box containing six cakes of soap from his luggage. He did not protest anymore because it seemed like that was how they operated here. On his way out, another customs official accosted him.

"Can you give me the gift you bought for me?"

"A gift I bought for you," cried Kofi, his eyes blinking rapidly, "you are kidding, right?"

The man looked at him and smiled. But Kofi was indignant when he spoke again; his voice was tinged with pained disbelief.

"Man, I didn't buy anything for you."

His head started reeling from this encounter. If this is how they treated visitors to this nation, then the tourism promotion of the government was dead on arrival, for no tourist would like to be treated in such a crude manner. He was genuinely astonished at the behavior of those customs officials. What sort of image were they portraying to outsiders if they acted with such impunity at the first port of entry? He was determined and made a mental note to bring their attitude to the powers that be. As a country, they could not afford such crude practices anymore. Putting that unpleasant experience behind him, Kofi made his way through the crowd of travelers who were now spilling into the arrival lounge. Several people had come into the arrival lounge to welcome their loved ones. Others were holding name signs to welcome their guests. He looked over all the signs, but none bore his name; his contact John Adams was not there to welcome him.

CHAPTER 2

HOMECOMING OF SORTS

The traffic at the arrival hall gradually thinned and Kofi was left standing there alone by himself. Suddenly, the situation dawned upon him; he had been abandoned at the airport by his party, the Freedom Convention Party (the FCP), who had invited him to serve in some financial advisory capacity, in their new government. After being in opposition for several election cycles, the party was finally handed a landslide victory in the last election. Due to his wish to return the trust placed in his party, the new president was recruiting some talented minds to help him move the country forward. That was when Kofi had come into the equation.

After leaving his homeland five years ago to study in the USA, he initially studied for a master's degree in information technology at the University of Denver. The quest for excellence and triumph was his burning ambition, so one degree was not enough for him. He applied further to the University of Utah where he graduated with a Master of Science degree in finance. He had just completed his internship when he received an invitation from the new Administration back home. He had opportunities for work after his internship, but his love for his beloved *Abibiman*, the country of his birth had seen him yearning to return.

Thus, when the new President came on tour in the USA, six months after his election, Kofi had joined the bandwagon. The President knew about him vaguely, for he had made himself known by offering his expertise during the electioneering period from his remote location in America. Such industriousness needed to be rewarded. His prize was a position within his administration. His talent for computers and his financial analytical skills were some of the services the budding government needed to fulfil their promise to their people. The President's desire was for him to come home and design a system that would help his government track expenses and advise on procurement and resource allocation. That was the passion of his heart but to get the opportunity to serve his beloved country was beyond intriguing.

That phone call had been a defining moment. It was what prompted him to get on board. If he was needed that badly, how come there was no one there at the airport to meet him. He could have despaired, but he was already here, and there was no reason to look back. He had to collect his thoughts. Hence now, as he sat at the airport, he encouraged himself to hold on until somebody came and got him. But alas, he had waited for several hours, and no one had shown up to meet him. They had probably missed him because of the flight change.

It was now well into the afternoon, and he had not eaten anything, so he decided to find an alternate source to get out of the airport. At that moment, he remembered his Auntie, his father's sister, who lived in *Sikakrom*. He went through his luggage to see if perhaps he could locate some correspondence, he had had with her some months earlier. After searching thoroughly, he found one, but unfortunately, it did not give any clues as to how to reach her. He sat there dejected until he remembered a conversation he had with her a while ago when she said she worked in a certain market in a suburb selling yams.

It was nostalgic to return to *Abibiman*. Getting out of the airport terminal was a feeling like no other. He was greeted by the sun, high in the sky like a glowing medallion. The heat hit him and burned with such ferocity it permeated his very skull and into his clothes to his skin, causing him to sweat profusely. He noted that between the moment he had stepped into the open, and the short time it took to hail a taxi, he was already sweating with careless abandon. Having no address, he described the market where his auntie worked to the taxi driver. Thankfully the cabby was able to use his ingenuity to locate it. He had disembarked from the plane at 5 am local time. By the time he entered the taxi, it was 2 pm and he was tired, frustrated, and hungry. However, as they left the airport, he cheered up, anticipating very soon he would be receiving a familiar welcome from his auntie.

The afternoon rush hour had not started, but traffic was still heavy when they left the airport. It took them about thirty minutes to reach the market. When they got there, the taxi driver explained that people selling the same kind of items were generally grouped in the same location in the markets. So, he said, "Ask anybody you meet where to find the yam zone." When he got down, he followed the cabby's instructions. He asked a few people as he kept going on the hunt for the yam zone. That market was not so big so he figured he would get lucky. Luck smiled at him because one woman he asked knew his auntie, and she left her wares and volunteered to take him to her. She took one of his luggage and carry-on whilst he carried the other pair and led the way through an alley shortcut to avoid the congested streets. As they went through the alley, he started getting suspicious of the lady's intentions and began fearing for his safety.

"Was she leading him through those alleys to have him mugged, and his few belongings stolen from him?" He murmured to himself.

Eventually they exited from the alley, and he made a sign of the cross. As they emerged into the open space, they came upon his auntie deeply engaged in a bargain with a buyer. They were so deeply involved in haggling for a price acceptable to both parties; that she had not noticed them approaching. He was turning round to thank the kind lady who had guided him, when his auntie, upon hearing his voice, jumped up with a squeal of excitement.

"Is that you, Kofi," she squinted, "or I am seeing a ghost?"

She inquired breathlessly.

"Yes, it's me, Auntie, in flesh and blood," he responded relief flooding his face.

His Auntie was all over him, not knowing what to do: a hug, a touch, or simply to stare at the nephew she never imagined seeing in the flesh at this time. Finally, recovering from her shocked amazement, she hugged him in a warm embrace for several minutes and shouted excitedly to the other vendors.

"My nephew is back from America ooh . . . almighty God has brought my nephew from America."

She was wearing a *kaba* and *slate* with a piece of cloth tied over it. She untied that piece of cloth rapped over her dress and waved it in the air as she danced from one end to the other. At that time, the traders, those who were his auntie's friends, and there were many, all came and greeted him enthusiastically. Their warmth and friendliness made him forget his hunger momentarily.

"Have you had something to eat?"

She asked after the fanfare had died down, and without waiting for an answer, she hurriedly left her wares and rushed to get him some food. Aunt Belinda, his father's junior sister, lived in *Sikakrom* with her husband Mr. Mark Prosper, and two children, Abena and Kojo. She sold yams at the market to supplement the meagre salary of her husband who worked as a pharmacy technician in one of the pharmaceutical shops in town.

"I can't take you home right away because I need to sell a few more yams to be able to pay my suppliers," she apologized.

"It's alright Auntie," he accepted her apology resignedly.

It was not until around 6pm when they left the market; by that time, dusk had set in. His auntie and her husband could not afford their own house and lived in a rented two-room apartment space, otherwise known in this part of the world, as "a chamber and hall".

There was a storage room attached to their unit which they had converted into a guest bedroom. Because they lived in the capital, they would often have friends and relations to visit, all of whom would come and stay for a day or two. They would always ask the children to sleep in the living room. So, to ease the situation, with their landlord's permission, they renovated the storage space and added it to their accommodation. This small room would become their new guest's room. When he arrived with his auntie, they placed all his luggage there and told him this was going to be his room for as long as he stayed with them.

Although he had eaten earlier at the market, his Auntie Belinda told him not to go to bed because he needed to eat dinner. She busied herself outside in the compound where all the cooking was done to prepare dinner. Dinner was late because of the time they came home. Nevertheless, by the time it was being served, his auntie's husband was not yet home. She explained that he worked far from home and had to contend with unreliable transportation. He wanted to meet him before going to bed, however, at about 9 pm, when he hadn't still come, they showed him the little room. The room was so small, it was only able to hold a single bed and a dresser.

"Well, it is better than nothing, I have a roof over me and a pillow to rest my head." He murmured to himself, as he changed into his pajamas.

Soon after, there was a knock on his door; it was Abena, his auntie's daughter, who had brought a chamber pot along.

"Uncle please, take this you will need it in the night if you need to urinate," she said.

He took it and shoved it under his bed. He remembered his parents giving him one to use when he used to live with them in the village. When he was alone, he offered a prayer of thanksgiving to God for divine protection in bringing him safely on his long journey from America to *Abibiman*. Before he finally slept, he took a notebook which he always carried with him to make a to-do list; those he needed to do immediately, and those to be done later. His list included getting a driver's license, collecting his truck he had shipped earlier on from the port and making a trip to the village to see his folks. One other thing he could have put on was—finding a soulmate. However, he debated how that could be on a list because love operates on its own terms. So, although he contemplated it, he did not add it to his list.

He fell asleep in the middle of making the list, only to wake up some two hours later. When he woke up from his short sleep, all was quiet around the apartment except for the sound of a girl in the living room. He supposed she was probably studying, repeatedly reading out loud how to work on a computer. As he listened, the girl continued to babble away. He strained his ears if, perchance, he could hear what she was studying, but he could not make anything out. Hence, he returned to complete the list he was writing down when he fell asleep. When it was done, he put it away in his briefcase.

Afterward, he returned to sleep, but sleep was elusive all night as he struggled to relax in his unfamiliar surroundings. Not only was the room small, but it was also stifling hot. He decided it was too hot to wear pajamas, so he took them off and lay on the bed naked, but he had to put them back on a few minutes later when he heard a mosquito buzzing in his ears. He lay still in bed for a while, and then he decided to turn on the light so he could see the mosquito. His attempt was futile because the lights did not come on. Then he remembered that there was probably a power outage. So, he resigned to go back to sleep, vulnerable and at the mercy of the mosquitos. For after all, he was back to *Abibiman*, the land where everything malfunctions.

He did not know when he drifted off to sleep but he was awakened by the crow of a rooster. When he woke up, he was unsettled and, for a moment, wondered where he was and why he was sleeping in such a small room. It was then that he remembered that he was back to his home country, *Abibiman*. As he lay on the bed, in the little room, now there was not only the crow of a rooster, but also the whimpering of a baby. These noises had jolted him back to wakefulness and banished sleep; more than that they placed him in the heart of *Abibiman*, the land of his birth. There was no urgency on his part to get up from bed, so he lay still and silently absorbed the sight and sounds of his new surroundings. The repeated crowing of the rooster and the unyielding whimper of the baby all pointed to a brave new world.

The crowing of the rooster was the more intriguing because he had not heard that sound for the last five years. In America, roosters were not allowed to roam around, so they were unheard of. Here, they roamed around freely and often became people's morning call to rise, a natural alarm system of sorts. No longer would he need to set up an alarm when going to bed. Next his attention turned to the baby who continued to whimper nearby. Perhaps he or she was in pain or afraid because the mother was probably not in their room. Most likely, the baby was hungry or just wanted the mothers' attention. His guess was confirmed because after a couple of minutes the whimpering grew into loud wailing. At that moment, though he had not slept very much because of the sweltering heat, he realized sleep was out of the equation.

CHAPTER 3

AN UNWELCOMED
AFTERNOON VISITOR

O n this first night of his arrival, Kofi had tossed from side to side, rolling over and over on his bed. He could not bear the intense heat, made worse by the size of the room. If he slept at all, it could not have been more than a few hours. Now, he lingered in bed, intent on going back to sleep. He was suffering from jetlag from that long and arduous flight. However, with the uncomfortable heat, a baby whimpering, and the rooster crowing, any sleep was out of the question. Reluctantly he got out of bed, put on a pair of boxers, and went out of the little room to the living room. Sweat was running down his forehead. He looked around him, there was no one in the apartment. He probably overslept because the room was ghost-silent.

A bowl of porridge was on the dining table nearby, neatly covered with a white tablecloth. It was his food, he supposed. However, he first had to find a place to do his morning routine. He opened the door to the courtyard and stared into the compound. Not only was everything perfectly bare and empty, but there was a frightening hushed silence about the place. He stood there in the doorway in his pair of boxers, his hands akimbo and momentarily lost in thought. He wished he could take a morning shower; not just any shower, but a swim in a pool to cool himself down.

He had arrived at this place late in the night. But he had noticed a well in the middle of the compound when he came in. Slowly he ventured outside, immediately feeling the tropical sun burning his forehead. He felt the urge to stop, and it was a good thing because before him was danger. The next sight, when he looked ahead, was frightening, and momentarily, he was transfixed. There, before him, lay a black and shiny venomous snake basking in the sun. His impulse was to shout and run but he stood and waited as the snake lay motionless close to the well, oblivious of whatever was happening around it. He could not tell why he waited, but he was not in a hurry to confront his unwelcome visitor. When you don't have much going on, when you are afraid, you hide, you run, or you stand and wait. Kofi chose the last option, he stood there his brows raised, as he pulled himself together and waited.

He stood and waited for this uninvited visitor to move but it was in no hurry to oblige. The scary but beautiful reptile waited because it was enjoying this spot to bask in the hot burning sun. Kofi waited, not because he had nothing better to do, but because he did not want to attract trouble to himself. Confronting the snake could put his life in some misery. That, he was not prepared to do yet. He had a mission to fulfill. As is done in this neck of the woods, you wait, and you bide your time. Hence, he waited but not for any reason, except in fear of confronting this obvious danger. He had no wish to upstage himself before his work in *Abibiman* had begun. However, his wait was not for long. A young girl had seen the reptile before him and had run out looking for help. She returned with a burly man following close behind. He held a big stick in his hands.

"Massa, watch out."

The man shouted to Kofi as he approached, thinking he had not already seen the snake. The snake raised its head and hissed aggressively at the man with its venomous eyes, but it was trapped on that concrete floor. Kofi stood there and marveled at the scene unveiling before him, a snake with a raised head ready to attack and a man with a big stick determined to get the better of the beast. He struck out at the animal, and it jumped high into the air. The man hit it hard again, this time in succession. The reptile continued to fight, hissing and scuffling. Everyone is afraid of death even animals will fight instinctively for life. That was all the reptile was doing and no one could begrudge it. Despite its resistance, the serpent could not prevail. Finally, it landed heavily and lay still on the cement surface. The burly man fetched a machete with which he severed the head from its body.

"Bravo, Bravo."

Kofi applauded and clapped, hugely relieved. On this one occasion, a savior had surfaced just in time. In the days and months ahead, he would wish the same to happen when he began his work cleansing society. Little did he know it in that moment, but he was going to need more people to stand at his side and help fight the battle of eradicating corruption and bestowing on the people the true fruits of their labor. In the meantime, his mind returned to the present; to his redeemer who was making a ridiculous claim about dead snakes and what they were capable of doing.

"You have to separate the head from the body anytime you kill a snake," the man said.

"And why is that?" Asked the bemused Kofi.

"Otherwise, it can come back to life."

"Wow," unable to hide his amazement, "don't we learn new things every day?"

He never knew a dead animal could come back to life, but coming from a person who seemed to know what he was talking about, should he take it in good faith or with a pinch of salt? He was very skeptical of the claim and dismissed it outright. At the back of his mind, though, he was trying to convince himself that the advice could come in handy should he have the unenviable task of killing a snake in the future. For now, however, he was grateful to this fellow for sparing him his blushes. He should introduce himself to a man who acts with such bravery, but the call of nature was too urgent to stand for courtesies.

"Is there a restroom here somewhere?" He asked, the urgent need to ease himself clearly shown in his eyes.

"Massa, what is a restroom? Do you need a place to rest?"

"No, I meant washroom."

"Now, you are talking." The man responded knowingly.

He led him out of the building to the back, where there was a pit overlaid with logs with little spaces between them.

"This is the latrine for that house," he pointed to a house facing his auntie's, "your house and a few nearby," he said.

For the first time, Kofi felt really scared. He used to go to one growing up in the village with his parents, but that was so many years ago. What if he falls into this pit trying to use the toilet? The man saw that he hesitated and assured him nothing could possibly happen to him.

"You are not going to fall into it," he was amused at Kofi's display, "it is perfectly safe if you don't panic and slip."

"Has somebody fallen in before?"

"Not that which I know of, but I have heard of people falling to their death in a pit latrine," the man replied, smirking.

"That's helpful." He whispered more to himself than to his companion.

The man excused himself and hurried back into the apartment. After he got back from the pit latrine, Kofi went to the well. He stopped as he drew closer, thinking about the snake he saw earlier on. By now the man was gone, but the young girl was still around. He shouted to grab the attention of the girl.

"Do you have something to draw water out?"

"There should be a bucket with a rope tied to its handle there." She called back.

Kofi looked around, there was no bucket there. "There is no bucket here," he told the young girl.

"Maybe the landlord has it," she said.

She ran to an apartment unit and knocked. There was no answer at first so she knocked harder. A white-bearded man came out. He was probably in his late sixties, Kofi speculated.

"Grandpa, can I get the bucket to collect water from the well?"

"Hey Ama, have I not told you that little children can't draw water on their own?"

The man's address was directed to the young girl whose name was Ama. She responded by pointing to Kofi who was still standing there by the well.

"No, grandpa, it's for the *bra* over there . . ."

He took a few steps towards him and asked, "I've not met you here before, young man. Are you visiting with some resident?" He appeared ambivalent.

"I'm a guest of Auntie Belinda."

"Oh, you're the American *Boga*?" This time, there was no animosity in his voice. Rather he was animated at the fact that this young man was a returnee from America. In *Abibiman*, when you travel outside you become a Burger. People here started going abroad in the 1970s mostly to Hamburg Germany. Since then, *Abibimanfoɔ*, as people from *Abibiman* are called, have been traveling to different countries. So, there are England Burger, Japan Burger, or American Burger depending on which country a person emigrates to.

"Yes sir," he replied.

He appeared uncomfortable at the sudden change in the man's behavior. He stood there squeezing his hands into a fist. The landlord stretched his hands towards Kofi who unclenched his fists and warmly shook hands with him. The man smiled, his eyes glittering. American Burgers are more respected here than the other Burgers. He ran back to his apartment and brought the bucket.

"Here, this is how to use this bucket to get water out of the well." The landlord demonstrated how to draw out water from the well.

"Thank you, Papa."

Kofi said graciously, as he collected the bucket from the landlord. The landlord then left him to return to his apartment, whilst he went on to draw water from the well.

"Hey Ama, where is the bathroom?" He asked the little girl after drawing the water.

She led him to a shed that stood outside the apartment where residents took their bath. The floor of the bathroom was filled with big stones so that the water would drain down once a person took a shower. When at last he returned to the apartment, he sat down deep in thought. Life has not improved very much for some people in *Abibiman*, even for those who live in the city. There must be a way out for these citizens who toiled day and night and still had to come back to such a basic subsistence lifestyle. He was really a worried man. After enjoying the porridge his auntie had left on the table for him, he dressed to set off outside to visit the vehicle and driver's licensing office. As he was setting off the landlord was standing in front of his apartment and he called out to him.

"American *Boga*."

"Yes, Papa?"

As Kofi responded, the old man looked at him questioningly before speaking again.

"Your auntie told me about you, so I'm glad to see you . . . I can see you're going out. But when you come back, you should bring me the gift you brought from America."

He could see that the old man wanted to talk, but he had somewhere to go.

"Okay, I will see about it. Meanwhile I have to go to town to do something so if you will excuse me?" He asked politely at the same time as he made his way out of the apartment.

When he got to the licensing office, there was a long line. He stood in the line for the rest of the day, but it was never his turn until the close of business. He returned home tired and disappointed. When he got home, his auntie's husband was waiting for him.

"You must be Kofi?"

Enquired a well-built man presumably in his late fifties, with bulges that were visible even through his clothing.

"Yes, I am Kofi."

"I'm Mark, Mark Prosper, your auntie's husband. Please call me uncle."

"Great," he exclaimed, reaching for a handshake, "it's great to meet you, uncle."

"So, how was your journey," Uncle Prosper asked, smiling broadly, "I heard you got stranded at the airport."

"Yes, it took me a while to figure out how to get out of the airport."

"Well, you should have informed us to pick you up at the airport. Anyway, now you are here, and we are grateful."

Mr. Prosper had a reassuring look about him. Surely in this country where you lived day to day not knowing where your next meal was coming from, at least from how Kofi understood it from his parents, one needs a strong male in the house. His auntie was surely a lucky woman to have such a man around her. Additionally, you could tell he loved his auntie. Here was a man who came to them unannounced, but he was not the least perturbed. Kofi was really grateful for the welcome he had accorded him and he was determined he would make him proud someday. Now he could forget the unsettling snake encounter.

CHAPTER 4

PORT DELAYS

The second day of driver's license pursuit began and ended the same way as the first. But this time he had left for the Driver and Vehicle Licensing office early in the morning. He arrived disappointed that just as the day before, the lines were long and immobile. The problem seemed perennial, compounded by the *guro* boys who would repeatedly lead some people to bypass the line to the clearing officer's office. Their action stopped the line from making any movement.

So, another day, and another opportunity for him to get his license passed; he had wasted two precious days. Since he did not want to run out of cash, he decided that it would be better to take the local *Trotro* to save some money. So, he went to stand by the roadside. A few minutes after he got there a *Trotro* pulled up, and the driver's mate shouted.

"Baptist, Baptist."

He glanced at his wristwatch, and it was 4 o'clock on a Tuesday afternoon. He was puzzled.

"Why are people going to church on a Tuesday afternoon?"

Several *Trotros* came but they were all shouting,

"Baptist, Baptist."

For that reason, he did not get on. A man came by after about thirty minutes.

"How long have you been standing here? He asked Kofi.

"For about thirty minutes."

"Must be hard to get *Trotro* today then."

"Well, a few have been coming, but they are all going to Baptist."

"Where do you live?"

"The suburb close to the big market."

As they were talking a *Trotro* came. Again, the driver's mate shouted Baptist.

"You can get on this one," the man said.

When he got home, his auntie was already there.

"Where have you been Kofi?"

"The Vehicle License office."

His auntie did not say anything so he asked her. "Why do so many people go to the Baptist church?"

"Why?" His auntie looked at him in surprise.

"Well, when I was coming home, every *Trotro* was going to Baptist."

His auntie looked at him a ghost of a smile on her face. "Kofi, Baptist is a name of a suburb."

He broke into laughter and his niece and nephew who until now were holding on to their laughter joined him to fall about laughing with him. When he had alighted from the *Trotro* he had stopped at a phone store to buy a local SIM card so that he could receive local calls. He also had his number from Colorado so people could as well contact him through telephone calls routed through social media. He had barely finished setting up his phone when John Adams, the FCP's representative assigned to pick him up from the airport, called.

"What happened Mr. Hope?"

"What do you mean?"

"I was at the airport to pick you up but you were not on the plane."

"Oh, I missed my original flight."

"Well can you text me your address so I can come to meet you?"

When Adams hung up, he turned to his auntie's children who were the only ones at home.

"What is our address?"

"Uncle we have no address." Both children shouted.

Now he knew what to do, he texted Adams describing the location as best as he could. That out of the way, he changed into his nightwear and jumped into bed. The next morning, he once again rose early for another attempt to get his driver's license. He was hoping that he would be third time lucky. As on previous days, when he joined the line, there was no movement, but he now realized this was normal, so he waited and did not despair. Around noon somebody tapped him on the shoulder.

"Kisito!" He gasped.

"Kofi!" Kisito shouted back in astonishment.

Kisito Banda, was Kofi's long-lost boyhood friend. The last time they met was at the airport send off before flying to America. They had been friends since their days in secondary school and university together. Kisito was so surprised to see him there, but it was just the breath of fresh air and stroke of good fortune that Kofi needed. He was an employee of the Driver and Vehicle Licensing office. He told Kofi to follow him and led him straight to the office of the issuing officer. The office was big and spacious. He had a radio on softly playing a song:

Yɛ neɛ woho bɛtɔ wo
Mentie obiara asɛm

Yes, he was doing whatever he wanted, as the song suggested because he was freely getting money for doing something he was paid to do. Kofi didn't have to pay any extra money though because Kisito led him directly to the officer. In a few short minutes, the license that had taken him three fruitless days to obtain was now in his hands. Since his friend Kisito was working, they exchanged phone numbers before parting. Even with the help of his friend, it was almost dinner time when Kofi returned home. It had been another stressful and wearisome day.

At home, he took his small notebook from his briefcase and ticked off completed against the driver's license. Now he could turn his attention to the next item on his list; retrieving his Jeep Wrangler from the seaport. The Denver-based shipping agent had called to inform him that the container used for the shipment of his Jeep, had arrived at the port. He gave him the name of the agent to use for clearance of the shipment and its paperwork as well as how to contact him. He wanted to have this matter cleared before he had to start work, in the event his contact should call unexpectedly. Kofi's friends in Denver had warned him that import duties on SUVs and trucks would be very high so he had saved some money to be able to clear his goods from the port. Beside the ten thousand dollars he brought with him, he had also opened a US dollar account from his base in Colorado.

Early in the morning he took a taxi to the port. When he got there, he went to the clearance office to ask about the agent the shipper gave him. One worker at the office went outside with him and pointed to several kiosks sitting outside the clearance office.

"You will find your clearing agent in one of those kiosks," he said. He went to the line of kiosks and knocked on one of them. A young man came out.

"Excuse me, I'm looking for Junior."

"He's in the kiosk over there." The young man replied, pointing to a wooden kiosk further on from where they were.

He found Junior sitting at his desk wearing a brightly colored open-neck shirt and sunglasses, and he had a visitor with him.

"Please will you wait outside for me, I won't be long," he told him.

A few minutes later the other visitor came out.

"He's asking you to come in." The man said as he walked away.

He went inside to see the agent still wearing his sunglasses though he was inside his office.

"Hello, my name is Junior."

"Kofi Hope."

"Good to meet you Mr. Hope."

They shook hands and Junior gave him a seat.

"The shipper, Isaac, told me to expect you."

"That's correct, I have my Jeep in the container."

The agent took two documents from his desk. He handed the first document which contained information about his vehicle.

"Please make sure all the information in the document is correct."

As he was crosschecking the information, the agent was closely looking on and absentmindedly clicking a ballpoint pen open and shut.

"Everything looks good."

Kofi handed the document back to him. Junior then gave him the second document. It was the agreement that he was making with him. He took it and started to slowly read through. Momentarily he stopped reading and appeared to look on with a glazed expression.

"Please, what's this about storage?"

"Oh, sometimes there can be a delay and things have to be put into storage," he replied, "but you don't need to worry about that because it seldom happens."

As Kofi continued to read, the agent removed his shades and put the earpiece in his mouth, he was all smiles and charming. Nevertheless, when he looked at him, he noticed his eyes flicking down the paper.

"Take your time and don't rush through it, but I do have some other duties to attend to," he said.

Kofi ignored his urgings and buried his head in the document again. This was five pages that required careful scrutiny. He took a pencil from a cup that stood on the table and started to make marks against the main points in the document. All the while, Junior sat quietly but repeatedly checking his cell phone. When Kofi was done, he handed the document back to him.

"Thank you," Junior said taking a deep breath before looking at him intently, "I will see you tomorrow then."

With that their business for the day was done.

Kofi rose to leave, then turned to him and asked, "how many days are we looking at?"

"Days?" exclaimed the agent, "it could take weeks."

"Why?" Kofi asked with a look of astonishment.

"I don't know but let's meet tomorrow morning at 10am."

Kofi rolled his eyes, a resigned look on his face, but he managed a forced smile, "okay, until tomorrow then."

"Isaac trusts me . . ." Junior paused and looked at his visitor before continuing, "I always do good business for him."

As he said this, he looked at him again with an exaggerated smile. He returned home apprehensive of how long all this would take. He just wanted to get it over with. Next day he returned to Junior's office, who gave him his customary warm welcome and ushered him to be seated while he returned to his paperwork. He had some papers on his desk which he was studying. Repeatedly he placed them in his filing cabinet and brought out a new set of documents. This interlude of apparent and repeated aimless shuffling of files was unsettling Kofi. Eventually, the agent settled on one document, but curiously, when he returned to his desk, he put it aside and doodled absentmindedly on a piece of paper. Kofi sat there, clenched jaw, squirming uncomfortably in his chair. Junior looked at him and smiled sheepishly, before getting up and walking to his window.

"I am waiting for the clearance officer," he said his eyes blinking rapidly. As he spoke, he looked down at his feet and avoided eye contact.

"Why don't we go to the office to find out?"

"The office, ehh . . . ," he scratched his neck as his words trailed off.

After a momentary hesitation, he got up deliberately and invited Kofi to follow him. He gave a sigh of relief; he couldn't wait for this process to be over. When they entered the clearance office, the agent went to one of the officers sitting there and whispered something to him. The officer looked at him and whispered something back. He was trying to read their lips but they were speaking too fast. The officer handed the agent some forms which he brought to him to fill out and to attach a hundred *Sikas* as filing fees. Once the paperwork was completed; Junior stepped out of the clearance office leaving Kofi by himself in the waiting room. It was by now well into the afternoon and Junior did not return, so he decided to find something to occupy himself with.

Abibiman has one seaport that contained two harbors; one for handling the country's imports and exports and the other a fishing harbor. Whilst he waited, Kofi decided he should take a tour of the harbor complex to familiarize himself with its operation. As he made his way towards the harbor there were posted signs barring unauthorized personnel from going beyond a certain point which was guarded by a security post. The security guard on duty told him that they provided conducted tours and directed him to a nearby booth where he could purchase a ticket. Three big ships had docked in the main trading port. They were busily being unloaded by huge mobile cranes mounted on barges. The whole operation was a fascinating sight. The cranes would lift container after container onto waiting trucks which would transfer them into the shipyard.

From the main harbor, he also went to see the fishing harbor which was much smaller. That harbor was mainly for anchoring and maintaining a fleet of fishing boats. It was almost empty except for two small fishing boats that were tied up at the jetty. Several fishermen could be seen removing their haul of fish from one of the boats. When the tour was over, he returned to the clearing office. Still, there was no sign of his agent so he sat and waited for him. It was not until around 4 pm when Junior came running to the clearing office, rather breathless and sweating profusely.

"Oh my gosh, it's been one hectic day."

"Where have you been all this while, Junior?"

"At the harbor making sure the container is ashore safely."

As he said this, he blinked quickly and the corners of his mouth twisted into a comical grin. Kofi looked at him wide-eyed not knowing what to believe about him anymore. Junior didn't know he had been to the harbor to see the unloading of ships. He however decided not to call him out on his lies. To cut a long story short, this saga and the attendant drama continued well into a third week before Kofi was at last able to receive the keys to his truck, and only then after paying ridiculously high import duty and agent fees. In the end, the agent tagged on a storage fee which he grudgingly paid. He called his friend Kisito and he told him to come the next morning so they could get the registration out of the way.

The next day, he drove his Jeep to the Driver and Vehicle licensing office. His friend Kisito took personal charge supervising the process from emissions test to registration in a matter of minutes. When he watched all the processes involved in the vehicle registration process, he wondered why it couldn't be as efficient as the USA or even better. Here, the emissions testing, inspection and final registration were all at one location. The only reason why everything was slow here, he deduced, was that the will was not there, because people lack patriotism to render jobs they were been paid to do. They rather required others to not only pay the government issued fees but to also pay them for doing something for which they receive wages from the tax payer.

They were not ignorant of the fact that time is money and by withholding release of vehicles as long as possible the more desperate the owners became and more likely to part with what was effectively a ransom payment for release. Kofi was fortunate and happy that his friend Kisito had been able to help him to receive first class service, but his hope was that one day everybody would receive similar service, without needing friends in the right places. He thanked Kisito and drove away. Now he had his own independent means of transport. The long wait seemed to have been worthwhile. All he needed now was to hear from the FCP, so that he could begin doing what he knew best. He was so happy that finally things were falling into place.

As he drove, he kept humming to himself until he came to a police barrier. The policeman who walked up to him, was being melodramatic. He walked around his truck clearing his throat unnecessarily. When he got to the driver's side, he asked him for his license. Kofi handed him his temporary driver license he received a few days previously. The officer narrowed his eyes and looked at it and then back to him. He then put the license he handed him inside an open notebook and pretended to write something. All this while he kept stealing furtive glances at him. When the customary bribe was not forthcoming, he tucked the notebook under his armpit, stroked his chin, and waited for him to act. As for Kofi, he sat in the truck patiently waiting. The policeman then turned his attention back to him, with a smirk on his face. He wondered whether he was not smart enough to understand what he wanted, or he simply wanted to ignore him. Then he asked the ominous question.

"You know what to do, don't you?"

"What do you mean?"

"You must be a Burger, eh?"

The locals usually knew what to do when the police stopped them. For Burgers either they didn't know, or they didn't want to follow the norm. As for Kofi, he was simply confused because he was not expecting to be stopped. He knew he had committed no speeding or other traffic offence and all his lights and tires were in perfect condition. Moreover, at that moment he did not understand that all they wanted was a bribe to let him proceed. Later though, on reflection he recognized that all they wanted was money, but he was not willing to give it to them. When he hesitated, the police officer thought he was feigning ignorance, so now he decided to make things tough for him.

"Where is your fire extinguisher and warning triangle?"

"I beg your pardon officer, what is a warning triangle, and what do I need a fire extinguisher for?"

"Oh, so you are driving and you don't know you need those?"

The policeman went to the next driver and took an orange triangular object that drivers put on the road to indicate emergencies and shoved at him.

"This is a warning triangle."

"I never knew," Kofi replied when he saw the object.

"Well now you know. You go and buy these items and bring them to the central police unit and then you will get your license back."

"How am I going to drive officer?"

One of the senior police officers took a piece of paper and wrote in all bold caps: BEARER IS ALLOWED TO DRIVE WITH THIS PAPER AS EVIDENCE OF PROOF OF LICENCE FOR FOUR DAYS FROM THE DATE SHOWN ON THIS DOCUMENT. He signed and dated it, and gave him four days grace period to collect his license.

"Here, take this and show it to any police officer who asks to see your license, they will understand."

"They will understand indeed." He muttered to himself.

When the police officer handed him the note, he was blunt about it. It was matter closed for them. Hence, they left him and went to the next driver they had stopped. Kofi drove on from there to his auntie's place. He went straight to his little room and took out his notebook. He crossed out the task of getting his truck from the seaport. Now he was left with two main tasks on his list of things to do: going to the village to visit his parents and meeting the FCP to begin his work in *Abibiman*.

For now, however, he had to get his temporary license back from the police. For three consecutive days, he went to the station they directed him to go. Anytime he arrived, he was told the officer who took his license had gone on patrol. On the third day when he went to the station, he was given the same message. He knew what they wanted, and he was not prepared to meet their demand, he decided not to go to the station again. He would drive with his American license until the permanent copy of his license arrived in the mail. It had been a frustratingly long month but that was just the beginning of the rodeo.

CHAPTER 5

OFFICE INTRODUCTIONS

It was early morning; Kofi had just woken up and was brushing his teeth. Abena, sweat running down her face, dashed inside gasping for breath. "Uncle, Uncle, there's a car outside waiting for you." She announced breathlessly.

Kofi raised his head and run his hands over his neck. "Who could be looking for him this early in the morning?" As he stood there contemplating, John Adams the FCP's representative who was supposed to pick him up from the airport walked in.

"Good morning, I'm John Adams." The visitor stretched forth his hand for a handshake to introduced himself.

"Oh, you're the fellow who went AWOL?" Kofi said jokingly. Both men chuckled.

"Shouldn't you blame yourself for missing your original flight, Mr. Hope?" Adams finally replied.

Kofi brushed his remarks aside. "Anyway, no worries," seemingly changing the subject, "what brought you here today?"

"I've been sent from the office of the President to collect you."

Kofi looked around; a chauffeur driven car had been sent to collect him.

"Could you give me a minute to finish getting dressed please?"

He went inside his apartment, when he returned, he was smartly dressed and ready to go.

"I'm going to follow you in my truck," he told Adams.

"No, don't worry about driving Mr. Hope my orders are to bring you in the official government vehicle."

"Well, I might need it to return home."

"You don't worry about that, Mr. Hope. My orders are to bring you in. In the same way you are going you shall return. The driver will deliver you safely back home."

John Adams had been with the party since the days they were in opposition. During that time, he had always been around doing party business. The only time he was not actively involved was during a six-month leave of absence he took for a trip to the United Kingdom so he could study the mechanics of crowd control. Since his return, he had become a prominent member of the party organizing and assisting with crowd control in the party's rallies. He was thirty-five years old, a married man with two boys. Working with the party had increased his self-confidence. He carried an aura around him that made most people he met show him respect. When Kofi met him, he acknowledged that fact about him.

On approaching the car, the driver jumped up to open the door for him. After that, he came around to the other side and opened the door for Kofi. As they drove away, Kofi's mind turned to consider what the nature of his new job was going to be like. How much authority he would have to influence decisions as well as implement them. His thoughts were interrupted by Adams who volunteered the answer he was looking for, as if he read his mind.

"Both the President and the chief of staff are impressed with your CV."

Kofi had been away for only five years, but since he had gone straight to the USA after university, he did not need to look for a job. For that reason, he never really knew what a C.V. was because in America, they call it the Resume.

"C.V.?"

"Curriculum Vitae; Resume, the Americans call it." Adams supplied the missing link.

"Ah, I see."

"I don't know the details of your job but the chief of staff will explain everything to you."

The conversation then turned to personal questions about life in

America as he experienced it. Adams also told him he might not be needing his personal vehicle since he was going to be assigned a car and a driver. This was just the kind of lifestyle Kofi was determined to kick against. He had come down to help this country, so he wanted to be part of the people moving freely among them. The trappings of power did not interest him. The drive to the ministries was uneventful. Though the road was bad around his neighborhood, this time the ride was much more comfortable, so he did not feel it as much as the times he had ridden in taxis or by *Trotro*. In the capital district, they drove by several neatly constructed buildings that served the various governmental ministries. Traffic was heavy but because they were riding in the official car of the president they smoothly sailed through. As they entered the building, they were greeted by a tall balding man standing in the doorway.

"Are you Mr. Hope the Journalist?" He inquired; his right hand outstretched expectantly.

Kofi shook his hand warmly. "No sir, I am Mr. Hope the financial analyst."

The balding man just ignored his answer and went on. "I've read all your articles about how this country can be set on a sound footing. You speak well my son, you speak well." He reached forward and put his outstretched hands upon Kofi's shoulders then proceeded with his introduction.

"I'm the Honorable John Biney, the chief-of-staff, but everybody here calls me Chief," he bellowed, and then turned to Adams, "thank you John, I will take it from here."

He led the way to his office and Kofi followed him. "Sit down son."

John Biney pointed to a chair by his desk on which Kofi obediently sat down and waited for him to speak. Then the older man announced;

"The President is not at the office today because he had to take a tour of a business that was opening in a nearby city."

"Does that mean I will have to wait for him?"

"Not at all. I have all the details for you."

He got up and went to a fountain standing in his office to pour some water.

"You see your position is not a cabinet position, so you do not need approval from parliament." The chief-of-staff explained as he sat down.

A few minutes later, he got up again, this time he went to a cabinet and took out some documents. "Here, take these," he handed the documents to him, "the President has already outlined what you are going to do."

"That's great," Kofi said when he received the documents.

He saw that as a good idea because he wanted to plunge into work right away without any impediments in his way. The chief went over his job description as a financial staffer for the president. Kofi had to suppress the excitement he was feeling, because his assignment was well within the scope of his expertise. The orientation briefing took about two hours. After the session, the chief got up stiffly and spoke.

"Here, I will escort you around the facility and introduce you to the personnel."

They entered the break room and immediately encountered a group of people who were chatting noisily. His escort, the chief, entered the room to join the others leaving Kofi lingering in the doorway. Presently, the noise of conversation ceased and momentarily five set of eyes fixated on him. Being on the receiving end of these staring faces made Kofi uncomfortable and self-conscious. He stood there awkwardly, nervously shifting from one foot to the other while examining his surroundings. The room was obviously big and spacious. There were two sets of comfortably upholstered furniture. One corner of the room had a bar. On the wall adjacent to the bar, was mounted a 60-inch flat-screen TV which was broadcasting the news. Kofi heard the announcer saying something about past government officials who were being tried for corruption. He was saying that their case had been determined by the attorney general to be a criminal case and would be tried by a panel of three judges.

"That is good news." He whispered.

"Were you saying something, Mr. Hope?" Asked the chief who had returned to his side.

Kofi did not reply, instead his mind was still on the news item. At least people are being held accountable for their actions while in government. He hoped the president would follow the same direction when it came to his own ministers. Only that way, was there any hope that systemic corruption could be eradicated from this society. Now he noticed the chief standing beside him, and he turned his attention back to him and the other five people assembled there. He presumed they were Presidential staffers who were probably on their lunch break. There were two men and three women in the room. One of the men was heavily built and stout. The chief was about to speak but the heavy-built man noticed that the newcomer hesitated, so he noisily got out of his chair and warmly took him into his arms. The embrace was comforting and reassuring.

"Joseph Baiden is the name," he said enthusiastically, "welcome, man, welcome to the team."

You could tell the fellow was happy to see him.

"Hey Nick," glancing in the direction of the other male who was in the room, "looks like you have a club member here."

The man was quiet, a half-smile on his face, but he said nothing. As he sat there, fury was surging through him, but he managed to control his emotions. He got up, shook Kofi's hand halfheartedly and announced,

"My name is Honorable Nicholas Hamma."

The two men were like chalk and cheese. Joseph Baiden was flamboyant, obviously talkative, and capable of talking any person's figurative ear off. Hamma was the direct opposite, thinner, reserved and melancholic. The chief then took over.

"These are some of the women who work with me," he nodded in the direction of the three women who were sitting there. "Ladies, this is Mr. Kofi Hope, the nerd we were all waiting for."

Two of the women smiled at him and chorused. "Hello."

The third woman simply sat there sullenly with a faraway look in her eyes.

"Miss Barbara Hilson," he pointed to the most sophisticated looking of the three, "is the presidential spokesperson."

He recognized her from her numerous television appearances. The chief then turned to the slimmest of the three ladies,

"And this is Miss Ellen Bosan, our indefatigable presidential staffer, she is always the first in and the last out of the office."

He looked at her with admiration mainly because of what the chief said about her. She had a comely stem-thin figure and oozed ravishing charm. All the while as the chief was doing the introductions, the third woman remained seated with a frown on her face and her lips pursed. When he turned to introduce her, she forced a faint smile.

"Finally, Mr. Hope, let me introduce to you Mrs. Lucy Bukari, the women's organizer of the party."

She appeared distracted and just sat there cracking her knuckles. When he looked at her, she rolled her eyes at him and drew in a deep breath before turning her back to him. At that moment, a fourth woman walked in.

"Am I missing out on something?" She asked.

She was dark, and her complexion had an impeccable hue about it.

"Yes, you have," the chief replied, "here, meet Mr. Hope."

"Good to meet you, Mr. Hope," she was smiling broadly as she spoke, "my name is Maggie Husup but everybody calls me Maggie."

She then turned to Mr. Biney and said; "Let me take it from here to show Mr. Hope around."

She was the assistant to Barbara the spokesperson for the President. As she led him away, Ellen looked at her suspiciously as if to say she could not claim him for herself. While they were in the break room Maggie told him,

"There's always free coffee here so you can come and get some at any time. If you find none left, feel free to brew more."

Adjoining the break room was the cafeteria, which was big, clean and exquisite. It was exactly what busy political operatives needed to find refreshment after a hard day's work. From there, they went to see some of the offices mainly used by presidential staffers and other government offices. One of the offices was labelled, "Government Statistician". Noticing him pause in front of that office, Maggie spoke;

"This is the office of the government statistician, Mr. Asap, the fellow is a talkative so it's better we don't go in there."

Kofi would have loved to meet him. He was a fan of anything that had to do with figures. But he followed her as she led him back towards the office of the chief of staff. Before they got to the chief's office, there was an area that was labelled "No unauthorized personnel—strictly out of bounds". She gestured to that area and said, "this stretch houses the office of the president."

He was inquisitive and asked; "So we can't possibly go there?"

"No, we have to get clearance to enter the president's offices section."

"That's okay then."

As they got closer to the chief's office she said; "There's more to see at the chief's than just his office."

"How many offices are we looking at?"

"I don't know the exact number," she started counting on her fingers then stopped, "there are also several conference and meeting rooms, those designated for big meetings and smaller ones for smaller group meetings."

He nodded, he was impressed with the facilities and the tour generally. Maggie smiled broadly.

"Okay, now let's go back to the break room."

On their way back to rejoin the others, they met a fellow who Maggie introduced as a driver of the chief of staff. To his right was a meek, plain looking and shabbily dressed fellow who was licking his lips nervously. Sensing his friend's discomfort, the driver quickly took over and introduced him as his friend who had just come from the village to visit him. Maggie took the driver aside and engaged in muted discussion. When they rejoined them, the driver handed his apartment keys to his friend so he could go home whilst he continued working. When the driver left, Kofi remarked;

"I like your approach with the driver."

"Yeah, he should have known better because we are not supposed to entertain friends on the premises."

They returned to find an empty break room; all the staff having returned to their duties.

"Do you want to report back to the chief, Mr. Hope?"

"Yes, I think I'd better do so."

When he got to the chief's the women's organizer was there with him. He got up and came to him.

"Mrs. Bukari came here to see me, but I kept her waiting because of your induction tour."

"She doesn't work here?"

"No, she's based at party headquarters. Now if you will excuse me, I think it's polite to have some time for her."

"Of course."

"So, you can go home now and come back tomorrow to begin work."

Kofi shook hands and said farewell. He returned home overjoyed that work was about to begin. After dinner, that evening, he retired to bed earlier than usual, so that he would have a head start for work the next day. However, sleep was proving elusive, and he lay restless in bed. Soon the whole apartment was silent except for Abena who was reading her notes from school out loud again. He got out of bed and went to the living room to see what she was doing. She was reading how to start and close Windows on different operating systems such as Windows 7, and Windows 10. She was also reading about how to work a Mac; how to use different commands. She looked up in surprise when she saw him. Kofi stood there a faint smile on his face.

"What are you doing Abena?"

"I am learning for a test tomorrow."

"What's it about?"

Abena hesitated before answering innocently. "About how to work on the computer."

"Have you performed these operations you are learning about, on a computer before? Don't they demonstrate it at school?"

"No uncle."

"Really," he was flabbergasted, surprise coloring his voice, "some educational system."

Abena just looked at him without saying anything. In *Abibiman* the opinion of adults was always presumed right, and children dare not challenge them. Besides, her uncle might know better from all his education and travels.

"What kind of educational system is this;" He retreated into the little room, mumbling to himself; "Children being taught only the theory of IT without practical application; how can this prepare them for the real world?"

He was determined to stop this trend, at least in the life of one young girl. Back inside his room, he took out his old laptop and handed it to Abena.

"Here take this."

"Uncle, do you want me to use it for the test and return to you after?"

"No, it's for you."

"Oh, thank you, thank you, uncle."

Her eyes were now wide open, and her jaw dropped. She was now squealing with excitement, overjoyed to have her very own computer. Now she could show off to her friends. No, she would just tell them about it, she thought. She didn't want to run the risk of getting it stolen. With her mouth gaping widely, she danced on a merry-go-round, first in the living room and then into her parents' bedroom. When she returned to the living room, her parents were following her. Not only had she disturbed their sleep, but she also dragged them from their bedroom to the living room to thank Kofi. They took turns shaking hands with him and expressing their appreciation.

In all the excitement, Kojo had also woken up. He entered the living room and stood timidly in a corner watching proceedings from a distance. As the others were dancing, he looked on grimly, his hands folded on his chest and his face downcast. His eyes were misting up and he had an icy melancholic stare. When Kofi saw him and noticed his demeanor, he became dismayed. He had committed the unpardonable sin of favoring one child over another. He returned to his room and took an iPad which he had brought with him to give out as a gift to anyone who deserved it. There was no better time, he decided now was the time, and the boy deserved it. When he returned, the family had gathered around the computer to examine it. He handed the iPad to Kojo who was suddenly transformed. The tearful sullen expression was replaced with the broadest grin on his face. He gave Kofi a hug of appreciation.

CHAPTER 6

WORK BEGINS

On his second day at work, Kofi was told to report to Barbara in her office. Barbara was not only the spokesperson for the president but was also the liaison between the chief of staff and the presidential staffers. He noted this was an important person who he needed to study well. First impressions of Barbara suggested she was not only sophisticated but also complicated. She also displayed a certain eccentricity and unconventionality in some aspects of her life even if you have just met her. She seemed like the type of crazy woman a man would want to chase because she's attractive.

She spoke the Queen's English, with a noticeable English accent. Barbara had been taken to Great Britain by her parents. Just to hear her speak you might think she was British. The first impressions she made on Kofi were profound. She officially welcomed him to the team and encouraged him to do his best to further the agenda of the President and support his team. She told him that she was in talks with the chief of staff to allocate him an office as soon as possible so he could begin work. He thanked her and left her office. Emerging from Barbara's office, he saw Ellen and Maggie, two of the women he met on the previous day, standing in the lobby along with a third lady.

"Hello Mr. Hope." Maggie reassuringly mentioned his name when she saw him, as if to say I remember who you are.

"Hello Miss Husup." Kofi returned her formal greeting warmly.

"Good to see you again," she turned towards the third lady they were standing with, "allow me to introduce Rebecca, you did not meet her yesterday."

"Hello! pleased to meet you." Kofi acknowledged her politely.

"Hello!" The lady returned his greeting.

Kofi looked at her and instantly felt his pulse beating faster. She had a pair of arched eyebrows that looked down on sweeping eyelashes. Her ears were subtly framed with an upturned concave nose. He was buried in thought until the lady spoke.

"I'm Rebecca Odom a clerk at the office of the government statistician."

The government statistician? That struck a chord in his mind. That was the office he saw yesterday in his tour of the facility with Maggie.

"Kofi Hope, I'm the new guy on the President's financial advisory team."

"Hope, I like that."

As she spoke their eyes met and it sent a tingle down his spine. Rebecca also blushed and was struggling to conceal it. The women excused themselves to return to their offices. Rebecca's office was the furthest away. As she walked down the corridor, Kofi was able to observe her better. Her figure was beautifully twine thin. Her waist was tapered, and she had a burnished black complexion. Arguably, a rare gem in a land where people gloried in being fat and fleshly.

Kofi was past his twenty-eighth birthday, but he had remained single. His friends and those who knew him mockingly called him the "president of bachelors". He had never really cared about getting a girlfriend let alone getting married. Until now, no woman had ever had any effect on him emotionally. Were things about to change? As this lady walked away, he felt something he had never felt in his life. Now alone, he stayed in the lobby making small talk to the staff members as they passed. Nicholas Hamma came by and mumbled an unenthusiastic hello and went by to his office. Later Barbara also came by and told him the chief-of-staff would soon be in so he should be ready for him. When Barbara left, Joseph Baiden came. You could hear him as soon as he came through the doorway.

"There is our new guy. How are you doing, are you finding things okay?" He called loudly in his direction.

"Yes, thanks I'm doing well."

"So why are you sitting out here?"

"Waiting for the chief to assign me an office."

"Over there is my office," he pointed to a nearby room, "you're always welcome there to talk to me." He then hurried away into his office.

A few minutes later Mr. John Biney, the chief of staff came in. He skipped the customary exchange of greetings and addressed Kofi.

"Could you please follow me, Mr. Hope?"

They went by several offices. Mr. Baiden's office was big and spacious. Next after him was Mr. Hamma's office, which was a little smaller than Joseph Baiden's. They walked past Hamma's office to the next one. When the chief opened the door, his eyes widened, and his jaws slacked. Kofi could see the muscles around his closed mouth tense up before exhaling sharply. The room was messy with furniture strewn all over the place.

"This is going to be your office," Mr. Biney pointed out to Kofi. He looked at him and saw perplexity written all over it, so he said sharply.

"We were not expecting you this soon, so you see, we still need to do some work here in your office."

Kofi read from his reaction when he first opened the door that he was not expecting the office to look this way. However, he did not ask him any questions. The chief then led him to a small cubicle space adjoining his office. There was a young lady in her early twenties sitting there.

"This is Lisa, she is going to be your personal secretary." Mr. Biney announced.

Lisa was the personification of childishness. Certainly, a demure young lady. She was soft-spoken, shy, and meek, with girly features. Even if you observed her cursorily, you would draw that conclusion, and no one would fault you for referring to her as a girl. Her childlike manners were cemented by her taste for childish things, shown in her kidult clothes which she was wearing in an offbeat manner. She stood up and bowed respectfully to him.

"Please sit down miss," Kofi motioned to her.

"Now if you excuse me, Mr. Hope, I will leave you to get down to work," the chief-of-staff interjected and left.

Though the office was in disorder, Kofi noted that the furniture and other items were all new. The only item which was old was a cabinet that stood alone by itself in a corner. Kofi wasted no time and got straight to work to put things in order and with Lisa's help they quickly rearranged the furniture and everything else in the office. After about an hour the space was transformed into an immaculate and respectable office. It was only then that Lisa returned to her station. The day had gone by very quickly and soon it was time to go home. All this while Kofi had been fantasizing about Rebecca, the lady he had met in the lobby. He thought this was unusual because he had never felt so strongly or had been preoccupied like this about a woman before. As he made his way out of the building, there she was standing in the hallway with Ellen, and Maggie. When he passed them, he uttered a feeble;

"Goodnight, ladies."

So awestruck was he by Rebecca's adorable and loveable personality, he felt shy in her presence. When he was out of the sight of the ladies, he hurried down the stairway, in the hope that he would get to the elevator before Rebecca and her friends. To his consternation, the elevator was arriving when Rebecca and Ellen caught up with him. He found her gorgeous and indescribable and her presence breathtaking. They all crowded into the elevator; Kofi did not speak. He blushed shyly when his eyes fell on her gaze. He looked away quickly and pretended he was busy searching for his car keys. When they stepped out of the elevator, Rebecca smiled broadly at him. He also managed to return a feeble smile and headed for his truck. As he was putting the keys in the lock to open his truck, he felt that somebody was standing behind him. He turned around, and there was Maggie, a dimpled smile lighting her face.

"Sorry for sneaking up on you Mr. Hope, but I wanted to tell you I would like to take you to see the city sometime."

He hesitated a little to think about her proposal. Wasn't it a little too soon to accept a woman's invitation to go out? Would he not be encouraging her to take an interest in him? He looked at her, she was boisterous and alive. Probably that was her nature and there was nothing more to it. She was likely the sort of person who wants to be upfront and involved with people as she displayed the day before. After a moment's hesitation, he came around and responded somewhat enthusiastically.

"That's a splendid idea, Maggie. When do you want us to do this?"

"Will tomorrow be okay with you?"

"Yes, I don't have anything planned. Besides, why will I delay going out with such a gorgeous lady?"

Maggie blushed at the compliment and smiled broadly.

"Tomorrow then, it will be."

Since this was his first day on the job, he had a lot of paperwork to do. He had earlier planned to come to work early the next day to complete them. However, since he now had a date to go out with this girl, he rushed back to his office to take it home to work on. He worked throughout the night eventually going to bed around dawn. The next day he woke up with rings around his eyes, but he was satisfied because he would be able to go out with Maggie with a clear conscience, without having to worry about the down time he would spend on sightseeing. That day when he got into the office, most of the workers were already in. Nicholas Hamma was in his office when he passed by, and he waved at him and said;

"Hi Nick."

Hamma rolled his eyes at him but pretended he had not seen or heard him, instead, he made his way towards the washroom that was by their office. Kofi watched him go into the washroom then he went to his office. When he got to his office, Lisa was already there, and she gave him his schedule for the day. She had scheduled several meetings for that day. When he sat down, he looked at his schedule and smiled; he was going to be a busy person. Most of the people who visited came to officially welcome him to his new role as financial advisor. Around noon, Lisa ushered in a beefy and barrel-chested man neatly dressed in a three-piece suit. He wore a big grin and appeared pleasantly surprised to see him and he made little effort to hide it.

"Good afternoon, Mr. Hope," his eyes widened, and his brows curved, "my name is Mr. John Acres, I was expecting someone much older."

Kofi shook hands with him and introduced himself. In this part of the world, it is customary to give visitors water to drink before you sit down to talk. He told Lisa to bring him some chilled water from the refrigerator. When Lisa brought the water, he drank it hurriedly and reclined in his chair.

"Aaahhh!" he yawned loudly, "he who brings water brings life; water is life."

Kofi looked at him and smiled, "Would you care for some more?"

"No thanks," the man replied grinning, "I'm sure happy to see you in your new role, Mr. Hope. I hope you'll be as hard working and conscientious for the people as all the others are."

John Acres was a car dealer, who imported a lot of cars into the country. Therefore, he always needed to be in the good books of whoever was in control of signing off on import duties. They chatted for a few minutes before he got up and spoke.

"I must take my leave of you because there's some business to take care of." He took out a fat envelope from his suit pocket and gave to him. "This is to welcome you back home and to your new job, Mr. Hope."

Kofi took the envelope and opened it. It was stashed with notes of American dollars. Slowly, he closed the envelope and pushed it back to him.

"I'm sorry but I can't take this sir."

John Acres looked at him bug eyed. He had never encountered any government official who refused a gift from him. He pushed the envelope back towards him.

"It's from me to you, and you know, no gentleman refuses a gift."

Kofi looked at him sternly but without any animosity and spoke. "There's always a first time."

The man got up and strode across the room, his hands clasped behind his back. Then he turned around to look at him.

"Mr. Hope," frown lines were drawn on his face now, "it's customary in this part of the world to welcome people to their jobs with a gift."

"I don't mean to be rude, Mr. Acres but I find it highly inappropriate to accept a gift from people when I am working."

"What! so you won't take it?"

He got up and fidgeted with the envelope and then shoved it into the inside breast pocket of his jacket. He took in a deep breath before shuffling towards the door with his eyes downcast. Suddenly he looked old and haggard. If Kofi had looked at him a second time, he might have accepted his gift, but he was determined not to be corrupted by anybody, so he looked away to avoid further eye contact and when he had left resolved to instantly blot the incident out of his mind. Mr. Acres had stayed longer than he expected, so he was running late for lunch. As he was entering the cafeteria, Nicholas Hamma was also going out. He shouted a greeting at him just as he did in the morning.

"Hi Nicholas!"

Hamma's countenance changed suddenly. He was simmering with anger but showed no emotion or animation as he spoke. He retorted dryly but sternly, his irritation flaring. "Don't forget to call me Honorable next time you address me, Mr. Hope,"

A sudden coldness hit him at the core, and he felt a heaviness in his stomach. As the implication of Hamma's words sunk in a shaky smile crossed his face. Surely, to be forewarned is to be forearmed. Calmly he responded.

"I hear what you say, it's noted sir."

Growing up in *Abibiman*, Kofi had learned that you have to properly address your elders. But the world was changing, and such demands were seldom necessary in his opinion. These were just some of the barriers that must be broken if the country was to progress, because such archaic customs shackle the ingenuity and restrict communication on the part of young people, he thought to himself. He brushed off Hamma's rebuke and walked on to the break room.

CHAPTER 7

INSTANT ATTRACTION

Kofi's introduction to the presidential staff had rippled through the team like no other addition before. Whether young or old, there were none indifferent to his arrival. There were those who were young and wanted to rub shoulders with one so young and bright. There were those who were old and feared the new order might cause the old to yield. Here was a young man who was both energetic and smart, both well-traveled and knowledgeable. Within the team, only Barbara matched his credentials of having lived and studied abroad. Nevertheless, her educational accomplishments paled in comparison to Kofi's. He had studied more and traveled far more widely. He had visited the Caribbean, Canada, and Australia, besides living in the USA. For a young man of twenty-eight years, he had two distinguished master's degrees in computer information systems and in finance.

The person who seemed most impacted by his arrival was Nicholas Hamma, a party stalwart who remained faithfully with the party throughout their years in opposition. With only a modest secondary school certificate, it was his loyalty that had been rewarded and fueled his rise through the ranks. He was only elected as an Assemblyman, as they call positions on a city or town's council here. Yet even Assemblymen craved the title of honorable. For Hamma, it was this recognition that made him felt fulfilled. Therefore, if anyone should address him as Nicholas or even Mr. Hamma it was anathema to him. Hamma had little computer knowledge, so he was helping presidential staff to set up a few rudimentary computer operations.

He also enjoyed a financial role, having been kept at the presidency under the guise of serving as an assistant financial analyst; but he was more a person collecting donations on behalf of the FCP. With Kofi's arrival, he was told to vacate his office for him. Mr. Hope as the expert, they said, needed a place where he could get all the business of the president going. In anger and resentment, he had trashed his office before he vacated it. On the evening of the day Kofi was introduced to them, he went home in a rage. He told his wife that it was a 'small boy' who had taken his job. He berated him all week to his family anytime he returned home. That evening, he was seething with anger, such that even his children were afraid to approach him.

On the second day when Kofi had addressed him as Nick, he was so infuriated that his wife had to comfort him repeatedly to get him to calm down eventually. He saw his demeanor as arrogance. Why should such a person as young as that, have the effrontery and nerve to call him Nick? He concluded that young people these days have no respect for their elders. Though he seemingly accepted his wife's comforting words, he began in earnest to look at how he could implicate that young man in some fraudulent dealings so that he could get rid of him before long.

He smiled wryly, convincing himself that before long he would find a way out of his predicament. He presumed that this young upstart who had already taken over his duties and office might do more damage unless he could put him in his place. He would not allow his arrogance to boomerang beyond the walls of his office; he would find a way to contain him so that his influence was discredited and dislodged from the domain of the presidency. If he failed, others like him or even more self-conceited would come in and his influence would become even more entrenched.

Another person who was not directly impacted, but who also loathed the idea of Kofi working at the presidency was Lucy the women's organizer. The president had touted his credentials to the party faithfuls and had told them about his desire to rid the country of corruption. To Lucy that meant, she would be denied certain sources of income. She had thus vehemently fought against his coming. She was determined in any way possible to make his stay at the workplace as uncomfortable as possible. Unlike Hamma or Lucy, another person who seemed impacted by Kofi was the young staffer called Rebecca. She was completely dumbfounded and bamboozled by his charm and intelligence. She was not present in the break room when he was introduced, but boy, the whole week she had been on cloud nine. When she was introduced to him, her heart missed a beat. For very differing reasons, to Rebecca, Lucy and Hamma, the days ahead seemed critical. Crucial in how they would react to him or cope with him; how they would endure or fade. Now each of them perceived a test that would get them off their beds to come to work daily.

However, these challenges were of differing dimensions; to one it meant an opportunity to be appreciated and loved; to another it meant to be deprived of the means of making extra income; and to the last it meant to be demoted, humiliated, and loathed. It was a challenge they were all up to in their own ways. Rebecca was not from *Sikakrom*, the capital. She had come to university there and decided to stay and look for a job after her graduation. Her parents and youngest sister lived in *Mpoano* whilst her older sibling and brother lived in *Ohenekrom* with his young wife. She was twenty-five, single and did not even have a boyfriend nor had she even dated anyone before. She thought all that was going to change now because she could not hold her breath in the presence of the new addition to their staff.

Not only was he eligibly young, but he was also charming and the perfect gentleman. She had a little worry though. She saw all week how one of her colleagues, Maggie, was all over him. Maggie seemed more skillful with men, so she might be in for competition. She had even offered to take him on the tour of the city. She was hoping that he would not mistake her friendly gesture for love. That evening, Rebecca's friend from university, Ashley Ayusa visited her at home. Ashley saw that she looked radiant and asked her why.

"Today we had a new addition to our staff," she said.

"Is that why you are so happy?"

"When I met him for the first time," Rebecca exclaimed, clasping her hands in her laps, "my heart almost jumped into my mouth. I think I'm in love with him."

"Oh Rebecca," Ashley teased.

"Oh Ashley."

"Okay," Ashley clasps her hands and shrugged her shoulders, "tell me about him?"

"He's about five feet ten inches. He is fair in complexion, miles lighter than me."

"Oh yeah?"

"Not only that, but Barbara also told us he has two master's degrees. He is very smart, and he seems so polite."

"Did you catch his eyes when you met?"

"Oh yes, our eyes met, and we were lost in each other's gaze."

"That's a good sign."

"Now tell me, Ashley, how can I get myself into his good books?"

Ashley just stood there and grinned broadly. She had no magic wand to prescribe how to approach love. Fortunately, Rebecca did not wait for a reply. As she continued to speak, desperation was creeping into her voice.

"One of my colleagues seems to have taken to him also and has already put herself forward,"

"How?"

"She told us she was going to ask him to go to town with her."

"Well girlfriend, don't get too worked up with your colleague's advances," Ashley advised. "You see Rebecca, the way to win a man's heart is not to throw yourself into his lap," she counseled, "rather it's better to play a little hard to get."

"How?" She asked, not really clear on what Ashley meant.

"Don't make gestures that have sexual connotations but be proactive in the ways you react to him. Smile at him as often as you can. Offer to help him if he needs something." Ashley explicated on her advice.

"That seems a pretty good advice. I'll try and do my best."

"Yes, you must, you're not getting any younger."

Rebecca tilted her head in thought and said, "you know Ash, there's going to be a staff party. I wasn't planning to attend, but now I'm going. It might be a good chance to steal a look at my man."

"There you go, Rebecca, I like it that you have already claimed him for your own."

The two exchanged a high five.

"Hey Rebecca, why don't we choose something you can wear to the party?"

Ashley offered to help with the selection and she obliged to her offer.

"Great idea."

The two of them went into her wardrobe and selected a dress befitting the occasion. She smacked her lips in satisfaction. She was determined to be ready for the joy ride.

CHAPTER 8

AN OFFICE PARTY

Since Maggie said she wanted to take Kofi to see the city, he got ready and prepared to meet her. He put on a T-shirt and comfortable canvas shoes so he could easily move around. He walked to the location where Maggie said he should meet her. He arrived at their rendezvous in good time and waited for her. A few minutes later Maggie appeared well-attired in a low-cut dress. She walked briskly up the block, her face glossy, probably from applying too much make-up. Her slender eyebrows, velvety eyelashes and sea-nymph ears were on prominent show today.

Though she was heavy set, Maggie was not a beach whale. Her size notwithstanding, she was healthy looking, buoyant, and fit. She had protruding hips, plump shoulders, large lips, a flat nose, and dimpled cheeks. Her dark complexion was especially shining through this afternoon. She wore sunglasses that covered her eyes as she walked towards Kofi, her hips wiggling with slight exaggeration. The sunglasses obscuring her eyes, gave her an inscrutable somewhat mysterious appearance, and meant you couldn't read her facial expression. When she arrived where Kofi was standing, she smiled broadly, her dimpled cheeks looking glorious.

"Are you ready for the tour?"

"Yes, I am, let's go."

She reached over, took his left hand, and tugged it under her armpit. He wiggled his hands free and looked at her disapprovingly clearly in a protest mood.

"That was highly inappropriate Maggie."

Maggie just looked at him quizzically and giggled, appearing heedlessly indifferent to his reaction. He saw the look on her face, but he believed he had made himself clear with his action, so he didn't need to extenuate the issue.

"Sorry if I offended you," Maggie finally said, "anyway you are not thinking of driving, are you?" She asked.

"What do you have in mind?"

"If we walk, we stand a better chance of getting a good view of the city than driving."

"Okay, then let's walk."

They walked for a long time but at the rate they walked Kofi didn't feel tired. He was a little disappointed with what he saw. Though he had been away for a long time, he still remembered how this city once was. It had parks where both children and adults could go to have some fun. Many of its streets were lined with trees. Now he was disappointed to see how those trees that adorned the streets had all been removed. He remembered vividly how the city had deserved its reputation as a garden city. He was really astonished at how things had deteriorated.

"What happened to all the trees that lined the streets?"

"They cut them down to widen the streets."

"This is catastrophic, a faded glory."

If he was appalled by the lack of trees along the streets, He would be devastated by the next scene, when they came to one of the city's parks. He remembered as a student in this city some years ago, that the parks and gardens depicted its beauty and pride. Now it stood in ruins, mainly built up of shanty structures and the rest reduced to a rubbish dump.

"What happened to the park?"

"People built structures on them to live in."

"That was not my question. I meant how could people build these structures on the park. Where were the authorities?"

Maggie laughed derisively before speaking.

"The answer is obvious, Mr. Hope, more people are moving into the city, and they have no place to live."

Kofi was aware that because people moved to *Sikakrom*, it put pressure on its resources. Nevertheless, he believed that if there had been proper planning and enforcement of building regulations by the authorities, these issues could be properly addressed without spoiling the city in this way. They left the park area and came to a section of the city where the roads were almost washed away. The constant rainfall, coupled with the lack of care for the roads had reduced it into an undulating mass of hills and gullies. The worst of it was that there were no pavements for people to walk on so both vehicles and people scrambled for the same space. Often, the drivers cared less for the pedestrians, so you walked those streets at your own peril.

At this stage, both Maggie and Kofi were walking cautiously. He was concerned for Maggie because she was not wearing the right shoes for walking on such rough terrain. While they were treading with caution, they saw people who were speeding past them as if they were walking on concrete pavements and not on a potholed minefield. There was a pool of water standing in the middle of the street. One car carelessly drove through the water splashing it on the pedestrian passersby. Kofi's shirt was all soiled up as was Maggie's dress. The driver had sped away without any apology or a chance to admonish him. They left the road and walked through the neighborhood where the terrain was a little friendlier, but still craggy.

Leaving the street, they came across a sight which was beholding and dumbfounding. It was of a group of boys playing soccer on that rugged terrain. Kofi watched them in amazement kicking around something that looked like a football. Whilst Maggie kept going, Kofi just stood there and watched them enthusiastically kick their ball around. When she turned around, she saw him still standing and watching the boys. She beckoned him to move on but he hesitated not wanting to interrupt those children at play. A tall, but lanky boy kicked the ball with such power, it flew over the heads of all the other players; high into the sky and seemed momentarily suspended. Then it started to descend and landed at Kofi's feet. He snatched the "ball" and kicked it back to the boys. It was no football, it was an improvisation, made by the boys themselves with plastic stitched together by bits of string.

All this time, Maggie was waiting for him, so he hastened to rejoin her. It was a tiring workout for them because they did a lot of walking. Maggie didn't look as tired as he felt Kofi thought. While his weariness was betrayed by his subdued mood, Maggie could still manage to smile and make small talk and jokes as they went along. Seeing that Kofi was tired she suggested that they find a place to sit and rest. There was an ice cream store nearby, so they sat there to rest and to enjoy the ice cream. It was nice to sit and relax, but it was getting late, so they hailed a taxi to take them to their respective homes.

First the taxi dropped Maggie and then Kofi. When he arrived back at his auntie's apartment, he found his friend Kisito Banda sitting in the living room. Though his folks did not know him, they had invited him in and entertained him until Kofi arrived. After the initial exchange of greetings Kofi asked Kisito to go outside with him where they could find a place to sit and chat freely. He had told him on the phone that he was going to see the chief of staff of the President, so his friend was keen to find out if everything went well. Kisito was happy and looked at him with glittering eyes. He was still his old self, never jealous of his friends. From about the age of twenty when he knew him, Kisito had always looked out for his friends. Kofi drew closer to him and whispered.

"There was this sultry woman at the office today. She told me she is a clerk at the office of the government statistician . . ."

Kisito looked at Kofi interestingly. His phone was beeping so he put it on silent so he could pay attention to what Kofi was saying.

"Sorry about the interruptions," he apologized for the beeping, "you were saying?"

"She was so seductive . . ."

"I beg your pardon . . . I didn't get the first part."

"I was saying a lady at work caused me to grow moist with attraction anytime I came across her at the office." He walked towards Kisito to make sure he heard him this time. "Boy she is attractive I'm sure she has a special effect on men or maybe just . . ." His voice trailed away because he saw Kisito looking strangely at him.

"Kofi, you're of age now," Kisito looked at him with fascination, "probably this woman's attracted to you personally and not all other men."

"You're sure about that?"

"No, I'm not sure, but doesn't it take two to tango?"

"Yeah."

"Right, so the fact that you were attracted to her meant she was probably also attracted to you. It doesn't mean she's a flirt."

"You may be right."

"So, make a move. All things are possible for those who make a move."

"She's my colleague at work and it would be highly inappropriate to date her."

"It's not wrong for two neighbors to drink from the same cistern if they know how to draw the water."

Kisito was being philosophical. His comments drew a grim look from Kofi.

"Kofi, remember you're of age, you need to find a wife—does it matter where you find her?"

"Hmm."

"Come on Kofi, man up. If this girl's attracted to you, invite her on a date."

Kisito was probably right. How could he possibly ignore such a person whose presence had such an effect on him? Now that he was back home, can he continue to lead the solitary life he led in his time in the States when he was trying to get a degree, to give him a career? That evening, there was going to be a party for the presidential staffers. Kofi wanted to go because he knew it would give him a chance of meeting Rebecca. He invited Kisito to go with him, who declined because he had a few things to attend to. When his friend declined to come along, Kofi also decided he wouldn't attend either. However, after Kisito left, it did not take long for him to change his mind. He returned to the apartment, and his auntie quickly gave him his food which he ate hurriedly because he wanted to go to the party.

When he arrived at the venue there were several colleagues from work already there. He scanned the room but neither Rebecca nor Maggie was there. Maggie, he presumed was worn out by their walk and so decided not to go out again. He moved around and made small talk with some of the people who were there. By the time the party got into full swing there were still some empty seats. The DJ was this funny guy at work. He was making all these comical remarks and the attendees were laughing riotously.

The third song was playing when Rebecca came in the group of three men and a woman. She was wearing a traditional African dress, expertly sewn in wavy pieces. It had a certain classic appeal about it. What made it even classier was that she wore them in an unimaginable way. His heart started pounding when he saw her. For a moment, she was the only person that mattered in the room and in his heart. He was surprised the effect her presence was having on him, and it somewhat concerned him, particularly because she was in the company of other men. Could it be one of them was her fiancé?

Unlike most people here who have flat noses, she has a dainty nose. As she sat there with her companions, she would continually touch her nose, probably because it made her felt special. As Kofi sat there admiring her, he wondered idly if a nose did something to change a person's appearance. He was expecting her to look his way, but she never did. In all likelihood she didn't remember him, or she didn't care about him. He wanted to go over and say hello but felt shy and decided against the idea. Soon he decided to take his mind off Rebeca and enjoy the party. However, since he did not really know anybody, he sat there alone.

While he sat there brooding about his inability to connect with Rebecca or any other person in a more meaningful way, he began thinking that it was going to be a drab night for him. He saw one or two people he knew from the office and made light conversation with them. Then he saw Nicholas Hamma standing in a corner all by himself. He seemed uncomfortable and appeared like he wished to be somewhere else. As he watched him, he moved to the bar and ordered a drink. The lights were dimmed, and his attention turned from Hamma to the other partygoers who were dancing into the Saturday night. At that moment, as he sat there enjoying the beauty of the night and all the young people dancing the night away; he remembered with nostalgia the nights he had spent in Colorado going to some of the nightclubs there.

His thoughts returned to Rebecca, and he peered at the people on the dance floor to see if she was among them. She was not one of the dancers, neither was she sitting at the place where he saw her earlier with her friends. With people dancing and singing loudly, the place was not only becoming noisy but also hot. He decided to get some fresh air outside since he didn't have much to do. He stepped into the cobblestone backyard. A lady was standing there by herself. As he approached, it became clearer. He couldn't believe his luck, for the person standing in the backyard was Rebecca and she was alone. Momentarily, he didn't know what to do.

"Sorry miss, I didn't know you were here, I just came to get some fresh air. Now if you excuse me, I will go back inside."

"Oh, you are the new guy at the office," she queried, "it's Mr. Hope, right?"

"Yes, but you can call me Kofi, please."

"You don't need to go in there if it's too hot for you," she said.

There were some plastic chairs piled up close to where they were standing. Rebecca pulled one out for him and got another for herself, then spoke in a low tone but loud enough for Kofi to hear.

"I like fresh air and I wouldn't mind if you stay out here with me."

He pulled up the chair and sat down. At first, he didn't know what to say but Rebecca was a good conversationalist and she led him on. They got engrossed in conversation, chatting about a wide range of topics. She was smart, adept and possessed the skill to put any person at ease. The longer they chatted, the fonder they were becoming of each other. As the tête-à-tête continued, he realized they had been away from the others for too long so he came up with a suggestion.

"I think we should rejoin the party before people started wondering about us."

"Don't worry Mr. Hope," she smiled broadly at him, "nobody is going to miss us."

He began to entertain the belief that probably she had not come with any of the three men. The realization was dawning upon him that he was probably all alone with an available woman, the very same woman who had been preoccupying his thoughts since their first encounter at work.

CHAPTER 9

GIFT OF A FOOTBALL

The weekend after the party, Kofi awoke to find an almost deserted apartment. His auntie had gone to the market, the children were nowhere to be found. Only Mr. Prosper, his uncle was still at home. They ate breakfast together and he returned to his small room. It was hot and steamy in there and he wanted to be out and about. He called his friend Kisito to see if they could do something together. He sounded busy at the other end and told him he was out of town and would call as soon as he returned. Kisito was the only person he could really go out with but since he was out of town, he was left with little to do.

He sat on his bed restless and genuinely bored. He took a pen and a piece of paper and doodled. As he randomly scribbled ideas on the sheet, he soon came up with an idea to keep him occupied. There was more that he could do with his time and perhaps become more fruitful for himself and for others. He remembered the children who were playing soccer with the improvised football. He decided to take a stroll to the area to see them play. He put on his sneakers and left the house. About a mile away, he came across a hardware store. The young lady at the counter had an earpiece on. She was listening to music and drumming her fingers on the table with her head bobbing. She seemed very happy as she mouthed along the lyrics of the song. She was so engrossed with the music she didn't see Kofi standing right in front of her.

He just stood there observing her; wondering whether it was a good idea to be listening to music with an earpiece, while busy at work. Since he didn't want it to appear that he was looking down his nose on anyone, he just stood there. Just then an older lady, presumably the mother, emerged from inside the store. She scowled at the girl for ignoring a customer. She apologized for the girl's behavior and started attending to him. The young lady seeing her mother taking over, took a plastic bag from under her counter and put the football he bought in it. As she did this, she slyly winked at him flirtingly and directed a sideways gaze at him before handing it to him. He didn't want to read too much into the girl's behavior, so he took his football and just left.

As he walked away, he hummed to himself and then broke into a rhythmic whistle. His day had already started on a good note. He believed the whole idea of playing football with some plastic material was not appealing. So, he was determined to help those children in his own small way. Besides, he had developed a love for their game, and had the burning desire to help them. Many times, on his walks, he had seen them playing with the same improvised ball. What he admired about the children was that they didn't seem to care about whether or not they played with a proper football.

All they wanted to do was to play. Such resourcefulness was very appealing to Kofi. So, the weekend was a good time to go there to see them play. Just as he had thought, when he got there, they were joyfully playing. Those children never seemed to go without a day of playing football. He waved to them, but they continued to play. He saw that they didn't want to be interrupted so he let them be. They would dribble the ball from one end of the pitch to the other. They didn't seem to have any formations; wherever the ball went, they would all chase after it. They probably needed a coach, but if they couldn't afford a football, how much more a coach. One day when they had all graduated to become professional players, that aspect would be taken care of. For now, all they needed to do was to play; and play they did. After a while one boy miscued a shot which came in Kofi's direction.

When the ball came to him, he grabbed it just as he did the first time, he had watched them play. They were expecting him to kick it back to them, but he held on to it. Occasionally when the boys would play, the ball would hit an adult. Whenever that happened, they had to go and negotiate with that person to get their ball back. They thought this was one such moment. Three of the boys ran to him to ask for their ball back with the lanky boy leading them. He told them not to worry about their ball as they looked at him pleadingly. He then reached into his backpack for the football he had purchased and handed it to the lanky boy. He and his friends exclaimed overjoyed.

"Wow, thank you very much, uncle."

Here, in this matrilineal society every adult male is uncle and female auntie. All the other boys joined in the chorus.

"Thank you, Uncle! Thank you, uncle."

He indicated to them that it was nothing and he just wanted to help. He encouraged them to play well so that they could become future stars. He was aware that there were other children who had come out of this area who now plied their trade in the Premier league, La Liga, Bundesliga, and other famous European leagues. Once a boy was able to graduate to those levels, it was the end of poverty for him and his family. He was glad that one day some of these boys might rise to those levels perhaps because of his small contribution. They were overjoyed to get a real football. They shouted their gratitude as they ran off to continue playing. As Kofi walked away, he continued listening to the kids shouting instructions to one another until he was out of earshot.

His heart swelled up with faith and hope; the faith that these children would pull through and the hope that people like him and others would be able to help create a better future for all the children of this nation. His hope hinged on the fact that unlike millions of children on this continent who grew up in conflict zones, surrounded by wars and fighting, here there was peace and tranquility. Children here were not forced to become child soldiers and fight. Neither were they separated from their families because of war, religious strife, or natural disasters. He was convinced that in *Abibiman*, a country that suffered from no such challenges, they were free to grow up normally, which offered hope and a basis for a resurgence.

From here, Kofi continued his walk; he was energetically swinging his arms back and forth as he walked briskly away to attend to his other duties of the day. The warm feeling of assurance he had from seeing those children at play was captivating. He remained on a high all day, particularly recalling the warmth with which they received his gift. Continuing, he came across another group of teenage boys playing marbles. Traditionally in *Abibiman*, games of marbles are an individual competition. The players mold out of sand a circular structure which they cover with hard brown papers. Stones are placed at the tips of the paper to hold it firmly on the ground. It is played by two or more players but not exceeding six. Players ballot to see who will go first. Each player spins their marble on the platform. He stood there and watched them. It was quite interesting. He remembered that as a boy he used to play that a lot.

Like those who were playing football, these boys were equally caught up in animated excitement. Sometimes they would hail their winnings by shouting and making fun of the loser. Kofi stood there thinking somebody might become angry from such a treatment. However, for those boys it was all part of being a good sport. They never complained, they just concentrated on their game. One of the boys noticing him standing there to watch their game turned to him and asked;

"Hey mister, do you want to join our game?"

Kofi did not respond. He just stood there and watched them. These were boys in their teens, why should he interrupt their game? As he stood there in contemplation, the boys were still beckoning him to come and play with them. He thought it would be interesting, so he decided to join them. There was no umpire officiating the game, there was no middleman who sold marbles; the boys did everything on their own. Theirs represented a perfect world, one in which each person fended for himself but was treated as an equal. Why wouldn't adults be able to do the same? The world of adults had been defaced by the clamor for money such that they are not able to care for the next person next door without considering what was in the dealings for them. Kofi was tempted to join them and to participate in this utopia.

"Where do I find some marbles?" Kofi finally summoned the courage to ask them.

Marbles grow wild in the bush so anybody can go and get them. However, there are those who go to the bush to gather them and sell them at the market. Beside these sources, players also accumulated marbles through their daily winnings. One of the boys was going to sell him some marbles, but another player decided to give him three free marbles to start with. He encouraged him to buy more if he wanted as he progressed in the game. They were all sitting on small stools so that they could be closer to the playing platform. Since Kofi did not have one, another boy willingly offered him his stool and squatted on his haunches to play. He was astonished, here was a group of youngsters willing to share their gains with a stranger without seeking what was in it for them. Kofi stayed for about thirty minutes enjoying every second he spent playing with his newly found playmates.

The boys were full of smiles as they played. When they made a winning, they would poke fun at the loser. As the play went on however, one boy who wanted to sell some marbles to Kofi was losing all his winnings, he started chewing his lip and stroking his jaw. Kofi looked at him and offered him three of his marbles. The boy's face lightened up and soon he was all smiles again. Kofi thought this was perhaps the best and most exciting game he had played for years. Here were boys who could have taken advantage of a stranger's ignorance to get some personal benefit, but that was not their goal. Their goal was only to play and have fun. He was really at peace with what he encountered with those boys. Theirs was one of innocent and pure hearts. They were not interested in acquiring wealth on the back of others. They shared freely and asked for nothing back, the joy of sharing friendship with others was enough.

After what had seemed ages but was only half an hour, Kofi told them he had to leave. He had won some marbles, so he gave them to the boy who had first lent him some of his. They were sad to see him go, but they told him he was always welcome to play with them anytime he was passing. When Kofi got home, he was very tired but also very happy. He was happy that he was able to give the children the football, but he was even happier impressed by the selflessness displayed by the marble-playing teenagers. Their generosity and genuineness were the qualities the country surely needed. That night he slept soundly like a child with no cares in the world.

CHAPTER 10

MOB RULE ENCOUNTER

The work at the office had been demanding but always interesting. Often Kofi's mind was preoccupied with his next step. It was usual for him to think about work just before he went to bed and when he rose in the morning. Hence his dreams were all about work; his morning thoughts about how to get stuff done. He always thought about programs he could design, ideas he could implement; and goals he could accomplish. His prime objective had always been to get the best output from resources available to him. This morning was no different. Except that his thoughts were interrupted by strange loud noises outside. From his room, he heard a commotion going on outside. His planning could wait, he told himself. The noise was such that he could not focus clearly. He rose from his bed and walked to his window.

Some people were repeatedly shouting the word thief. He opened the window and pulled his curtains aside to see what was going on. He saw a man being manhandled by a mob. Some in the crowd were hitting him with sticks. Others were throwing stones at him. The fellow was struggling to get away but the crowd was too much for him to do so. He stumbled and fell on his knees, but the people continued to beat him. He fell in a heap and the mob started to drift away. The man laid there on the ground motionless. Kofi thought he was probably dead. However, as he watched on, he crawled on both hands and feet and got into a nearby sewer. Then as he watched, he saw three of the stoutly built men, the *macho* men they call them here, return. Two of them were each carrying a used car tire. The third was carrying a bottle full of some liquid. They thought the robber had escaped but then a young boy came and pointed to the sewer. The men lit a fire and smoked out the robber.

By this time, he was very weak, from the beatings and from the smoke, and was defenseless. Seeing the three macho men approach, he tried to get up. They helped him to his feet but did not help him escape. When he got up, they put the car tires around his neck one at a time until they had forced both tires onto his body. The man was weeping and begging them, but they did not pay any attention to him. They were behaving like men who cared little about law or its implications. The liquid in the bottle was kerosene. They poured it all over him. Then an unbelievable thing happened; they set him on fire. He wriggled and screamed but these *macho* men knew no mercy. It was more than Kofi could bear to watch. He lowered the curtain and returned to bed, shocked, and horrified at the cruelty of the mob and particularly of those three men.

Later in the morning, when he left the house to go to work, he saw the ashen remains of what used to be a man on the street. People stopped as they passed by. Some just continued to walk barely looking at the charred remains. The police did not come when the man was being killed. Perhaps they might not come at all. The charred corpse will probably lie there on the street and become food for the vultures. In *Abibiman* it seemed the police only worked for their self-interest. Their main duty was standing on the side of the road to extort money from unsuspecting motorists. Since the country was as good as having no police, what would put an end to such barbaric practices as mob rule where the crowd, rather than a court of law, administered summary justice and execution. Later in the day he learned that the poor man had only stolen a chicken from a neighbor's coop and look at the harsh punishment meted out to him by the angry mob.

The next day, he woke up early to embark on his usual morning walk. It was a routine he had established since he got into government to keep in shape. His motivation was not to fall prey to weight gain because he went by car everywhere. If he chose not to drive, his assigned driver would come and pick him up. When he returned home, he still felt he needed to do more walking, so he decided to start taking a bus or *Trotro* to work. As he was walking to the roadside to catch his ride, he met the same lanky boy, to whom he had donated the football. He was with a young man of about twenty-five years old. The younger boy approached him smiling blushingly.

"This is the man I was telling you about uncle."

The lanky boy, whose name was Suleimana told his companion. It was then time for Suleimana's companion to introduce himself.

"My name is Yakubu Oedrago."

"Nice to meet you, my name is Kofi Hope."

"Wow," Yakubu exclaimed, "you have a unique name Mr. Hope."

Leaving them, he broke into a trot in order not to miss the bus because of the time he had lost. Fortunately, the bus was just arriving at his stop when he got there. Meeting Suleimana and his uncle took his mind back to the neighborhood. The boys having to play football on rough ground with an improvised ball was one thing; the summary lynching of robbers was something else. He longed for a more humane society that would put an end to the cruel and inhumane treatment of their fellow humans whatever their alleged crimes. He was determined to work for justice, to make the people understand. It would take some time, but he was determined to take on that task. People should simply respect the rule of law, so that when others break it, they would allow the due process of the law to deal with them, and not take matters into their own hands.

His fears were that unless law enforcement authorities faced up to the challenge, those barbaric practices would never be uprooted from society. His fears, though, were not unfounded, for in a few days' time, that barbaric incident was to repeat itself. This happened on one Friday morning. It was one of those days when he decided to ditch his official car and truck and take a *Trotro* to work. A few yards away from his apartment he saw about five people dragging a man from a nearby house onto the street. As they dragged him, they were shouting;

"Thief! thief!"

There was tension all around, and the fear of death hung in the air. The feeling was so overpowering and nauseating. The incident of two days previously flashed back at him, as if it was just happening. He remembered it vividly, because that man was killed not too far from his present location by an angry mob, right outside his window. Was the incident about to be reenacted? There is nothing a depraved people will not do. A helpless people finding their hopes and savings taken away from them by some unscrupulous people masquerading as politicians, and with it their sense of self-respect, will resort to extremes out of frustration at their economic woes. As they approached where Kofi was standing, he raised up his hands to stop them.

"What's going on, guys?"

"This guy is a thief." One of the young men told him, shoving an MP3 player at him.

"Oh, I see, then you need help to take him to the police."

Kofi realized the situation was dire unless he intervened. He decided that he was going to reason with them to take the right course instead of taking the law into their own hands. He then suggested.

"Let me assist you take him to the police."

"No mister." They replied in unison.

"Why not?"

"The police are in business with the thieves, as soon as we leave, they will just collect some money and let him go."

The crowd was gathering as the group around the man continued to shout thief. He was confused. He had to act fast before they killed him like the other fellow a few days ago.

"So, what will it take for you to forgive him?

"Who's talking of forgiving him?" One of them asked.

"You know to err is human," Kofi said.

"And to forgive is divine," one of them responded, "but we are not God, in fact we cannot compare ourselves to God." "If you pay for the MP3 we will let him, go," said another.

"But you have it now, why do you want money for something which you still have in your possession."

"Mister, we thought you wanted to help?" Another spoke up.

"Okay, listen here. How much is the MP3? I will pay for it."

The boys hesitated so he thought that was an encouraging sign. He took out his wallet and gave them a fifty *sika* note. One of the boys took it.

"Mister this will not be enough for all of us."

Just then, there was a young man passing and they waved at him. When the newcomer got to where they were he asked.

"What are you guys gathered out here this early morning for?"

"This fellow, stole our MP3," he pointed at the man who they were about to lynch, "and this gentleman is giving us fifty *sikas* to let him go."

The man turned around to look at Kofi and recognition dawned on him. "Ah Mr. Hope!"

"Do you know him, Yakubu?" One of the boys asked him.

The new arrival was Yakubu Oadreago, the uncle of the lanky boy Suleimana, the soccer player. Yakubu encouraged them to take the money and release the robber. At this, the mob fell quiet. Seeing that the anger had subsided they took the money Kofi offered them and released their victim. The man looked strangely at Kofi and took off running, but not before Kofi had noted his features. He was a burly built man about five feet nine inches tall. He had a big mark across his left cheek and had a haggard face probably wearied from years of being homeless, often without food or shelter. As soon as Kofi was sure the man was safe, he put his wallet back into his back pocket and left the mob that had assembled. Fortunately for him when he reached the main road a *Trotro* stopped for him. As Kofi sat down there was a young man in the vehicle who smiled at him, and he smiled back. Soon the mate asked the passengers to pay their fare. Kofi reached into his back pocket to get his wallet, dismayed to find it was not there. Though the astonishment was depicted on his face the driver's mate was unconvinced.

"I'm sorry, I think somebody took my wallet."

"Mister, I'm not buying that lie. Pay your fare or I call the police."

"Mate don't talk to him like that. Do you know who you're disrespecting?" The man who had smiled at him shouted at the mate.

He took his wallet and paid Kofi's fare for him. When they alighted from the *Trotro* he approached Kofi.

"You don't seem to remember me? I'm the driver of the chief who was introduced to you by Miss Husup."

"Forgive me for not remembering you," Kofi replied, "and thank you very much for bailing me out of that situation."

All day Kofi's mind returned to the homeless man with the haggard face. But for his intervention that man might also be dead by now. He was worried that he would not be able to make any progress in his desire to help the poor people of this country. After all, what can one man do to repair the years of injustice and meet the needs of the people? He wondered if he could work to affect this country in any positive ways. He knew the problems were only increasing. He had been shocked by the statistics showing more and more people were moving from the rural countryside into the urban towns and cities. However, it seemed the government was not able to provide adequate housing. Soon the urban areas will be overcrowded with people who will barely be able to make ends meet. Marital splits, alcoholism, and drug abuse were resulting in greater homelessness and an increase in petty crime. The haggard-faced vagrant was representative of a wider problem. There was a growing social burden to the nation of rapid urban expansion.

He wondered if anyone in Government understood the problems of this phenomenon, still less had any ideas for tackling it. It should be a concern of anybody elected by the people to lead them. But were they really concerned? From that moment, he decided he had to do more to help change minds, because this was not a fight he could handle alone. However, if he managed to elicit support for his course, more people would become aware of what needs to happen to change people's attitude and way of life. His one concern though was the attitude of the politicians whose only desire was lining their own pockets. It was obvious that the greediness of these politicians was only contributing to inequality, but they obviously seemed oblivious of the discord their actions were impacting on society in so many negative ways. Since his return from America, Kofi had discovered that there was so much corruption he had struggled to come to terms with it, let alone formulate ideas to find a way around it. Greed, corruption, and injustice not only stalked the corridors of power, but was also evident at the grass roots level, amongst the life of the poor who most needed help.

The ones who suffered most were the poor folks who toiled day and night but had little or nothing to show for it. Perhaps his work should start with them. When they are alerted, they would know the right course of action to take. It was only in that way the war against corruption could become successful. He needed a popular movement to take up the cause. In the past though, like his peers, he could have offered various reasons to explain away poverty such as political instability, bad economic policy, an over-reliance on tropical commodities, lack of a manufacturing sector to create added value jobs and save imports, the colonial history, distance from major markets, poor health and education, lack of basic infrastructure. The list was endless. He could have gone on and on. But could the same reasons be tendered as an excuse today? It was obvious that a framework for the rule of law had been established with the introduction of democracy to this country after the coup d'états of the previous century. What was now needed is the willpower to enforce the laws of the country. This though seems like a mirage, because the police, those entrusted with enforcing the law seem embroidered in corruption just like all other institutions.

Their impropriety was largely responsible for small-scale bribery becoming entrenched in the fabric of this country. How long will this country continue to be impoverished because its wealth has all been stolen, plundered by people who are supposed to be custodians of the wealth and resources of this beautiful country? That night Kofi had a strange dream. In fact, it was more of a nightmare. There were several wearied-looking men like the robbery suspect he saved, all looking at him. They were shouting for help and pointing to him. This time, they were not free, they were all in chains, hair disheveled and wearing tattered clothes. He awoke to find himself drenched in sweat. He was panting heavily like a person running away from some thugs. He lay in bed thinking about the dream until he drifted back to sleep.

CHAPTER 11

IN JAIL

Time had crept up on Kofi; he had always thought he had much to do so he had been giving his all. It was already the third month since he started work, and he thought he hadn't worked hard enough. Another thing that worried him, though it was a lesser priority, was his accommodation. Barbara was still waiting on a vacancy at the senior staff residency to allocate him an apartment. Hence, he was still commuting to and from work living at his auntie's place. He was conscious of not wanting to be a burden to her, though she had never complained at his extended stay. Every day he went to work early and came home late. He and Ellen were always the first ones and the last to leave the office.

On this day, he realized he did not have enough A4 paper to print some documents, so he sent Lisa to Barbara. Her assistant, Maggie, was out on an errand, so she asked if he could send Lisa with his driver to go and buy some office supplies for himself. Lisa was gone for a while, but since he didn't want to waste any more time, Kofi went to Hamma's office to borrow some. There was a young man there with Hamma whom he introduced as a friend. Lucy Bukari, the women's organizer, was also there. When he entered, she was speaking but she stopped in the middle of her sentence and took a pamphlet that was on the table. She basically ignored Kofi's presence and continued to scan the pamphlet. Hamma had a song playing in the background as he worked.

Yɛ neɛ woho bɛtɔ wo
Mentie obiara asɛm

He stopped to think, where had he heard this mischief-laden song before? He scratched his chin and held on to his forehead. He was searching for the place where he had heard that song before. Then as he stood there, he remembered the licensing officer. Was Hamma of the same mindset? That he wasn't going to listen to any advice from any quarters? Hamma noticed his hesitation, but he could not connect it to the song; he simply stared at him. The sight of Kofi standing there looking bemused gave him an edge of irritation as did Lucy. After his moment of hesitation, he remembered what he had come to Hamma's office for. He took some sheets of printing paper and left. Unlike Lucy, Hamma's male visitor had wanted to make conversation with him, but his attention was elsewhere. When he left the man, the lanky boys uncle Yakubu, told Hamma he knew him.

"How do you know him?"

"Oh! Our steps have crossed a few times."

"Okay elaborate."

"He bought a football for my nephew, and a few days ago, he paid to free a robber who was going to be lynched by a mob."

"He did?"

"Yes, he did. He gave the money to me, and I disbursed it."

"You have to go to the police."

As Hamma spoke fury welled up inside. His young visitor though was calm and was reluctant to take the action he was suggesting.

"But why?" he yelled, a lopsided grimace on his face, "was he not simply being a good Samaritan?"

"Good Samaritan my foot," he blinked rapidly, "what that man did was criminal."

Yakubu turned to Lucy for support but from her expression he could see she was sympathetic to Hamma. Nevertheless, he felt obliged to ask her opinion.

"What do you think Madam Lucy?"

"I think you should do as the honorable Hamma has suggested."

"What is in this for me honorable?"

"You get one thousand *Sikas*."

The man's eyes were bulging, "one thousand *Sikas*?"

"And I will add a thousand *Sikas*." Lucy added.

"When do I get this money?"

"Text us your mobile number and we will send the money to you right away," Hamma said.

A few minutes later when he checked his phone's mobile money account, the money was in. He smiled broadly as he got up to leave.

"Consider it done honorable."

"There must be no games. . . . you know me." Hamma told him as he walked across the room to the door.

When he left, Hamma and Lucy looked at each other and exchanged a high five.

"Partners in crime." They said in unison.

It was early morning. Kofi was eating breakfast ready to go to work when he saw Suleimana, the lanky boy he had given the football to. Behind him were two policemen and a civilian. He thought he had seen the man who accompanied them before but could not recollect where. As they drew closer, Suleimana pointed to him and then ran away.

"Excuse me, are you Mr. Hope? The police asked when they came to him.

"Yes sir."

"Well, we are here to inform you that you are under arrest for being an accessory to robbery. You have the right to remain silent. However, anything you say can and will be used against you in the court of law."

They recited to him his Miranda rights, as if they had any intention to give him any. Kofi looked in disbelief at the police, a ghost of a smile on his face. Then he asked them;

"What have I done to warrant arrest?"

"For accessory to robbery," he pointed to the fellow they came with, "this man was a witness."

One of the policemen put Kofi's hands at his back and handcuffed him. Now it was apparent to him that this was no laughing matter; but when had he been an accomplice to robbery? Just then his auntie came running outside shouting;

"My nephew is innocent; my nephew is innocent."

"Woman, we will leave that to the court to decide." The policeman offered.

At the same time the other policemen glared at her for daring to challenge their decision. She was adamant, she was not going to allow them to take her nephew away without a fight.

"If you think he has done something wrong, you leave him to me, and I will bring him to the station myself."

The police simply ignored her protests and pushed Kofi from behind gesturing to him to move. When Auntie Belinda realized that they were determined to take him in, she knelt on her knees and held on to the right leg of the policeman who handcuffed him as if her nephew's life depended on it. The policeman was already incensed by her challenge so he would have none of her pleas. He hit her with his drawn baton. She fell into a heap, but the police paid no regard to her welfare. They just left her there to bleed. Then they led Kofi away and bundled him into their car ignoring his protestations. Once at the police station, he was searched; his phone, keys and some cash confiscated. They gave him paper and pen to write his statement. He looked at them with a gaping mouth, his eyes widened. Was that the right thing to do? To ask a man to write a statement without the privilege of a lawyer. No, he was not going to do any such thing. The policeman walked across the room to where he was seated. He had this intimidating look about him. When he spoke, he was brimming with hostility.

"You are going to do just as I say."

Kofi ignored his threat and just sat there calmly. That seemed to have enraged the officer more. He smacked him on the face and then returned to his seat. Though he walked away from him, the policeman's anger did not subside. Rather, he was becoming aggressively angry. He was looking to force a confession, but Kofi was not prepared to grant him one. He remained tight-lipped since they were not going to grant his request for a lawyer.

"Are you thumbing your nose at me?"

"No, I am just claiming my rights as a citizen."

All this time, the policeman had a cigarette dangling from the corner of his mouth. Kofi did not like the smoke that went into his eyes, but he couldn't tell him to put it out. He came over to him again and this time took the cigarette from his mouth. This time he threatened to stub the cigarette in his face if he didn't submit to their request. After he sat down, a second policeman entered. He repeated their request to write his statement; he was much calmer, but Kofi again declined and calmly declared.

"I don't mean to be rude, but every accused person should be given a right to a lawyer."

"Criminals like you do not deserve a lawyer," the policeman asserted.

"Criminals like me?" He asked in bewilderment, "isn't a man presumed innocent until proven guilty?"

They poked fun at him. Now they were getting frustrated with him for not complying with their orders. They left him sitting there as they withdrew to a corner of the office jingling money in their pockets. They were perhaps sharing their loot of all the free monies they got standing by the roadside to harass drivers. When they returned to him, one of them tugged at his earlobes forcing him to grimace. They pushed him to his chair, but he fell on the floor. He got up from the floor and held high his head; he was not going to be made to feel humiliated because of their maltreatment. He was not going to be defeated; nor be crushed. At this point, the police realized they couldn't get any confessions out of him, so they put his handcuffs back on and put him in a cell even smaller than his small room in his auntie's apartment. The air in there was thick with the smell of sweat. The walls had graffiti scribbled all over them. There was no chair to sit on so he sat on the floor starring at the wall.

After a while, he felt the urge to use the toilet, so he called the police. They uncuffed him and led him to a dirt-ridden room with a dirty toilet bowl. It appeared like it had not been cleaned for ages. He looked from the toilet to the policeman and back at the toilet. Suddenly, he felt like throwing up. The officer was just standing there, a triumphant look in his eyes. Kofi waited until he was gone, then climbed onto the bowl. When he finished, he tried to get out, but the door was locked from outside. He banged on the door and a stern-looking policeman opened it. He put the handcuffs back on him and led him back to his cell. Apart from his cell being hot and stuffy, the sweltering heat made it tough to be in handcuffs. He pleaded with the officer to unshackle him, but it only gave him cause to make a mockery of him.

"You're a tough guy, aren't you?"

He did not say anything, he simply looked at him as he made his way back to his desk. He was in the cell for a while when one of the policemen brought him some food. When he looked at the food, it was so disgusting he lost his appetite. He kicked it away and went back to sit on his bed. The policeman looked upward and shook his head; then he turned round, shrugged his shoulders, and walked away. Kofi could contain hunger, but he could not contain thirst. Sometime later, he was very thirsty, so he banged on his door to get attention. There was no response. After banging on the door for a while, he clenched his jaw and let out a loud shriek. This time, two policemen ran to him thinking he was trying to do something to himself.

They found him sitting silently on his bed and his chin quivering. One of the policemen turned back; the second clenched his fist tightly and signal to him that the next time he hears a shout he was going to punch him. When the second officer also turned round to leave, he asked him for the water. They brought him water in a dirty plastic cup. He wanted to refuse it, but he was so thirsty. He held it closer to his nose and it was so smelly he put it down in a corner. After some hours he got thirstier, so he went for the water. This time he closed his eyes, held his nose, and gulped it down with great effort. That was the only thing that got into his belly the whole day.

On the second day when the police opened the cell door, he was sitting in a corner with his head on his chin in a resting position, and his jaw was clenching. They took him to their desk, uncuffed him and asked him to write his statement. Again, he refused to do so without proper representation. The police saw that they could not compel him to write a statement, so they threatened him with more punishment if he did not oblige. He was still unyielding, so they returned him to his cell. Soon hunger and thirst overpowered him, and he passed out and fell into a deep sleep. Beads of sweat stood on his face as he woke up from his slumber. He was really confused, he scrunched his forehead and stepped away from the little bed he was lying on. He peeped through the little hole in the door of his cell. He could see the clock in the hallway, but he couldn't read the time properly.

The last time he looked, the hour hand was at six; this time it had moved to seven, it couldn't be just an hour, it had probably gone a full cycle; it was another day. He sat up, drenched in sweat, he wondered how long the police were going to keep him there. The only people close to him; his auntie and his uncle had not been there. The man had traveled at the time he was arrested; his auntie was also left on the ground lying in a pool of blood. He didn't know her situation now. Without his auntie, he was not sure his colleagues at work would know about his situation. He was in this state of deep thought and confusion when he drifted back to sleep. He was woken by a key turning in his door. When the door swung open a policeman was standing there, and his auntie was behind him.

"Kofi are you okay?"

He couldn't see properly; he was feeling dizzy for going days without food. He tried to overcome the dizziness by shaking his head and forcing out a smile.

"Yes auntie, I'm okay."

The policeman left them alone. Auntie Belinda entered his cell and sat by him on his little bed. She apologized for not coming promptly but said she had been admitted to the hospital.

"Do you have some food with you?" He enquired.

She took out a loaf of bread and a sachet of water which was in her handbag. After he finished the bread, he drank the water. Now he started to feel better and regained some energy. They sat there and chatted like two lost relatives. Then he told her to go to his office to see Barbara.

"Kofi, shouldn't we keep this to ourselves?"

"No, Auntie, Barbara is a good person, and she is my boss. She will know what to do."

Just then the policeman returned. It was time for her to leave. Auntie Belinda got up and left. At the door she turned and assured him everything would be alright.

CHAPTER 12

THE PLOT THICKENS

It had been three days since Kofi reported for work. Now people were really getting anxious; why would a person who really loved his job choose to stay away for three days without letting anybody know about his whereabouts? Word was going around in the office that he had been arrested as an accomplice to robbery. When Rebecca heard this news, she did not know who to believe. She was yearning to go and see him, but she had no idea if the rumors were true or not. Probably he was sick and had been hospitalized somewhere? She had no way of knowing; she worried severely. Though everybody was wondering what was going on with him, for Rebecca it was a haunting feeling. She had fallen in love with him at their first encounter, although she did not know anything about him yet, let alone know where he lived. She had tried to call him several times, but it seemed his phone was turned off. All day she felt tortured that she couldn't go out there and look for the love of her life, nor get him on the phone.

Tears welled up in her eyes as she considered the possibility of something bad happening to him. The other workers also wondered about him. It was not like him to keep away from work. They made efforts to locate him, but no one knew how to get hold of him. Adams was the only one who knew where he lived but he too was not at work; he had travelled on government business. After lunch, Barbara was in her office when Maggie came to tell her a woman wanted to see her. She was busy working on some documents, so she asked her to wait outside. When she was done with what she was doing she went outside to find the visitor. She found her sitting there holding her head in her hands and sweating excessively. As she raised her head, she saw Barbara standing in front of her. To hide her anxiety, she took out a handkerchief that was tugged on the breast of her blouse and wiped her face. Barbara saw her discomfort but did not say anything initially.

"Please come inside," she said.

The woman got up and followed her to her office.

"Maggie, Maggie," Barbara called out. She came running to her. "Please get some water from the refrigerator for my visitor."

Maggie went out to the lobby and returned with some cold water.

"Thanks," the woman said as she took the water. She finished one cup and Maggie refilled it. This time she took a sip and put it down.

"My name is Belinda, I am the auntie of Mr. Kofi Hope," she said.

"Mr. Hope," Barbara leaned forward, "is he alright, we've been so worried about him."

"He got arrested."

"Arrested?"

Just then tears started trickling down the woman's face. At first it was only a tear, but she could no longer hold it in, and she broke down, weeping openly. Barbara handed her a tissue which she took but that did not end her continuous crying. All this time Barbara just sat there and looked on. After a while, she stopped crying, wiped her nose with the tissue, and composed herself. There were prominent lines between her eyebrows underscoring the stress she had been under in the last few days.

"Why was he arrested?" Barbara asked.

Auntie Belinda began narrating the story of Kofi's arrest, while Barbara leaned forward in rapt attention with a half-opened mouth. Intermittently she would nod to show her understanding and empathy. While Belinda was speaking, who should enter but Hamma? He stood in the doorway hooking a thumb in his front pocket with a look of bland indifference. Unlike Barbara, he was happy for the arrest, so as he stood there, he sported a careless vacant and an almost bored expression.

"Could you please wait outside for me," Barbara told Belinda once she had concluded the story of the arrest. Barbara then turned to Hamma and retold him the story, even though she knew he had already eavesdropped on a part of the conversation.

"I had earlier heard through the grapevine that Hope was in police custody for accessory to robbery," Hamma said.

"What Nicholas!" Barbara exclaimed aghast; she pressed her lips together and grimaced, "When did you hear this, Nicholas?"

Hamma winced. Though he resented being addressed by his first name without the title Honorable, he could not argue with Barbara. She was too powerful.

"Yesterday," he replied.

"So why didn't you tell me this before?"

Fury surged through Barbara, and he could see the anger plastered all over her face; she stormed out of her office almost pushing him over. When she got to the parking lot, she found Belinda sitting on a stone. She was looking a little more cheerful now. They got into Barbara's official car and drove to the police station. The police all came to their attention when Barbara entered.

"I have come to post bail for Mr. Hope," she told the police.

"Are you talking about the criminal who was brought in three days ago?"

"You mean the government's financial analyst?"

"He works for the government?" The policeman exclaimed; his mouth wide open aghast.

Barbara just stood there watching him; she was not smiling and that made the policeman yet more anxious. Behind her Belinda was grinning gleefully at his shocked embarrassment. The officer looked away from them and started picking the cuticles and skin around his fingernails with his incisors while he tried to come to terms with the situation. He was genuinely surprised that they had arrested a government official. The officer apologized profusely for the arrest. However, he explained that they had been compelled to make the arrest by a high-ranking government official. The officer got up from his chair and tugged at his trousers. Deliberately and slowly, he took Kofi's phone and keys (but not the money which he had kept), along with another large bunch of keys from his desk and proceeded directly to Kofi's cell to set him free. When Kofi emerged, Barbara was horrified. Three days of not eating had taken its toll on him. He looked emaciated and he had dark circles under his eyes showing the stress he had been under.

"How, Kofi, what did they do to you?"

He was too weak to speak. He just looked at Barbara sullenly and then at his auntie.

"Looking at the situation he is in, it would be better to take him to hospital," Barbara suggested.

After settling Kofi at the hospital, the official car dropped Belinda home. She had suggested that they must find a change of clothes for Kofi. Barbara sensed the older lady had gone through a lot, so she offered to take him what he needed. The two ladies entered the apartment. Barbara waited in the living room while Belinda went into Kofi's room to find his clothes. She forgot to close the door after her, so Barbara could see right into the room. When she did, her heart sank. She was shocked at how small it was, and marveled at how Kofi always came to the office every day always smartly dressed and never once complained about his accommodation. Barbara looked at these humble circumstances and concluded that he could have had nothing to do with any robbery. Here was a humble altruistic man, who rather gives his money to people so that they would let a robber go. How could the police arrest him for being an accomplice to robbery? It made no sense at all.

The injustice of it was playing on Barbara's mind on the drive back to the hospital. Once there, she gave him his clothes, and sat by his side for a while. She was beginning to admire him for all he stood for. The next day when she went back to visit him, she found he was much recovered. She had him discharged and dropped him off at home on her way to the office. She told him to come and see her when he reported to work and went on her way. Barbara could not wrap her head around how Kofi could be arrested for helping a person to escape a lynching. She had spent all night thinking about it. It bothered her to know who this government official was, who had given instructions to get him arrested.

If the arrest was surprising to her, when she later found out that the government official was none other than Hamma, she was even more confounded. She believed there should be a congenial atmosphere at work where every member of the team was supportive and could give of their best. She was determined to tackle this blot on their teamwork. She was going to make sure that every team member was supportive, not disruptive.

However, she decided not to bring the matter up with the chief of staff or the president—at least not yet. The next day when she got to work, she went into Hamma's office.

"How did you hear about Mr. Hope's arrest?"

"We have connections?"

"Honorable, were you instrumental in his arrest?"

"Well, I knew a friend who knew a friend?"

"What's the meaning of that?"

"Shouldn't children know their rightful place in the house? He wished for war, now he has it."

"Nicholas, this is below your dignity."

Saying that, she stormed out of his office in a rage. She was appalled at Hamma's behavior, and her forehead puckered. She couldn't wrap her mind around the reason why Hamma would get Kofi arrested. As she turned to leave, Hamma deflected his head away from her, but his eyes followed her. When she turned around and saw Hamma still watching her, she forced a smile, although she was not happy with him.

"Stay away from Mr. Hope," she warned.

Hamma took a sideways glance at her, "and if I don't?"

"I am not joking with you, Nicholas. . . . and be careful not to mention the arrest to the chief or the President otherwise I am going to expose your treachery," she said.

"That's fine with me," he replied.

"Consider yourself at war with me if anything like this ever happens again," she said as she turned round to go.

When she left Hamma's, she called the girls and informed them what happened to Kofi. Then she warned them not to mention the arrest to anybody. What was more, she went to great lengths to admonish them to make him feel welcome when he returned to work. Rebecca left the meeting reassured, but a little uneasy. She imagined that probably even Barbara liked Kofi. She realized it was not going to be easy and she probably would have a fight on her hands to win his love. Meanwhile, when Hamma got home, rage was pounding in him like a drumbeat. His wife noticed the change in his demeanor, but she did not say anything. Later in the evening she found him reclining in his sofa chewing on a toothpick.

"You didn't look so happy when you came home tonight, Nick, what's up?" she asked.

"It's about that loser called Hope," he replied.

"What about him, Nick?"

"All the women are drooling over him," he swallowed hard, "I was really astonished at their reaction."

"Why's that Nick?" She asked, unable to hold her astonishment at her husband's reaction.

"They were all asking, 'where is Kofi, where is Kofi'?"

"That's understandable, the fellow went missing."

"Yes, but even Barbara, who appears to like no man, warned me to stay away from him otherwise she was going to deal with me."

"You mean the President's spokesperson?

"Yes."

"You need to be careful then, it seems you're in a war you're bound to lose."

Hamma had a grave look about him now, his edge of irritation had returned. He picked up a tops pillow and threw it at her. He was peeved at his wife for daring to challenge his decisions. He scowled at her;

"Watch your mouth woman."

After his wife ran off, he sat alone in silence thinking about what she had said. For a twenty-eight-year-old newcomer, Kofi Hope was very powerful. Even if his wife was right, he really didn't care; one thing he knew, he was going to let him see fire. Nobody can tussle with Honorable Nicholas the Hamma and prevail, he consoled himself.

CHAPTER 13

A PLACE TO CALL HOME

It was a gloomy April morning, but Kofi was in an ebullient mood. He had just returned from jail thanks in part to his auntie and to Barbara. He had spent a day and a night in hospital, but now he was feeling strong enough to go back to work. When he got there Ellen was already in her office working. She called out excitedly when she heard his approaching footsteps.

"Is that you Mr. Hope."

"Yes."

When he drew into sight, she smiled broadly at him.

"Sorry, what happened to you. We were all so worried about you," she said.

"Thanks, Ellen. That was surely a blip. But I'm glad everything worked out finally."

The feeling of relief and gratitude was mutual. He found her affable and a delight to have at the office, as she also did. The teamwork and good example set by these two were key to the success of the establishment. Both were hardworking and always the first at the office. Ellen was single and charming; but if any man thought they could take advantage of her good looks they would be deceiving themselves. For one thing though friendly and helpful, she was no pushover. Those were not the only reasons why he liked her. The two of them seemed to share a similar work ethic, but that was where it ended. His love was for Rebecca though he had not been able to make it clear to her. Presently he turned his attention back to her.

"Call me Kofi," he said.

"No, Mr. Hope, in this country, one must learn to address people properly. If I call you Kofi others might take it the wrong way."

"It's alright with me," he replied, "I was used to everybody calling me Kofi in America. I had grown accustomed to it."

He already had a backlog of work before his arrest, but losing a week of work did not help matters. He had decided to come in extra early today to try and catch up on his schedule. He plunged straight into work because there was a lot to do. Mostly it was paperwork he needed to study to get acquainted with his duties. Lisa had been helpful pointing out what he needed to do each day. She helped him set up a roster to follow to make best use of his time. He was a person who always appreciated what others did for him. He wanted to continue that habit because he knew it would get the best out of the people he would be working with. He praised her efficiency and greatly appreciated her input in his growth into his new job.

"You look very young and yet you are so efficient," he observed.

"Really," she smiled shyly, "how old do you think I am, sir?"

"Twenty-three."

"Close, I'm actually twenty-four," she teased.

He decided that it was okay to let matters end there because he wanted his relationship with her to be purely business and nothing more. They continued to work in silence. After working for a while, he sensed she was tired, so he asked her to take a break, whilst he continued to work. He was scrutinizing some spreadsheets when she came back in.

"There's a visitor to see you, sir," she announced.

"Do they have an appointment?"

"No sir."

"Okay make an appointment for. . . ."

In the middle of his sentence, a lady barged in with an ear-to-ear grin on her face. She was a young woman in her late twenties or early thirties; immaculately dressed to depict her standing in the society. He gave her an icy stare, but she seemingly took no attention. Instead, she strode gracefully across the room all the while staring at him with half-lidded eyes. She could see he was displeased to see her barge uninvited, but she was undeterred.

"Good morning, sir," she announced in a sweet and soothing voice.

"Good morning, madam." He motioned with his hands to a seat in front of his desk. "Won't you be seated?"

Gently, she pressed her dress from the back, with both hands before taking her seat. When she sat down, she emptied the contents of her handbag on his desk, took out a big brown envelope and handed it to him. When he received it, he turned it over several times in his hands.

"What is this envelope for? Madam?" He squinted his eyes to look inside the partially opened envelope.

"Go ahead, open it," she said.

He gasped when he found a stash of dollar notes in there. It was déjà vu all over again.

"What is this for?"

"It's a welcome token sir," she replied jubilantly.

Just as he did with the Acres fellow, he pushed the envelope back to her.

"I cannot take that," he said.

She rolled her eyes at him, "What, you don't want this?"

"I have already given you, my answer."

With a furrowed brow yet still managing a dimpled grin, she said; "Are you sure of what you are saying? This is money that can make your life here comfortable."

"Thank you anyway, but it would be most improper for me to take gifts."

Her jaw dropped and she just sat there pouting at him. This was the first time a government official had refused a gift from her.

"Actually, you're not the only one I do this to. All the other officials take money from me, so it's not something out of the ordinary."

"I don't mean to be rude, but you've overstayed your welcome. Now please leave before I call the police," he said.

Her eyes crinkled as she picked up her envelope, a quizzical smile on her face. Her audible exhalations were displayed in a pronounced sigh as she walked out of his office. It was already almost past lunchtime when he got up to go to the cafeteria. On his way he heard his lady visitor speaking to Hamma in his office. A little further down he met Lucy Bukari.

"I heard you were arrested, Mr. Hope," she said.

"Who told you I was arrested?"

"Barbara."

"Are you sure?"

"You don't seem to believe me," she said, a shaky smile on her face.

"So, should I ask her?"

"No, Mr. Hope, that won't be necessary."

He didn't want to be delayed further. "Excuse me, madam, I'm running late," he said.

When he reached the cafeteria, it was almost deserted. The only person there was Rebecca who had also come in late. Any feeling of anxiety or animosity created by his encounter with Lucy evaporated when he set his eyes on her. She was standing near the kitchen sink with her back to him. In the daylight she looked even more attractive than in the night at the party. Her curvaceous figure silhouetted well by a close-fitting dress perfectly tailored to bring out her contours. She glanced over her shoulder and saw him standing a few yards away from her. She then turned round and tilted her head backwards. As she did this, spools of her neatly braided hair plunged around her photogenic face. The braids seemed to hide a swan's neck, which was elegant and smooth. She dashed him a broad smile and gently pushed her hair backwards.

"Are you alright Mr. Hope, I was so worried about you," she said.

He gave a light-hearted smile and looked at her, reflective and adoring. Suddenly a calm cheerful feeling descended on him. She stood there still wearing her broad and beguiling smile lighting up the room with her oyster-white teeth. As they stood by the kitchen sink and chatted, he stole any opportunity he got to glance at her. Once she lifted her fingers to scratch her face, and he couldn't take his eyes off them. They were clean, slender, neatly manicured and bore nails which were perfectly filed and decorated with an innocuous polish meant to represent her pristine upbringing. He longed to reached out and touch her, but his mind went back to the party, and her male companions. Couldn't one of them be her fiancé. If they were, how come none of them sought her out when she was in the courtyard, and left her alone for such a long period?

"How do you feel now, Mr. Hope?"

"I feel perfectly alright."

She never once took her eyes off him as they spoke, neither did she bring up the topic of the arrest.

"Do you want something to eat?"

"Yes, I think I do."

"Well sit here and wait for me."

"Thank you very much," Kofi said graciously when Rebecca brought the food.

"You're welcome."

"How much do I owe you for the food, Miss Odom?"

Rebecca looked at him questioningly. "It is to welcome you back."

"Well, thank you," Kofi said as he looked admiringly at her.

"What?" Rebecca asked as she returned his admiration.

Their gazes were locked at each other; they were both in dreamland; but then she remembered the break time was long officially over so she said;

"Mr. Hope if you will excuse me, I have to get back to the office."

As she was marching out of the cafeteria she called out; "It's great to see you back."

By now the place was almost empty except for two people who had just entered, sitting there and talking over their late lunch. It was the chief of staff and the Attorney General. Kofi moved to a table away from them but just within earshot. The Attorney General was talking, but when he saw Kofi, he paused. The chief signaled to him that it was okay to continue.

"The trial is going to begin after I return from my working trip to the UK." He was saying.

"Have you decided whether the case should be tried by the bench or at a jury trial selected from the people?" The chief queried.

"Nope."

The chief turned abruptly towards Kofi and noticed that he was staring their way. He whispered something into the ears of his companion, and they changed the subject. As he sat there, Kofi wondered what case they were referencing. It could not be any other trial but that of the former government officials, he concluded. He was interested in that case because in his opinion it would serve as a warning to incumbent ministers who were still involved in corrupt activities. His only hope was that the President would extend the net to catch people in his administration who were also steep in corruption. He finished eating just about the time when they also left the cafeteria, but he waited for them to leave before returning to his office. After lunch he was in his office working on some papers when he received a message from Barbara to come to her office. When he got there Maggie was also there.

"Thank you very much for all you've done for me," he said.

"It was a pleasure to help Kofi," she said smiling, "by the way, the chief of staff has finally been able to assign you a flat."

"That's amazing, just great," said Kofi.

"Maggie will take you to see it whenever you're ready."

He turned to Maggie; "Okay Maggie, I'm ready whenever you are. Shall we go now?"

Maggie led the way to the parking lot where his assigned driver was waiting for them. They traveled in silence to an upscaled area of town. When they got there, the driver waited in the car while he and Maggie went in to inspect the flat. It was a beautiful three-bedroom flat with a big balcony in front and a garage. It was already fully furnished. All he would need were some personal items for cooking, as well as curtains and bedding. When they were done with the inspection, Maggie handed him his keys. Now he had his own apartment. Finally, a place to call home.

CHAPTER 14

TRIP TO THE MARKET

The next day at lunchtime, Kofi, overhead Rebecca asking Ellen if she wanted to go shopping with her after work. Ellen, however, said she had something to do so she couldn't go to the market. Kofi saw it as an opportunity to get to know her, and since she did not drive, he volunteered to drive her so he could also get some items he needed for his new flat. Rebecca thanked him but declined the offer. However, at the close of work, he pulled up at the curbside and waited for her. She was surprised when she saw him waiting for her.

"Hello Miss Odom."

"Hello Mr. Hope."

"I'm waiting for you as I promised."

"I thought I told you I would go alone?"

"I don't remember you saying so," he lied.

"But the market is no place for a man," she protested.

"Really?"

"You know, the open market's too chaotic for a man like you to go to."

Rebecca's fears stemmed from the fact that the central market in *Sikakrom* was reputed to be the largest in the whole region. Shopping there was hectic, the place was notorious for pick pockets, and she perceived somebody not used to going there would find it a tough place to go.

"A man like me, what are you talking about?"

"I didn't mean it negatively; oh well, if you insist." She could see the look of disappointment on his face, so she jumped into his truck and sat next to him in the front passenger seat.

"But I must warn you the market is no place for a man, Mr. Hope," she repeated.

"Please call me Kofi," he said.

She looked at him and was genuinely surprised. Men in *Abibiman* do not subscribe to being called by their first names. She probably thought either he was different, or he had just adopted the casual ways of the Americans.

"Okay. If you say so."

As the truck pulled away, and they were out of earshot, it was time to express her true feelings about his arrest.

"Sorry, I couldn't express my sympathy for your arrest the other day."

"It's alright Rebecca."

"You know, Barbara warned us not to speak about it to anybody."

"She did?"

His mind went to Lucy the other day on his way to lunch. He knew she was lying about learning about his arrest from Barbara. She was hell-bent on causing deep resentment amongst the presidential staffers, but he knew better than to believe her lies.

"You don't know she cares for you? She was as worried as any of us, she kept asking Maggie about you until your auntie came to her," Rebecca was saying.

"Oh."

"I was worried about you too."

He saw the agonized look on her face, so he touched her left hand that was on her lap with his right hand to comfort her. He squeezed it gently for a moment before letting it go. She wished he would have kept the physical contact. But it was early days yet, so she kept quiet instead of encouraging him to go on.

"If you don't mind, we could get some items for my new flat at the market?" He asked turning to glance at her.

"I wanted to suggest you would need help finding things for the flat but decided against it. I didn't want to give the impression I was being too pushy or nosey,"

She directed him to the vicinity of the market, and they found a convenient parking spot. She was perky and upbeat. Her designated work clothes were tight-fitting enough to outline her curvy form and delightfully bouncy breasts. As they drove, he would steal furtive glances at her. At one point their gaze met. As they stared at each other she wore an expression on her face that he was unable to articulate hovering between appreciation, wonder, and skepticism. She broke the silence.

"Did you used to go shopping in open markets when you were in the USA?"

"Yes, I did. In the US, the open markets are called flea markets. I usually went there whenever I needed to buy cheap plantain which was sold by the Latino vendors."

She was fascinated that he would go to buy plantain in a flea market, so she asked. "Do they have plantain in America?"

"Yes, of course. It's mostly eaten by the immigrants from Central and South America who are called Latinos or Hispanics," he explained.

"Are the vendors male or female?"

"It's a mixture of both, but there are more males than females in the flea market."

"Interesting," she observed, "here in our markets, there are more women than men sellers."

They found a place to park the truck and then started walking to the big outdoor market. They were walking at arm's length by the time they were entering the market. Kofi observed that this market was much bigger than the one his auntie sells from, and bigger than the flea markets he used to go to in Denver. It was also much more crowded and noisier. Most of the sellers here were women with rented spaces selling different kinds of merchandise. They ranged from used goods, low and high-quality items, such as collectibles and antiques, fresh produce, baked goods, plants from local farms and vintage clothes.

"Mr. Hope, sorry Kofi, you have to follow closely because you can easily lose me in this crowd," Rebecca warned as she hurried forward.

He took her warning as a command, so he obliged silently and hastened after her. Try as he might, he struggled to keep pace with her because she wasn't giving way to anyone, whereas he instinctively yielded to a passerby when they were competing for the same confined space. He was struck by her energy and assertiveness. As they went on, he began to come to grips with negotiating a path through the hustle of street market shopping. No wonder she warned him beforehand. She would stop by one stall after another to ask for the price of stuff but never bought anything. He was still finding it hard to keep space with her so he called for her to slow down but she couldn't hear him over all the noise. Fortunately, she looked over her shoulders and realized he was not directly behind her, so she stepped into a store entrance to wait for him. Kofi, however, did not see her and just kept going.

"Kofi! Kofi! Kofi!"

Rebecca shouted when she saw him passing but her voice was swallowed up by the cacophony of noise, so she reached out for his arm. At this point, she had sweat streaming down her face, but they were still glowing.

"Oh, I didn't see you standing there."

"Surely, with the crowds and the way business is conducted here it's always noisy so you've got to keep up otherwise we'll be separated."

Trading here was hectic, involving a lot of bargaining. The vendors and buyers haggle for merchandise until a price agreeable to both parties is reached. Rebecca seemed skillful in bargaining for prices. She astonished Kofi who watched her patiently as she bargained her way through all the items she bought. Presently, they came across some food vendors selling snacks and drinks. At this point Rebecca was feeling very thirsty and she thought Kofi might also be.

"Are you thirsty Kofi?"

"Yes. It's thirsty work walking through this scorching sun, trying to keep up with you," he replied teasingly.

She bought two bottles of Guinness Malt. The vendor opened two bottles and started pouring their contents into two plastic bags. Kofi was distracted by two women fighting over a customer; when he turned around, he saw what the vendor was doing and protested.

"Please can't you leave the drink in the bottles?"

The vendor looked at him puzzled. "These bottles are not mine," she said.

Rebecca saw his look of confusion so intervened to explain; "She has to return the bottles to the wholesaler who sold her the drinks so she can get her deposits back."

He was puzzled, this was not the practice before he left for America, but he went along with it. They continued, sucking on the sachets animatedly like two kids. A little further on, there was commotion. A woman was shouting.

"They're coming." Other women hearing the alarm joined in.

"Quickly, they're coming."

Several women darted out of their stores and started running in different directions as if trying to hide.

"Why are the women running?" he asked Rebecca with a perplexed expression.

"There are workers from the Internal Revenue Service going around the market and collecting taxes from the vendors."

"But that's a good thing."

"Well, the vendors don't see it that way. Those women you saw running don't want to pay the tax that's why they are running," she explained.

"Oh really?" Kofi covered his mouth to smother a laugh.

"Some of these vendors play games with the tax collectors."

This time he laughed out loud. "They do?"

"Yes, often when they see the tax people coming, they will run or hide somewhere until they're gone. Sometimes the police have to come in to help collect the taxes."

"Why would they be running because they wanted to avoid paying taxes?" This was one of the funny side of things in *Abibiman*.

"You tell me, Kofi."

"This is where the city authorities should devise a scheme to register and easily identify the traders so that no one could run from the law."

"I agree, it's long overdue."

"But you know, whether the women like it or not, taxes keep any economy going. In the USA even buyers pay taxes on things they buy."

"Well, we have something similar here called Valued Added Tax, but it's not on everything you buy."

Just then they heard a man shout behind them.

"Give way! Give way!"

They turned around and it was two men who were pulling a wooden trolley loaded with lots of different goods. As it passed, two other trolleys carrying heavy sacks of rice followed. They only went forward a few stores when they heard another shout.

"Mind your backs, Make way!"

This time it was a much bigger trolley. It was fully laden with furniture. Two men were pulling it, and another two pushing from behind. The strain they were under was obvious. Not only was their load heavy but it was also cumbersome, requiring extra vigilance to stop it from toppling. All four men were sweating underlining the strain they were under. By now it was becoming apparent that this was the lane used predominantly by delivery trolleys, so Rebecca suggested they move to another part of the market. She had been mainly buying foodstuffs so when she was done, they went to the area dealing with hardware and other household items, so that Kofi could buy some items for his flat. He discovered he didn't have enough money on him to buy all the things he needed, so they only purchased some essentials. After this they headed to the truck. It was a relief to escape the crowds and noise. When they sat down in the truck Rebecca asked him a question that had been on her mind all afternoon.

"So, Kofi how are you finding life in *Abibiman* now that you are back?"

"It's good. I'm feeling at home, but I'm still studying the system."

"What about work, do you like the people there?"

"I like all the people at work, especially Ellen," he looked at Rebecca who looked puzzled, so he added, "and of course you."

She wore a perplexed look at the mention of Ellen's name, but her face relaxed a little when he mentioned her too.

"Do you get along with everybody Kofi?"

"Yes, I like to think I do." He didn't want to bring up Hamma.

"How do you see the chief of staff?"

"Well, he's okay, but why do you ask about him and not the President?"

"You know he is your boss, and you directly report to him and not the President?"

He had not thought about it that way before, but Rebecca was right.

"Well Kofi, around here, his word is law," she remarked idly, "even for those of us who work directly with the President, you dare not step on his toes."

They drove alone mostly in silence, making occasional small talk all the way to Rebecca's house. She thanked him for taking her to the market and apologized for making him tired.

"Not at all," he protested.

"Would you mind going with me to my apartment so that I can cook something for you?"

"Oh, thank you very much, it's a nice idea but I'd perhaps do it another time. Better still what about I invite you out on a date for dinner?"

He could see that she was startled. She hesitated for a moment before replying.

"Okay. So, when shall we do this?"

"Any date and time of your choosing."

"All right then. I'll leave you now to go home. Rest well. Goodbye."

He watched her until she was inside, then he drove away.

CHAPTER 15

HUMILIATED

Kofi was very appreciative of the role Barbara had played to release him from jail. He thought there was going to be a court case, but Barbara told him not to worry because she had got the case expunged. She assured him that there was no record of the arrest, and there was nothing to worry about. It appeared she had pulled all the right strings. Out of respect for Barbara he decided to let it go. He was hoping that the matter would be taken to court so that he could prove his innocence. But then this was *Abibiman* where people could be arrested and charged for no reason whatsoever. Hence, it was probably good that the matter was done with.

He was worried about one thing though. Who was behind the arrest, and why and how did they get the lanky boy, Suleimana to lead them to him? What about Yakubu? What was his role? He determined that he would find the boy or his uncle and asked about their involvement. Finally, he settled on finding Suleimana as it might be easier to find him than the older man. He drove to the neighborhood where the boys were playing football on his way to work and parked his truck. He asked around if anybody knew Suleimana. They pointed him toward the other end of the street. The road that led to the direction they pointed to him was reduced to a mass of ridges and gullies. He did not want to risk driving further, so he locked the truck and set off on foot. It was also littered with refuse. It appeared people never took the time to dispose of their waste properly here. Stinking water from makeshift bathhouses was running everywhere.

Amid this squalid environment, there was buying and selling at every corner. He had to hold his breath to keep walking but the majority of the people who lived there were oblivious of the stench. As he plodded along, he wondered if the politicians knew about places like this. He was sure that they did not have any inkling of what it might be like to be genuinely destitute. There was no obligation for the bigwigs to go wandering around in slum areas of their constituents to get acquainted with their situation. He was really getting angry and depressed as he kept walking towards the direction the children pointed to him. With the people living in such an environment, it was sad that his colleagues wantonly dipped their hands into the national coffers to meet their own needs instead of supporting people who lived in such abject poverty.

He was convinced that if he desired to be an activist for the people more trips like this to observe their plight first-hand would be necessary. It was the only way he could become a credible advocate for these poor and downtrodden citizens. Those children pointed to a certain direction, and he had been walking that way for a while. He continued to ask more children he saw as he went forward. It looked like Suleimana was very popular in the neighborhood. After a little while he asked another group of children. They knew him and pointed to a little ramshackle house at the end of the dirt-ridden street. Several children were gathered in front of the house, and they made way for him to go inside. An overweight woman was sitting in the compound of the little rickety house washing clothes in a bucket with her hands. He greeted her politely and asked about Suleimana.

"So, tell me, who are you?" The woman asked.

As she looked at Kofi, she was puzzled that such a well-dressed man would know of her little Suleimana. Then it occurred to her that he might be the man who bought them a football.

"Are you the fellow who gave the children the football?"

"Yes ma'am," he replied.

The woman stared hard at him fury surging through her. This time it was not a look of mystery but that of scorn.

"Can you wait for me sir?" She suggested.

The woman got up, wiped her hands with one of the cloths she was washing and dashed into her room. Kofi didn't know what was going on with her, so he just stood there and waited. Shortly after she went inside, the woman returned, carrying a bucketful of dirty water perfectly balanced on her head. It was water she had collected from her cooking. She was waiting for her children to come home so they could dump it in the drain outside their house. As she got closer to him, she lifted the bucket off her head, and poured its content all over him.

"Oh! Oh!" Kofi shouted, his mouth gaping widely.

"Pee! Pee! I'm trying to get the boy to stay home, and study and you buy him a football. See, now he doesn't stay at home."

Now Kofi stood there smelly and drenched. It would take a good shower to get rid of the foul smell. Even after doing all this to him, the woman would not let it end there.

"Useless man," she marinated in resentment, "what is it you want with my son?"

By all indications, her action was likely prompted by sheer jealousy and resentment of seeing another person so well dressed whilst she floundered in poverty. Suleimana never stayed at home before the football gift. Football or no football, he just couldn't be pinned down. In her indignation, the woman had shouted so loud that the children who were outside rushed into the house when they heard the uproar going on inside. They saw Kofi just standing there all wet, the water dripping from all over his body. They chuckled at first then broke into a belly laugh. You could see that they were trying to stop themselves from laughing. However, one of the children had broken into laughter, before the others all joined in and laughed hysterically. Kofi felt humiliated. His head was spinning, and he couldn't think straight. Why would anybody treat another person they barely know this way? He just turned round and started back down the road towards his car.

She kept following him clapping and shouting;

"Meddler", "meddler."

Behind her were the children who were having fun at his expense. She was creating quite a spectacle with all her shouting. Other people came from their houses to watch a man dripping with water and a woman following him shouting slurs at him. When Kofi slowed down, she slowed down, when he quickened his steps, she did likewise; but he refused to break into a trot which would have discouraged her, instead he walked in quick strides. In this community you dare not do that, because one wrong step, one wrong move and you would be mistaken for a robber, a thief. People stopped him to ask what was going on. But he had no desire to stop and explain. He was in such haste to get away from the woman he did not see a girl carrying oranges approaching until they collided. Her oranges ran all over the place. It took the generosity of the kids who were following him to help her pick them up. All the while, the girl was crying about the oranges and wondering what her parents would do to her when she returned home.

As for Kofi, he just kept walking. At this point, the stench was too much for him to bear. He took off his shirt and threw it away. There was a scramble for it on the side of the street, which broke into a fistfight. In the ensuing melee, the people's attention was no longer on him. This discouraged the woman, who turned around and returned to her house. Finally, he was able to escape her attention and insults. When he reached his truck, he breathed a sigh of relief: he had been to the lioness's den. He drove back home to have a shower and a change of clothing. All this had happened in the early hours of a busy Monday morning, so he had no choice but to go to work despite his harrowing experience. He got to the office almost at the same time that Ellen was getting there.

"You're early today, Kofi," she observed.

"That's right. I left home early today to attend to some business."

He was enthusiastic in his response, but he alone knew what he had gone through. He wanted the incident of the morning to vanish from his memory, so he was not going to look sad. They walked side-by-side to the office, talking about mundane things. When they got inside Kofi headed towards his office to begin work for the day.

"Must you go so soon Kofi?" Ellen asked.

It was apparent she wanted to talk. She didn't seem to have any true friends at work and often sorted out Kofi to speak to since his arrival. Today, he was not interested in talking.

"Yes," he finally replied, smiling broadly, "I have work to attend to urgently."

"Don't we all, Kofi, but sometimes, you have to get a little time to talk to your friends."

"Okay, if you insist," he said resignedly.

"There is nothing urgent Kofi. As you can see, the other workers are not yet in. Must we be the only ones to kill ourselves with work?"

"Is that Ellen talking or am I dreaming?"

Kofi lingered on for a little while. He went with her to the break room to brew some coffee. When the coffee was ready, he grabbed a cupful and headed towards his office. This time, Ellen did not object. He had some expenditure records he needed to finish studying, so he went straight to them. First, he looked at the account statement for the office of the president. There were a lot of phone calls made to overseas locations. Some of these calls would go on for hours. He sat there and wondered why calls were made to certain numbers repeatedly. He dialed one of the numbers on the bill from his cell phone. A girl picked it at the other end. He disguised his voice and asked who he was speaking to.

"May I know who I have the pleasure of speaking to?"

"My name is Sarah Biney, a student from *Abibiman* here in Canada."

That rang a bell to him. She was the daughter of the chief of staff.

"Oh, Sarah do you live in Toronto?"

"Yeah, in a Toronto suburb called Scarborough."

"Well Sarah, I was trying to reach a girlfriend of mine who lives in Brampton, so sorry for taking some of your time?

"No problem."

He dialed three more numbers to the UK and the USA. There were several questionable expenditures on the accounts. These included hotel bills and some payments to some brothels in Canada and the USA. After finishing his inspection of the accounts, he sat there confused and beside himself. These government operatives all have their children attending prestigious schools overseas. That was okay if they were supporting them from their own resources. However, the phone bills suggested they were using government funds to support their wards. These people were using the office phones to make private calls to their children for hours on end, all at public expense. What about expenditure listing brothels? Should the people be made to pay for somebody's profligacy?

By now, his anger was mounting; this government, while busily prosecuting the former officials, was clearly no saints themselves. He found it difficult to understand why they often put up mock prosecutions involving current government operatives as a show of parity in their dispensing of justice? But justice never comes because, in most cases, at some point during the prosecution, the government controversially discontinued the cases and quietly let the matter drop. On the other hand, this government had dealt ruthlessly with the operatives of the previous government. This is clearly a case of selective judgment. Kofi was pretty sure this was not the first time this had happened. Probably, the operatives of the former government are suffering now because the actions of the government made them believe they were above the law. That is exactly what this present administration is doing. In all estimation they felt secure in how they plunder the wealth of the nation.

What disgusted him most was the façade they put up before and during election campaigns. Even they seemed to recognize that there was a limit to how long they could take the people for granted. He knew from experience that in most developing countries, as in *Abibiman*, the officials were not above embezzling funds they contracted as development loans from some Western countries and institutions. It was so hypocritical that their experiment with and exploitation of the system would be halted during the electioneering period lest the people discover, punish, and vote them out.

Though he had only been working with the administration for a short time, he was already appalled about their approach to tackling the economic woes of the country. How long would *Abibiman* continue to suffer at the hands of its own citizens who are supposed to know better. He was determined to bring all the cases he was uncovering to light because the law is no respecter of persons. As he sat there and contemplated this troubled predicament, it seemed he had fallen into a trance only to be roused by Lisa announcing there was somebody to see him. It was the President with the chief of staff and Barbara. He stood up when he saw them.

"Good afternoon, Sir," he said.

"Good afternoon, Mr. Hope," the President and his companions replied.

"Mr. Hope, the President wanted to visit with you," Barbara explained.

"If the mountain does not go to Mohammed, Mohammed will go to the mountain," the President explained mockingly.

"Sir . . . excuse me sir . . . ? Kofi struggled to explain why he had not been to his office.

"It's okay Mr. Hope, I know you are busy."

Kofi explained what he was doing and how far he had come. He told him he was building a system aimed at weeding out corrupt practices from the system and making every team member responsible. The President expressed his appreciation and left.

CHAPTER 16

WOKEN BY AN ANGEL

In *Abibiman*, if it was not raining, the sun would soon be up high and shining. Rainy days are not terrible because they cool the temperature, but sunny days are always better. When Rebecca got up it was sunny, but it was not a particularly hot day. Once she peered out of her window, she saw that the sky was bright blue and cloudless. She was convinced it would be a beautiful day to be outside; for a good day in the sun was always soothing to her. She took a stool which she had stacked under her bed and went outside to sit and enjoy the bright new day. Though the sun was shining brightly, there was an area with considerable shade. She positioned her stool in the shaded area and sat down to read a book.

Sometime later, the shade she was sitting under continued to diminish as the sun rose higher and relentlessly moved in her direction. With that development, she decided it was time to go back inside. She had left her phone in the room when she went outside. She saw there were several missed calls, about six of which were from her friend Ashley. She had her friend on speed dial, so it was very easy to call her back and the call went through first time.

"Where have you been, girlfriend?" Ashley enquired. She was relieved though because she thought something might have happened to her. It was not like Rebecca not to pick her calls.

"Sorry Ash. I was just sitting outside reading."

"How are you doing dear?"

"Great," Rebecca replied chirpily, "everything's great."

"You sound very happy, what's going on."

"Everything."

"What's everything?"

"Work, life, everything is going well."

"Good, some specific examples?"

"Went shopping with him."

"Him? Who?"

"Kofi, of course."

"Who is Kofi?"

"Oh, Mr. Kofi Hope, the new employee."

"You mean your dream man, the American Burger?"

"Yes."

"How did you manage to catch him so soon?"

"I wouldn't put it that way. He only wanted to see how the market has changed since the last time he was there."

"Don't be too modest Rebecca why didn't he go with anybody but you?"

"It gets even better."

"Yes?

"He wants to take me out on a date tomorrow."

"Wow! That's my girl."

"Thanks, girlfriend."

Ashley suggested it would be a good idea to shop for a new dress and visit the beauty salon. A few minutes after hanging up, she got into a taxi to Rebecca's. The two went to the mall to look for a new outfit. Rebecca tried different types of dresses and settled on one she felt would make her attractive to Kofi. From the mall, they went to the beauty salon. Rebecca chose to have her hair braided. After several hours, the braids had only half been completed so Ashley left her to go back home. It was well into the late evening when she returned home, worn out by all the time she spent having her hair done. However, she was extremely satisfied with her new hairdo and the dress she bought. She was so pleased with herself; she didn't notice her weariness. She slumped into her loveseat to salivate the time she would adorn herself with her beautiful dress to meet the man of her dreams. She was the happiest person in *Abibiman*.

Kofi sat in the restaurant where Rebecca told him to meet her. It was past the hour mark, and she still was not there. He began to wonder whether she would show up or not. He thought that she was probably just caught up in traffic. As he sat there pondering her whereabouts, he dozed off. He was awakened by a tap on his shoulder. When he opened his eyes, it was Rebecca standing in front of him. She was grinning broadly displaying a set of dazzling, angel-white teeth, exquisitely dressed and stunningly beautiful. Her hair was superbly braided and appropriately adorned with beads and her arched eyebrows with the sweeping eyelashes looked even more prominent.

Everything about Rebecca tonight made her appearance desirable. She was a completely transformed person from the work colleague at the office. Her face was shining, her lips suddenly appeared puffy and were seemingly pleading for a kiss. He stood up and smiled at her but he did not hug her. All the while as he stood, he contemplated whether to kiss or hug her in greeting; would it be too much of an ask on a first date? Was his fascination and amazement an overwhelming sense of love, or of delusion? He had never felt that way in his life before, so though he stood there motionless and mortified, he was also very happy. Rebecca felt uncomfortable at the silence, so she gently cleared her throat and fluttered her eyelids rapidly at him. He looked at her questioningly.

"What's on your mind Kofi? You seemed to be deep in thought," she asked.

Even after she spoke, he remained speechless; he simply looked at her and marveled. He was obviously struggling with his feelings, not knowing what to do or say. He was resisting any desire to sweep her off her feet; but Rebecca was looking so pretty he couldn't keep it to himself.

"You're looking so beautiful," he finally whispered.

Rebecca pretended she did not hear him. "What did you say, Kofi?" She wanted to hear him say it again.

"I said you are beautiful," he whispered again.

As he said that, he could feel her presence in an enticingly new way. Her constellation bright brown eyes were gazing at him now and absorbing all the plaudits he was giving her.

"Thank you very much Kofi," she was smiling broadly now, "you are so kind."

He reached out, took her hands and held on to them.

"We are not just going to stand like this all night, are we, Kofi?" Rebecca asked after a while.

"What about we order some food and sit down to talk?" Kofi suggested.

"Great idea," she agreed.

As they waited for the food they talked about the weather, life in *Abibiman* and some mundane small talk safe subjects. He had really no dating experience, so he was feeling self-conscious, clumsy and awkward and did not know what to talk about. However, as they sat down to eat and the evening wore on, he started to relax and grow in confidence. He started talking enthusiastically, as he found Rebecca an easy person to get along with. She had sensed his initial shyness and discomfort and wanted to make him feel good about himself. She was the one asking the questions.

"Can you tell me a little about yourself?"

"I was born in a little village in the province."

"Thought you had never been to a village?"

"Why?"

"Well, you look so clean, so polished and refined" she smiled broadly as she said this.

"Thank you, that is a compliment coming from a pretty lady like you."

A favorite song of hers was playing now so she invited him to the dancing floor. Her dancing was refined and exquisite while Kofi's was disjointed and out of step with the music. The evening passed by quickly and soon it was time to go home. They rode together in his truck, first to drop Rebecca off before he went home.

"I'm so glad you agreed to go on a date with me, Miss Odom," Kofi said, trying to be formal.

"It was a pleasure being with you Mr. Hope," Rebecca returned his formality mainly out of sarcasm. He smiled at her mockery but said nothing about it.

"Well Rebecca, would you like to go on another date in the future?"

Rebecca hesitated and considered the ramifications of a rushed answer. He saw her dilemma so to avert an awkward silence, he added;

"Don't you think it will help us get to know each other better?"

"Well, I must say it was a pleasure to be in your company Mr. Kofi Hope. On the face of that, a future date would be very agreeable," she replied finally.

This meeting came sooner than Kofi had envisaged. It was about a week after their outing. He was going through his morning routine when he got a telephone call from her. It was both their day off and she had nothing to do with her time. She suggested that since they were not working, she wanted to come over so they could take a stroll around town. He was still unpacking his stuff, but he thought that could wait.

"Sure," he agreed without hesitation.

As Rebecca hung up, he sat down and contemplated whether she had also fallen in love with him. At any rate, he had no problem because there was nobody, he wanted to be with more than her. It did not take long for Rebecca to get to his place. They drove to the center of town and parked at an accessible place. This was different from his walk with Maggie where they mainly navigated the neighborhood. They found a car park to park for a fee so that the truck would be secure and easily accessible when they decided to go home. They walked in silence for some time. That gave Kofi the time to observe the passers-by. He saw people of different races and nationalities. He noticed that there was a marked improvement in the lifestyle of people, and the city was more cosmopolitan. Before he left for America, you hardly came across other nationalities. This time it was different. Additionally, people seemed more affluent and better dressed than he could ever remember. Judging by this outward appearance, it suggested times were improving.

He saw more men immaculately dressed in three-piece suits and shiny black shoes. He wondered how they could be comfortable dressed like that in the hot scorching sun. Others were dressed casually just as they would do at home. Those were probably people who were simply walking around or going to jobs that did not require a formal dress code. The women also came in different shapes and sizes. Here again, there was a contrast from his time here before. In the past, most women were big and fleshy. Today however, there were many more slim and younger ladies. Just as they ranged from slim to medium to well built, so the ladies all had varying skin tones. One woman, he noticed, was unusually dark in complexion which seemed to have a beauty unique about it. Her hair was thick and kinky as if coiled into small, tiny balls. She had protruding hips and bulging buttocks that made her tempting to look at.

They came to the main bus, or as they are known here, lorry station, where people were busy at work mingling with and selling to travelers. Some were selling food drinks and other items to travelers; some drivers mates were shouting for passengers, while others sold herbal medicines. The unique sights and sounds, the different activities, filled Kofi with an overwhelming sense of awe and admiration. What might appear chaotic worked remarkably efficiently.

"What are you thinking about, Kofi?" Rebecca asked, seeing him lost in thought.

"Nothing, I'm just admiring the different people we keep coming across."

"Why?" She smiled affectedly.

"Why?" he asked puzzled.

"I meant there's nothing different about them. Don't you see crowds of black people in America?" Rebecca asked surprised.

She did not seem to share his sense of awe because she was so accustomed to the scene it was unremarkable to her.

"Kofi, have you always been so congenial in your life?" she asked, probably to get him to talk more.

He told her a little more about his childhood, moving from the village to live with other people. As a ten-year-old moving away from home, he became socially disoriented. This had prompted his guardians to pay closer attention to his movements and actions. However, the more vigilant and stricter they became, the more resentful and withdrawn he turned out. It was only after the age of eighteen when he realized his guardians had been working for his good. With their help, he studied hard and was eventually able to go to university and then to America.

"Oh Kofi, sorry you had to go through all that. In *Abibiman*, most children get uprooted and have to leave home and that's not ideal," Rebecca acknowledged, "but I'm very proud of you for how far you've come."

"Well thank you," he responded touched by her compliment.

"You are a determined person, Kofi," she smiled at him, "see how you grasped the opportunity presented to you with both hands."

"What do you mean Rebecca?"

"Pursuing education when you were in America. Most people when they get the chance to go overseas, only work to make money but you didn't do that."

As they were walking, they passed a restaurant.

"Let's eat dinner before we go home," Kofi suggested.

"Why not come back to my house so I can cook something for us to eat?" Rebecca asked.

"No," he put his index finger on her lips.

"Okay you win," she said without putting up a fight.

The restaurant was small but very clean. They went in and found a table close to a corner by itself. This time around, when the waiter came, he invited Rebecca to order first. He also ordered the same dish as her. When they finished eating and were heading out, Kofi saw an ice cream shop.

"Hey Rebecca, care for some ice cream?"

"I'm trying to keep my weight in check."

"If you ask me, I'd say you're thin enough to eat ice cream."

They both broke into laughter, and she reluctantly acceded to his suggestion

"Okay if you say so."

They bought some ice cream and headed for his truck. They talked freely about their dreams, hopes, and aspirations. It appeared they had known each other all their lives. It was a good evening, but now they had to go home; they were both visibly tired.

CHAPTER 17

PICKLE AND A NIGHT
ON THE SOFA

K ofi dropped Rebecca at her apartment before he went home. It had been a good day. It felt like he had known her all his life and couldn't imagine his life without her in it. He didn't want to go back to unpacking so he decided he would take a shower and go straight to bed. Barely had he finished bathing than she called him on the phone.

"Hello Kofi, please I was just calling to make sure you got home safely."

They stayed on the phone for hours. Telephone calls in *Abibiman* were very expensive because you had to pay per minute. However, at night most companies give free airtime. That night, their conversation went on and on. If she decided to hang up, he would bring a new topic; if he decided to hang up, she would bring a new topic. It was getting well on towards midnight when they finally hung up and went to bed. When Kofi awoke, he was a little bleary-eyed and sore from turning in so late. Rebecca however, slept a little more because she did not start work as early as he did. After eating breakfast, he packed something for her also and drove to her apartment. She was still sleeping when he got there. It took a couple of knocks before she woke up and came to the door. She looked tired and had dark circles under her eyes.

"What are you doing here, Kofi?" A yawning and sleepy Rebecca managed to ask.

"Can I come in?"

She stood aside to let him in. She was still in her nightie. As a junior staff, she did not qualify for staff housing. All she could afford was a studio apartment. She had a curtain separating her bed and dressing area from her sitting area. When she let him in, she rushed to her dressing area for a piece of cloth, which she tied over her nightie because it was transparent. She didn't like the man she loved to see her in the state she was in, but she did not complain. She reasoned that he was only doing a good deed in coming over to give her a ride to work. She took a bucket and went outside her room. When she returned, she had taken her bath already. She went to her dressing area and stayed for what seemed like eternity. When she re-emerged, she was dressed and ready for work.

"I brought you some breakfast, so don't bother to prepare anything," he told her when she came out.

"Do you sleep at all Kofi?"

"Why?"

"Didn't we speak on the phone till nearly midnight?"

"Yes, but I'm an early bird."

She took the food he brought her, gratefully. It was in a food flask, so it was warm enough. He had made scrambled eggs, two sandwiches stuffed with diced onions, pickles, lettuce and tomato. She took a bite of the sandwich and realized it tasted different from the ones commonly made in *Abibiman*. She didn't like the taste of the pickles, so she started to take them out.

"What are these?"

"Pickles, made from salted baby cucumbers."

"I don't like the taste of it."

"Try it you might get to like it. When I first went to America, I was invited to a friend's home and was offered a pickle sandwich."

"Did you like it?"

"No, but now I do, I think it's good for you."

Rebecca tried to eat it, but you could see her grimace as she bit on the pickles.

"It's not as bad as I thought," she said when she was done eating.

The drive to work took a longer time because the diversion past Rebecca's place meant there was more traffic than usual. However, they made it in good time. After work, Kofi found Rebecca standing in the lobby about to get outside, as he came by. He wasn't sure if she was waiting for him hoping for a ride. Since she did not say anything, he waved goodbye to her and went outside, only to return shortly afterwards. She was still standing at the same place, her hands shoved into her front pockets.

"Did you forget something Kofi?" She asked when she saw him return.

"The clouds are gathering," he replied, breathing heavily, "It looks like it's going to rain. Come on let's go."

He looked at her and hoped his explanation was good enough. As for Rebecca, she didn't say anything. She just looked at him alluringly and with a quirk of her lips, agreed to follow him.

"It's going to rain so I came back to get you," he repeated.

Outside and looking up at the darkening sky, she realized he was serious about the inevitability of rain, so she followed him to the Jeep.

"Thanks for coming back to get me Kofi," she said.

"You're always welcome, fair maiden," he replied without looking at her.

Rebecca looked at Kofi intrigued. She did not know what he implied by addressing her that way, but she did not want to cause any fuss. They drove on in silence for a while until Kofi broke the silence.

"My first trip with the President is coming on in a week's time."

"Oh, yeah?"

"And since tomorrow's a holiday, I intend to use the long weekend to visit my parents in the village."

"Oh, that's sweet. Can I come with you?"

"It's too treacherous a journey for a woman to undertake."

She smiled and looked at him slyly almost as if she was flirting and flatly dismissed his assertion.

"Let's look at it this way. You just returned from America, and you can safely go to a village. I've lived in *Abibiman* all my life, but I cannot go to a village? Who are you Kofi? A chauvinist?"

"Oh, oh, oh, don't take it that far," he protested.

"I didn't mean it in the wrong sense," she said.

"OK, you are in, but don't say I didn't warn you," he cautioned her.

The sky had darkened by the time they got to Rebecca's apartment.

There was no way she was going to allow her loved one to go out there into the impending storm.

"You cannot go out there and drive home, Kofi," she advised, concerned shown in her voice.

"No, I must go home," he insisted.

Rebecca did not raise any objections. So, she let it appear initially.

"Okay I will see you off to your truck."

"No, you don't need to see me off, the rain will soon start," he protested.

She didn't give in to his protest though, so they started walking to his truck.

"Can I take a look at the keys to your truck?"

He unsuspectingly gave them to her. When she took it, she turned around and began walking back to her apartment.

"Hey come back, you have my keys," he protested.

"Catch me if you can."

As she said that, she started running towards her apartment with his keys in her hands. He then had no choice except to follow her into her apartment. Just like the morning when he picked her up to go to work, she went behind the curtains as soon as they entered. When she resurfaced, she had changed into casual clothing. The only place she could cook dinner was in the compound of the apartment building, but with the rain approaching, that was not possible. She stood there confused with frown lines drawing on her pretty face. A picture of Rebecca with a man and a woman, probably her parents, hung on the wall. Whilst Rebecca stood there and contemplated what to do, Kofi walked to the picture and took it from where it was hanging on the wall.

"That was me and my parents taken on my sixteenth birthday. I remember I didn't want my siblings in the picture, just me and my parents," Rebecca explained, her brow relaxed and free of the frown there a moment before.

"Sweet sixteenth," Kofi said.

"Why sweet sixteenth?" She asked.

"In America the sixteenth birthday is a big thing. They call it sweet sixteenth. It always gets the teenagers excited, so they celebrate it big," Kofi explained.

"I'm not sure I knew about the concept at the time; however, I felt that it was a special moment since I was soon going to transition from adolescent into adulthood," she said.

"You're very lucky, Rebecca," he said smiling, "I never had any experiences like that since I was not living with my parents at the age of sixteen."

She moved closer to him and rubbed his back. "I'm sorry Kofi," she said.

"No, I'm alright, but am happy that you have such memories you can always cherish," he said.

He replaced the photograph on the wall and went over to her dining table. It was overlaid with a beautiful, embroidered material.

"Do you like my tablecloth?" she asked flirtatiously.

"Yes, it's beautiful."

She smiled broadly at him. "I made it myself," she said.

"Wow that's amazing," he exclaimed, genuinely astonished that she could do that.

Her mind now turned back to dinner. The frown lines returned as she considered her next step to prepare dinner for the night. She ducked into her dressing area again and came out with a small electric stove.

"I bought this for emergencies like tonight," she said.

She turned towards Kofi and handed his car keys back to him. He took his keys back and smiled at her. She blushed and smiled back at him showing her oyster white teeth.

"Don't worry about food because cooking conditions are not the best," he told her.

"I hope, Mr. Kofi Hope recognizes Rebecca is a true *Obibini* who cannot allow her guest to sleep hungry?" she said coquettishly.

He didn't say anything. He just watched as she hurriedly prepared a very sumptuous dinner for two. They sat down and ate together. It was the first time he had sampled her cooking and he enjoyed it. As they were eating, the rain continued and became heavier. By now he was getting worried. There was intermittent lightning that kept flashing across the sky. Occasionally, they would be followed by a deep rumble of thunder. This frightening phenomenon was accompanied by a gusty wind that shook everything in its way. Rebecca's roof was shaking with the repeated rumbles. At a point the shaking stopped but the rain intensified, the noise on the corrugated iron roof sheets was deafening.

The water from the rainfall got trapped on the ridges and started leaking through different parts of the roof onto the floor. She ran into the courtyard, and he followed her to get some buckets to collect the water that was dripping through the spots where there were holes in the corrugated iron sheets. They had not known each other for too long a time, but that didn't matter. They felt comfortable in each other's presence and company. The rain continued well into the night. Though he wanted to be home and sleeping on his own bed, he knew she wouldn't allow him to go out there and drive home in such weather, so he stayed. Besides, not only was the next day a public holiday, but they would be travelling together, so it made sense to stay the night. After they had eaten, they sat down to play a game of *ludo,* a popular game commonly played in many homes in *Abibiman.* They played two rounds, both of which she won. She was gracious in her win and did not make fun of him. Soon it was time to sleep.

"Please I have made the bed for you," she said.

"And where are you going to sleep?"

"The couch."

"No, I can sleep on the couch," he said.

She took a bed sheet, which she had never used, to make a bed for him on her couch. Sleeping after rainfall was always enjoyable for him. He slept soundly even though he only had an unfamiliar couch for a bed.

CHAPTER 18

MEETING HIS PARENTS

At about four-thirty in the morning, Rebecca was already up. She gently tapped him on the shoulders to wake him up also. Then they drove to his flat to prepare for their journey to the village. When they got there, they both took their shower. Afterward, whilst she prepared breakfast, and some food for the road; he also packed their luggage and put the extra food into the truck. Then they sat down for breakfast.

The sun had not come up when they set off from *Sikakrom*. It was still dusk. Slowly as the dusk gave way to daylight, God's morning star arose like a fiery ball in the sky. Sunrise though brought its problems. Since they were driving eastward, it shone into their eyes and made driving difficult. However, on the brighter side, with sunrise, the beauty of the scenery became more evident. The road was mainly asphalted in the urban area surrounding *Sikakrom*. However, as they left the built-up area behind, the road became serpentine and rocky and seemingly meandered into the great unknown. Driving on it even in a robust off-road jeep required care to avoid the potholes. Their route was dotted with towns and villages as they drove on. In places, there were patches of grassland and steppe underscoring the pressure the once forested land had been subjected to slash and burn by loggers and farmers to clear it for agriculture. This exploited land soon gave way to thick forest.

From afar, it seemed impenetrable, but as they drew closer it dazzled with splendor bestowing on them a soul-swelling experience. In this rainy season it was obviously in full luxuriant growth, with its canopy forming lances of molten-gold beams that swept to the ground. It was sufficiently nourished from the abundant rains that have been falling lately; a magnificent sight to behold. The soul of this pristine rainforest still intact was clearly not yet suffering from the avarice and ruthlessness with which others, even in *Abibiman*, had been exploited. Kofi wondered how long it would be before this area too would be plundered for its timber and abundant mineral resources. He felt such an untouched area should be protected for its scenery, biodiversity and as a tourist attraction.

As they went further away from *Sikakrom*, the road meandered through rugged terrain, but it was no obstacle to the Wrangler. It rambled on through alternating rocky outcrops and flatter low-lying marshy areas, but the vehicle negotiated it all with ease almost as if it was driving on asphalt. It helped eliminate the obstacles that would have ordinarily impeded their progress. Only occasional trucks and animals being herded slowed them down. They saw men and women walking by the road mainly going to work on farms. The men often were only carrying their machete while some of the women carried pans on their heads with their babies tied with pieces of their clothing to their back.

"Do you know in America women and men carry their babies in front?" Kofi said.

"Really, how do they do that?"

"They put them in baby carriers and tie them around their midsection with the babies lying on their bellies."

She had this whimsical look on her face but did not say anything; she was having difficulty imagining such a strange method of carrying babies. After several hours of driving, they came upon the first larger town on their route; it was the municipal capital, a sign they were getting close to his parents' village. He remembered this town because they would stop there whenever they were going to the village. His parents did not own a car, and this was the last stop for the bus that brought them from *Sikakrom*. When they got here, they would wait for the smaller local *trotros* that went to the village. Today it looked noticeably cleaner, and the streets were nicely paved. He was really astonished at the transformation that had taken place in that town.

"What happened to this town? I mean why is it so much cleaner than the smaller places we passed through?"

"They appointed new and progressive people to the town council who had aggressively being tackling the problems of the town," she answered.

"Isn't that amazing, I wish all the towns could be like this."

Suddenly she remembered they had not bought any bread for their host.

"Hey Kofi, we didn't buy any bread for your folks," she said.

"Is it something we have to do? We have other things to give them."

"You're right Kofi, but in the villages, they hardly get any bread to eat. So, when somebody is coming from *Sikakrom*, they always expect that you will bring some."

They pulled over so they could buy bread from vendors standing on the roadside. Hardly had the vehicle stopped than a group of traders crowded around them vying for attention. They were women and young boys and girls each selling different produce. They pleaded with them to buy something.

"We're only buying bread," Rebecca told the vendors to disperse the crowd.

All the other vendors withdrew leaving about four bread sellers all pleading with her to buy from them. She bought about forty *Sikas* wealth of bread distributed among the sellers. All the sellers were happy because it was a lot of bread. As the couple took off, they all waved at them.

"Have a safe journey," they said in unison.

As they pulled away, he had a word of praise for her.

"That was a good thing you did back there."

"You've got to spread the smiles on the faces of those unfortunate people," she said.

He nodded in approval. It was unfortunate that there were not enough jobs for everybody so that they literarily had to run after moving vehicles in competition to make sales. The road from the municipal capital to the village was quite a challenge to drive. In places it was reduced to one lane width for traffic going in opposite directions. Not only was it narrow, but it was muddy, and rugged. Since there was no shoulder, finding a place to pass oncoming traffic to go through was a tough ask. Progress was slow but they completed their journey in daylight. By the time they ventured into the village, the setting sun cast a deep red glow over it. It was ready to cascade out of view. However, they had enough daylight to have people come to them and give directions to his parents' huts. They made their way there without difficulty.

The whole village sprang to life and was aglow in fanfare. They knew who their guest was. Every one of the villagers wanted to come and see this man who just returned from America and works for the government with his gorgeous girlfriend. Several women who were wearing the traditional *kaba* and *slate* untied their third piece of cloth and spread them on the ground singing and dancing. They circled him jiggling and wiggling their waist at him.

"Step, step, step, on my cloth, Kofi *Boga*," they sang repeatedly.

As the women danced around him, Rebecca stood there beaming at their display. She was not jealous; she was only happy for him. The men also became particularly fascinated with her. They told her not to worry about the village women because they were only glad, their kinsman was back from abroad. The children were not to be left out; their appeal was with the Wrangler. They circled it to have a closer look. After the initial exchanges, Rebecca left him with the adults and went to the children. As for Kofi, he was trapped, surrounded by the people who were all trying to embrace him and gain his attention.

After the fanfare died down, his parents and some elders from the village sat down with the couple for the traditional welcoming rites. They gave them water to drink and then asked them the purpose of their visit. In *Abibiman* you would always be asked to give a reason for a visit even if people knew why you were there. It fell to Kofi to be the narrator at this time. All eyes were upon the couple. He introduced Rebecca as a colleague at work who was kind enough to accompany him to visit his parents on his maiden return trip to the village. As the conversation continued, there was one woman who stood behind by herself waiting patiently for everybody to leave. Her head was downturned, and the corners of her mouth were drawn down. All the while as she stood there, she had an empty stare in her eyes. At last, the reception over, when everybody left, she approached Kofi. She had three children with her. As she began addressing him, she bowed down slightly.

"I'm sorry to disturb you sir," kneeling on one foot as she spoke, "I wish to discuss an issue with you."

He looked at her wondering what was so urgent for her to approach him at such a time before he had settled down or rest from his arduous journey.

"Couldn't she have waited for the morning? How tactless can a person be?"

"How may I be of help to you?" He asked.

"These children are my children from my previous marriage," she began.

It turned out that her first husband had died and left her with them, a widow with three children. She was, however, lucky to have found another husband who had been wonderful with the children and accepted them as his own. Besides her three children, she had another two with her second husband. With five children and just a little income from their farming, things were tough on her. Her visit to Kofi that evening was to plead with him to take her eldest child to the city. The child was about seventeen or eighteen years old.

Kofi looked from the woman to his parents and to Rebecca who was surrounded by the wide-eyed children who were asking her questions about the Jeep. He felt they were all pleading with him with their eyes. Whilst the woman was pleading, Rebecca and his parents seemed to be saying no. He wore a frowned expression. He was sympathetic to the plight of the woman and wanted to give any help possible. At the same time, he needed to be careful not to incur the disapproval of his parents and especially Rebecca.

"I would've loved to take one of them on the return journey to ease the burden on you, but we've only just arrived, so I need time to settle before making such a major decision," he told her.

He took a hundred *Sika* note from his wallet and gave to her.

"Kofi, be careful with the villagers else they will take all the money you have on you," his mother told him when the woman had left.

After she was gone, at last he had time to sit with his parents and talk. Rebecca stepped away to join the children who were still standing by the Wrangler. She was out of earshot, so his parents asked,

"Is that the woman you intend to marry Kofi?"

"Yes, I would love to, but I haven't asked her to marry me yet," he replied.

"If that's your intention then you should make it clear to her while you're here, so that we can go to perform the marital rites," his father recommended.

After dinner his mother led them to one of those huts and showed them where they would sleep. The floor was not cemented. It was only decorated with clay to give it a homely feeling. The bed in the room was made from four cone-shaped laterite structures overlaid with wood and Raphia mats. Rebecca had brought a blanket and bed sheet with her so she used it to complete the bed. Since there was only one bed in the room, he asked her to take it whilst he slept on the floor.

"No Kofi, you simply cannot sleep on the floor," she objected.

"Why not?"

"There are all sorts of insects, and even rodents that crawl about on the ground in villages in the night."

"Okay, then I know what to do."

He went outside to ask his mother to give them extra pillows. They used those pillows to divide the bed into two. There was no electricity. The only source of light was from kerosene lanterns. Though his parents lived in this village, he had not stayed there much since he spent most of his time in *Abibiman* going to school in different towns and cities. Thus, his memories of village life faded. When they were ready to sleep, he took the lantern and extinguished it.

"Why did you put out the lamp, Kofi?" Rebecca asked him.

"I find it hard to sleep with the light on," he said.

"Well in the village no one turns off their lantern. They only turn it down to dim it so that if they need it in the night, they just turn it up," she replied.

There were no matches to relight the lantern, so Kofi went back to his parents to do it. When he returned, he was smiling.

"How did you know all this Rebecca? You're a city girl."

"Last year I went to a village for the first time in my life with a friend," she replied.

"Boy friend?"

"Come on Kofi, it's time to sleep, but to answer your question, it was a girlfriend," she said. She dimmed the lantern and then felt her way back to the bed.

They went to sleep divided by two pillows tacked between them. She resolved not to bring up any topic at risk of drawing them closer to indulging in something sexual. In *Abibiman*, chastity was required of young women, and she was determined to observe it.

CHAPTER 19

LOVE DECLARED

It was in the middle of the night, Rebecca suddenly felt sharp stings all over her body. She yelled and jumped, hitting her legs against their makeshift bed, and sending Kofi tumbling onto the floor. As he limply got up, he looked around and saw the faint figure of Rebecca holding on to one foot and jumping on the other.

"What's the matter?" he asked.

Then he sensed burning pains all over his body. He scrambled on his legs and feet to the lantern that stood in a corner dimly lighting the room. He turned up the wick. As the lantern's flame glowed and illuminated the room a horrifying sight was revealed. There was an invasion of epic proportions by soldier ants, marauding and chewing up everything in sight. They were all over the room, in their clothes and bedding, on the walls, and on the floor. They were at their predatory best stinging and biting them with such venom. They ran outside the hut, but the army of ants was there also. Now outside, they heard other people also come out of their huts. The whole village had been invaded by the ants.

Kofi threw caution to the air and took off his pajamas. Rebecca did the same but none of them had time to look at the other's nakedness. They were both screaming, jumping, and shaking their clothing. After Kofi put his pajamas back on, he turned around to see how Rebecca was doing. She had managed to rid her nightie of the ants and was standing there petrified. As they stood there, they would stamp their feet to keep the ants from climbing unto them. There was pandemonium with people running all over the place; the women were clutching on to their babies, the children were crying their eyes out. A man's voice shouted over the noise.

"Calm down everybody, we will soon have things under control."

It was Kofi's father trying to calm nerves. With the help of the other men of the village they fetched spraying machines to spray the huts and the vicinity of the village with insecticide.

"Now everyone can go back to sleep."

A voice boomed when they were done; it was Kofi's father taking charge again. One by one the villagers ventured cautiously back into their own huts. Kofi's father came over to Rebecca and put his arms on her shoulder.

"My in-law, sorry you have to go through this, it is okay now so please go back to sleep you will be alright," he said.

Kofi put his arms around Rebecca and led her back to their hut. When they got back to the room, he turned the lantern up, he no longer thought he would be bothered with the lamp on. They slept soundly after that. When they woke up in the morning, there were swellings all over their bodies from the ant bites. They took turns to scrub down their bodies so that they would not suffer any side effects from the ant bites. Strangely, the villagers did not display any effects from the ant bites. When they came outside, they saw them already going about their duties as if nothing happened to them in the night. Kofi's parents were also up. They came to the couple when they saw them come outside.

"Sorry, what happened to you in the night," his father apologized.

"Please, stop apologizing because it was not your fault," Rebecca told him.

Kofi's mother turned towards him and spoke. "Your father and I are going to the farm please take care of my daughter-in-law for us," she said.

When they left Rebecca turned to Kofi and smiled. "Your parents are very nice people," she said.

All the villagers, including Kofi's parents, soon left for their farms, leaving them alone by themselves. Since they were left alone, they had to find something to do with their time. There was not very much to do in the village though. Initially their plan was just to catch up on the sleep they lost in the night. However, on their way to the village, they had seen a lake close by, so Rebecca suggested they go there to see it. His parents had breakfast already prepared so they ate and set off to the lake.

Arrows of sunlight bathed the woods as they emerged from his parents' hut and walked towards the lake. As they advanced towards the woods, withered leaves from the trees were falling at their feet. They danced and pirouetted from the naked trees in a shower of color, warming their hearts to the bright new day ahead of them. The problems of the night were a million years behind them. Their world now was calm, and serene. It was a world in which no other person existed beside these two young people who had found each other. Walking to the lake was a short trek. They sauntered through the bush ambling beside each other until they came to the lake. It was glass-clear and still, and it seemed untouched by the pollution of the city.

There they sat, buried in the euphoria of each other's presence, and the glittering lake before them. They were on a journey of discovery and the tranquil environment made it easier for them to forget the world around them to concentrate on each other. The sun was like a celestial fireball in the sky. Its beams scorched the land and sent the lake a-glitter with golden sparkles. Above them in the distance sky birds were hovering around and chirping melodiously as they flew by. Below on the lake, speckled trout arced into the air and plopped under the water's surface, seeking to grab a fly or mosquito from the platoons of them hanging over the lake. Rebecca and Kofi were absorbed in the serenity of the moment. They sat by the lake, lost in thought, except for the knowledge that they were overwhelmed by each other's presence.

Kofi who had never really had a woman for a friend, thought his relationship with Rebecca was about more than just friendship. He strongly felt these were feelings that signposted the way to marriage. However, he never brought up the subject of marriage. He dared not mention it because their relationship was still young. They spoke about many subjects. Rebecca was buried in her thoughts. Kofi's parents might like her. She looked at him sitting beside her and she felt good.

"Why did your parents call me their in-law, do they know something I don't?" She enquired gently.

Kofi looked at her and replied with a laugh and a smile, but he did not say anything.

"Can you please tell me more about yourself, Rebecca?" He asked her, to change the subject.

They had been going together but he realized he still did not know so much about her. Like the person she was, Rebecca never spoke much about herself. She always gave the limelight to Kofi since they met.

"OK, I'm the second of three siblings, one male and two females," she said.

He sat up straight and attentive as she started to tell him about herself.

"My brother is twenty-seven years old, married and living with his wife in *Ohenekrom*." *Ohenekrom* was *Abibiman's* second-largest city. "I'm twenty-five, and I have a bachelor's degree in mass communication with a minor in statistics," she continued.

"Now I know why you work at the statistical office," Kofi said smiling broadly, "what about your baby sister, where is she?"

"She lives in *Mpoano* with my parents."

"Isn't she lucky to be home sucking Mommy's breast," Kofi chimed in.

"She's eighteen, isn't she too big for sucking breast?" She replied jokingly.

Kofi sat there thinking, at twenty-five, Rebecca was ready for marriage. It was the age when most single women actively look for partners. He was probably the lucky one to get this pretty unassuming woman for a wife. Rebecca turned to him.

"What are you thinking about Kofi, it seems you are far away somewhere?" she asked.

He turned towards Rebecca. "I was just thinking about you."

"What were you thinking about me?"

"Pretty," he said.

"What about pretty?"

"You, you are the pretty one," he replied.

Until now, he had been tempted to hold back, but he couldn't do it anymore. He looked at Rebecca who now had her gaze focused on him.

"You know I love you, Rebecca, don't you?" He asked.

Rebecca was taken aback, but it was what she had been hoping for and expecting from him all along. They had been going together for about six months now and he had never said he loved her. Now that he had said it, she couldn't say anything, she only nodded. They spoke for a long time mostly about each other and their aspirations; it seemed they could stay there all day, just to talk. After a while Kofi changed the subject. His mind went to the television announcement about the trial of the ex-government operatives before he joined the administration.

"What do you think is going to happen to the former government operatives on trial?" he asked.

"The outcome is obvious. In *Abibiman,* the attorney general prepares the deposition and determines what form of trial it should take."

"Why do you think the outcome is being determined?"

"In most of the cases I have seen, he goes for the bench trial. Usually, three high court judges sit in to determine their fate."

"Three is a good number, if there is one dissent then there will be a mistrial."

"Not necessarily, but what I know is that these ex-ministers are going to fight hard, but the facts are there for all to see. Therefore, they will not come out innocent," she observed.

"If we don't give them a fair trial, it will be a travesty of justice," he responded.

That elicited a whimsical smile from Rebecca.

"Now tell me Rebecca, do you think any of the people at the office hate me?" He changed the subject again.

"Why will anybody hate you, Kofi?"

"I don't know. Just asking."

"I believe that everybody likes you, particularly me, Ellen and Maggie."

He didn't want to probe further, instead he switched the talk to Hamma.

"Do you see how Nicholas Hamma behaves towards me?"

"How?"

"He clearly demonstrates a bossy and unpleasant demeanor towards me. Whenever, I address him he insists I call him honorable."

"Well, he's an elected official of the party. All those elected want to be called Honorable."

"But don't you think Hamma demands it more? I have always perceived that his actions are intended to cause deep resentment amongst his colleagues. I've noticed that whenever he is not present there is an air of freedom and love, but when he is there the atmosphere changes. He resents me for some reason."

"Kofi, you've only being here for a few months, and you've made all those observations?"

"Haven't you noticed how whenever he comes to the break room, he chokes the air out of the room, and the atmosphere becomes subdued?"

"Kofi, don't take it to heart, but please be careful of Hamma if he is behaving in that way towards you."

Rebecca was aware how Hamma infantilizes people at the office like he was the only adult there. However, she was not willing to bring that up and make Kofi feel inadequate in a way. What she told him, rather, was that Hamma might be bitter towards him because he had to make room for him to come in because of his superior qualifications. Kofi now understood why Hamma behaved the way he did. He took his job. However, he wished he would not blame him for that, since he was only here for the good of the country. For her part, Rebecca also knew it was Hamma who got Kofi arrested, but she was not going to tell him that. It was early days yet, she thought. What if things did not work out between them and he confronted Hamma? She concluded she was not going to be a gossip and spill out everything. As they were talking, it suddenly became overcast. The sun, which a moment ago was like a celestial fireball was now muted, wax melt yellow but shafts of light still poured through it.

"It's time to go Kofi," she exclaimed.

Hardly had she spoken than a mighty sparkling lightning bolt flashed across the sky. It was soon followed by a deafening thunderclap that caused them to run helter-skelter. Just then the rain started. They ran as hard as they could laughing at the same time. They were like two little children who had no cares in this world: except the urgency to get away from a rampaging beast in the woodlands of a mysterious forest. However, at this time, there was no beast chasing them. By the time they got to the village they were well soaked down to their bare bottoms. Kofi, who had a bigger towel, gave it to Rebecca to wipe herself down whilst he waited outside in front of the hut, for her to finish changing. The thatch-roof mud houses were being twisted by the heavy rainstorm.

The rain relieved the sweltering heat of the day, but it left the whole village inundated by muddy flood waters running all over the place. Kofi and Rebecca, hurried to the Jeep and sheltered there. In the comfort of the truck Kofi took Rebecca's hand and told her again how much he loved her. Rebecca returned his gaze, just like she did before by the lake but this time she told him she also loved him. As they sat in the Jeep and professed love for one another, they felt safe and assured that one day they would cement their love with marriage. When the rain stopped, they returned to their room to discover the mayhem. There was debris blown all over the room. They were, however, not the only ones impacted by the rainstorm. Everybody in the village suffered the same fate, and some even worse. They spent a greater part of the evening cleaning their room before they could go to bed. The rains seemed to have disrupted their evening, but it was a precursor to a good night's sleep, because they contributed in keeping the soldier ants away.

CHAPTER 20

A HUNTING TRIP

In the morning when Kofi and Rebecca woke up, the sky was peaceful and serene, a welcome sign after the heavy rainstorm the night before. It was time to go back to *Sikakrom* and to their world. They prepared feverishly to set off so they could be home and ready for work the next day. They were preparing to leave when three of the young men who were among the crowd to welcome them came to see them. After the initial greetings they went straight to the subject of their visit.

"American *Boga*, we came to take you and your wife to go hunting in the forest," one of the men said.

Kofi and Rebecca exchanged a knowing look, but they did not correct them that they were not a married couple.

"We are getting ready to go back to *Sikakrom*, so we will have to do that the next time we come," Kofi replied.

One of the men bent over with his hands hugging his shin, another was looking down at his feet whilst the third stood there cracking his knuckles; all of them looking disappointed. They had wanted to allow the couple to experience village life at its best, but if they had to go, they could not do anything about it. Rebecca noticed the disappointment in the men's faces and winked at Kofi. He took the clue, so he asked the men to excuse them while they discussed their next step.

"What should we do, Becky," Kofi asked affectionately.

Rebecca blushed; it was the first time he had called her Becky. The name Becky brought nostalgic feelings, of love and affection. Growing up, when her father was angry with her, he would call her Rebecca Odom. On any normal day, he would call her Rebecca; but when she did something good or if her father was in a good mood, he would call her Becky. So, when Kofi called her Becky, she felt like throwing herself into his arms.

"We can go hunting with the men and still be able to leave sometime in the afternoon," she replied.

Rebecca's answer seemed to have finally settled the issue, so they called the men in.

"Okay, we will go with you, but we have to do it quick because we have to go to work tomorrow," Kofi told them.

The men were already prepared, so they waited for the couple as they changed into appropriate clothes for the forest. One of the men was dressed in khaki trousers and shirt with boots fit for the forest. The other two were wearing old jeans bought from the used clothing market stalls common in *Abibiman*. Conditions for the walk to the forest were a little daunting for Kofi and Rebecca but did not deter the farmers. The ground was wet and damp from the rainfall, the day before. Curled brown leaves were half-embedded into the ground, seemingly trampled by the farmers who had gone that way in the morning before them. The weeds along their path had collected dew making their clothes wet. Kofi thought the presence of the dew meant conditions were probably not right to go hunting. His perception was wrong though, because to the locals, the morning dew on the weeds was always seen as a sign of good health and of good fortune for the morning. The farmers always expected the early morning dew to grace their day and give them a feeling of bliss and sustenance. It refreshed the soul and gave people healthy bones. As they plodded on, Rebecca noticed a grimace on Kofi's face and pitied him.

"Are you alright honey?" She asked, her voice laced with compassion.

"Yeah, I'm good," he responded, trying to allay her fears.

After they had walked for some minutes, they left the path they were on and entered the forest. They were entering a place where there was no path, so they walked in single file now, following the lead of the farmer in khakis. As they made their way slowly through the untrodden vegetation, they fought with the occasional low lying bushes and twisted branches that reached down and touched them. The leader, as well as the other two farmers were holding machetes. They would cut the ends of the branches that were impeding progress. Kofi and Rebecca on the other hand had to use their hands to push aside the remaining branches.

When they entered the forest proper the scenery changed. Low shrubs formed an understory beneath the tree canopy. In parts the understory was thinner and some trees had shed their leaves blanketing the forest floor. The smell of dead tree stumps and rotting leaves was prevalent here. In sections, the forest was dense and humid with lush green leaf trees. The couple had a sense of foreboding as they ventured forward. Rebecca held on tightly to Kofi's hand as they moved on.

"Are you okay honey?" he asked her.

"Yes, but I prefer holding on to you," she replied.

Kofi shouted ahead to the leading man in khakis. "Why is the forest here so dense and humid, and seems untouched by human activity?"

"Ah, that's because this is not a farmer-owned forest. It's government land which is managed as a forest reserve."

"So why are we here?"

"This forest sees little human activity so it's the best place to go hunting. On our farmlands there are no animals present."

"But don't you need a license to hunt on government land?"

"I never heard of anything like that." One of the men in jeans said innocently.

Kofi was puzzled. So, these forests are not regulated, and people treat them as their personal property. No wonder they had walked for a while and had not come across a single animal. It appeared like all the game in this forest had been hunted and killed already. Despite what he saw as this unregulated exploitation of the forest it was still beautiful. There were so many different plant species that had adapted to the humid and damp environment that existed there.

"I was never aware that the forest had so many species of trees." Kofi remarked.

"Yes, there are many" The man in khaki said, his eyes lighting up with pride, "they survive on plenty of rainfall and they are not in short supply around here as you can see. In the months of June to August they receive enough rain to keep them green throughout the year."

"This forest is everything to us. It's the most precious gift we have inherited from our ancestors," added another man in jeans who had not spoken.

"If it's so important to you, then you must take good care of it," Kofi chimed in.

"American *Boga*, you don't know how much care we give to these forests," the man in khaki replied.

Kofi admonished them to take proper care of the forest because it was only then would it remain useful to them. Taking care of it, he told them include managing it well, stopping illegal tree felling and making sure nobody encroached on land reserved to sustain the ecosystem of the area. He told them that it was only then would they be protecting the land for posterity. One of the men in jeans spoke animatingly about the beauty that abounds in the forest. The many different types of trees, some big, some small all of which makes the forest a great place to visit.

"What is that gigantic tree over there?" Kofi interrupted, his curiosity aroused about the size of the tree, with its buttressed trunk. It was the biggest they had come across the whole morning.

"That is the *Kapok* tree, there are a few in this forest, actually they are only found mainly in these forests." The farmer in khakis boasted.

For Kofi and Rebecca, this hunting trip was like a guided nature tour. When they left the dense and plush green vegetation, they came upon a cleared area where the forest had obviously been touched by fire, where until recently the thick tree canopy had stood, all that remained were charred tree stumps; the area was open to the sky looking austere and sad. It was a complete departure from the dense, thick forest they just passed through.

"What happened to the forest here?" Rebecca inquired.

"Well Madam Rebecca, some farmers have no place to farm so they come here to cut down a section of the forest to cultivate it."

"That's too bad," Kofi interjected.

"The forest rangers when they come here on patrol, they say the villagers are encroaching on the forest. But we do not see it as encroachment. After we use the land, we let it go fallow as you can see here."

"That's not good enough," Kofi observed.

"No, it's okay because the farmers take care of the land. What is damaging is illegal logging."

"There is illegal logging here too?" Kofi asked.

"Oh yes, some of it's by locals with chainsaws, others are by big companies who bring in machines to fell and strip the trees and drag them away through the forest which further damages what remains."

His statement was concerning to Kofi. How as a country could they maintain the beautiful ecosystem that the forest provided without compromising the trade in goods such as lumber and medicinal products that were constantly harvested from the forest. It was a big eye-opener for him. The next time the presidential team met he was going to table an idea where all stakeholders in *Abibiman* can be vigilant against the many illegal activities that go on in the rainforest. He concluded that if they don't do that soon the well-known trees of the forest would only be spoken of in textbooks and by the elderly.

They were now in the heart of the forest and their leader told them they were coming to an area where they could begin hunting. Thus, they ventured forward. As they did so, there was a smell of fallen leaves mixed with distinct aroma of fetid earth. Kofi and Rebecca held their breath so they would avoid the putrid odor, but the villagers prodded on oblivious of the rotten smell in the air. As they drew closer it became clearer, it was a pool of marshy water with a collection of different leaves fallen from adjoining trees. Nearby a small creek hidden by the canopy of trees gurgled gently into the marshy water. The men motioned to the couple to keep still and quiet. They stopped to listen hoping to see some animals there, but it seemed the forest had hidden all the animals that would come and drink from the creek.

As they moved away from the swamp, the smell changed to damp moss. The dearth of animals in the forest was apparent. Though they had by now done quite a trek through the forest, there was none in sight. When Kofi thought their journey was perhaps in vain, the farmers identified some holes on a little hill they claimed harbored some animals. They weeded around until they discovered two other similar holes. The men remarked that the holes were bush rat burrows, and they could easily hunt for them there. They blocked one hole and lighted a fire on the second hole. The aim was to smoke out the bush rats. As they continued to kindle the fire, the bush rats came out of the third hole dazed, so it was easy for the men to catch them. That move took Kofi down memory lane; to the time when he stayed at his auntie's and a man was hunted down in similar manner. Suddenly he was stricken with sadness.

Using the method of smoking out the animals, the men were able to catch six large bush rats. Then they set out to return to the village. Their homeward journey took them through a beautiful valley drowned by hafts of sunlight clearly separating the forest from the village. It was around noon when they returned from their hunting trip. As soon as they got to the village the men ran to prepare their game while Kofi and Rebecca bundled their stuff into the Jeep and took a quick shower. Later the men brought them their share of the game. At about two in the afternoon, they set off to drive back to the city. The whole village had then returned from their farms, and they came to see them off. Some children ran after their truck until they disappeared down the road.

The return trip was hazardous and unsafe than when they were going to the village because of the rains the day before. Since the road was not well-traveled, it had become muddy and unfriendly. Before they reached the municipal center, they had to tow two lorries that were stacked in the mud. At some stretches, it was narrow and perilous and almost impassable. In places the terrain was rugged and impenetrable, but the wrangler plowed along proud and boisterous. Eventually after six hours they arrived at *Sikakrom* clearly worn down and exhausted.

CHAPTER 21

THE PRESIDENTIAL TOUR

The week after Kofi and Rebecca returned from their visit to the village, it was time for the scheduled visit of the President and his team. It was going to include a week-long tour of three Provinces. Kofi was part of the delegation, but Rebecca was not. The night before the trip, he packed a few things before going to bed. The morning for the trip dawned bright and promising. Kofi was eagerly looking forward to it, particularly because he was going on his maiden Presidential tour; moreover, he would be treated like a VIP. A sense of optimism filled him in anticipation of a great week ahead. Though he had not been able to complete the paperwork needed for the trip, he knew Lisa would have it ready by the departure time. Just as he thought when he got to the office, Lisa was already there putting things together.

"I've prepared all we need to take with us on the trip sir," she told him when he entered the office.

"Thank you, Lisa, you're so helpful," Kofi said.

With their paperwork together, they went outside to join the delegation who were already waiting. Hamma was standing in the doorway of his office watching people rushing in and out. As Kofi passed him, he cast a scornful look in his direction. Kofi ignored the disdainful look.

"Good morning, sir," he chirped warmly.

Hamma continued to stare off into the distance as if no one had spoken to him. He wished that Kofi would return the same animosity just as he did often, but it seemed he was always nice. He blew the air after him to wish him an uncomfortable journey. Meanwhile, when Kofi and his secretary reached the parking lot, some of the cars in the fleet were already there. However, they discovered a few of the entourage had not yet arrived. Since everything did not seem in place, Kofi went in search of Rebecca to say goodbye to her before leaving. As they were talking Rebecca's boss emerged from his office to see her.

"Did you want to speak to me sir?" Rebecca asked.

"Yes, I did, but I see you've got a visitor," he replied.

"Oh, Mr. Hope wanted to give me a message before he went on the trip with the president."

"Is that the same Mr. Hope who is the new financial analyst."

"Yes," Rebecca replied.

Kwame Acres stretched his hands for a handshake with Kofi.

"Mr. Hope, I have heard so much about you," he said smiling at him.

"Sorry we have not met until now, Mr. Acres," Kofi said.

They shook hands and Mr. Acres turned to Rebecca and spoke.

"Please come to my office after Mr. Hope has gone."

He turned round and went back to his office. Kofi and Rebecca walked outside just when Lisa came running towards them.

"The fleet of cars are in," she said.

He turned to Rebecca; "OK, it's time to say goodbye honey."

Rebecca then stretched her arms and looked at Kofi questioningly. He seemingly did not catch the clue so Rebecca asked; "You're not going to leave without giving me a hug? Are you?"

"You bet I'm not." Kofi replied as he hugged her in a warm embrace.

When he released her, Rebecca overcome with emotions just stood there watching him, while fighting back tears. He walked a few steps and looked over his shoulder to see her blowing kisses at him. The drive to the provinces was fascinating even though it was long and arduous. As they left *Sikakrom*, they travelled along the main roads for several miles. It was asphalted in long stretches; straight and endlessly boring. Several miles later, it suddenly curved and meandered dangerously through hill country such that it posed certain danger and a trap to unwary drivers lulled into a false sense of security by the earlier unending boringness.

The first leg of the tour took them to a newly created Provincial capital.

It was small and sparsely populated. However, it was the sort of Province the administration had to create to open up large sections of the country to development. Because it was new, there were several projects being undertaken by the administration. For that reason, the chief divided the delegation up into three groups. One group was to go with the President to inspect some infrastructure projects that were being undertaken in the province. The second, led by the Minister of Trade was to inspect a local factory just constructed for the manufacture of fertilizers. The third group, led by the Minister of the Interior was to oversee a massive solar plant that was under construction. Kofi was in the last group inspecting the new solar installations project.

The visits to those projects were to show the nation what the administration was doing and to also put the contractors on their toes. It highlighted the somewhat importance the administration attached to development projects in a bid to open up the entire country to the outside world and to civilization. Later in the day, the President and his team met with all the contractors and subcontractors undertaking the various development projects. He gave a short but rousing morale-boosting speech to congratulate them on their work and the efforts they were putting in to open up the country.

> Thank you, friends, for the good work you are doing.
> You are aware the great importance we as a nation
> attach to the work you are doing. My administration's
> goal is to arrest the infrastructure deficit facing the country
> and you are the ones at the forefront of bringing this about.
> The success of these projects, on time and within budget, will
> allow this government to secure more funding to undertake
> similar projects in the other Provinces.

The speech was impromptu, but it was a well-rehearsed line. Kofi trailed off as the president continued to speak. It was a speech he had heard him give on several occasions. Nevertheless, he did not dismiss the speech because he saw hope in it. The president spoke for about thirty minutes. His speech, coupled with the projects themselves were heartwarming to his audience. For Kofi it was an occasion to feel pride in his country. At last, there was a savior for the people to dig them out of the poverty and the grimness that had generally dominated their national life over the past few years. He was greatly comforted not only by the site visits, but by the desire of a president who knew about the plight of his people and had the desire to arrest it.

Whatever joy Kofi had did not last long. His optimism was to be dented by the government operatives who were with him on the trip the succeeding evening. The following day, the group left the Provincial capital to another budding town within that Province. They had meetings all day with stakeholders in the town. Afterwards there was an open-air meeting in which the President and some party leaders as well as some members of his cabinet spoke to the people. They were now on the fifth day of their one-week tour, having spent four days in the first and second Provinces. On the fifth day, it was time for celebrations. When business was done for the day, Barbara announced that it was a night for a special dinner.

The host had prepared for the delegation to enjoy dinner right at the rally grounds instead of going to their hotel. Moreover, since most of the dishes were local, it required an early dinner. There was boiled plantain and yam; various meals made from corn and finally *fufu* and goat meat soup. Most of the men, as did Kofi went for the *fufu* and goat meat soup. It was spicy and delicious. As the men ate their *fufu* and spicy goat meat soup, they reveled in their ill-gotten wealth. There was a song playing loudly in the dining room. The same one that the Licensing office official was playing but with a slight twist to it. It was saying they will not take advice from anybody.

Yɛ neɛ woho bɛtɔ wo
Yɛntie obiara asɛm

The ministers and party leaders had to talk loudly to be heard over the loud music.

"I don't think I would have enjoyed this food as much at home," remarked the Minister of Health.

"I don't enjoy my wife's cooking anymore,'" the Minister of Transport announced.

141

"I bet you enjoy that little girlfriend of yours," the Minister of Trade hypothesized.

"Hey Kwame, you have a girlfriend?" Somebody asked him.

"Shh, walls have ears. I don't want the old girl to get mad with me."

"Don't worry Kwame, we all have skeletons in our closets," the Interior Minister assured him.

"Somebody tell me, what do you think of that journalist who has been accusing some of us as being corrupt? The Minister of Trade asked.

"I don't worry about such hungry people. Whoever goes hunting without helping themselves with the game?" Replied the Minister of the Interior.

"The fellow is just hungry, so he just wants to find others to blame," one other Minister interjected. His remark was accompanied by an uproar.

"Mind you fellas, the election will be coming soon, and these poor folks are the ones who are going to vote for us." The Minister of Education cautioned.

He had been quiet all the while as his colleagues were poking fun at the electorate. Like the Minister of Education, Kofi remained silent throughout the entire discourse, appalled at the ministers' blatant misconduct and their open acceptance of it in the presence of each other. He felt out of place and alone amongst them. His thoughts went back to the rally from the previous stop, with its big speeches and big promises, which kindled hope and optimism. He contrasted that with this evening; the indulgent lavish feast of free corporate hospitality, laid on by the hosts, the idle boasting of his colleagues; their dismissal of the journalist's complaints about their lifestyle; their open display of lack of respect for decorum and the rule of law. Their boorish behavior disheartened him. How could the ministers undermine all the good work of this president on a mission to banish poverty from the ranks of the people?

"People, I've always told you that this is your chance, when you get into government, it's a once in a lifetime opportunity. Make hay while you have the sun," the trade minister advised.

"I agree with you friend, I'm working on my third house," the Minister of Transport reported.

Kofi was horrified at the way they glorified crime and idolized wealth gained on the back of the poor people of this land who had entrusted them with authority. That they could poke fun at the peoples' plight as they eked out a living from absolutely nothing, made it even more shameful.

"I've been accused in the media of having an ostentatious lifestyle, but doesn't that come with the trappings of the office I'm holding?" Questioned the Minister of Tourism.

"Ostentation my foot. Should I put my life on the line every day for nothing?" Queried the Minister of Local Government. Then he turned to Kofi.

"Hey Hope," he was smiling broadly, "why do people always talk about equality? Don't they know that some are more equal than others?"

He wanted to blurt out in anger, he looked at the men, and Barbara who was sitting two tables away from him. She was looking his way and speaking to him with her eyes to be restrained. He thought to himself;

"These people are watching me, so I must be careful how I react."

He took the cue from Barbara and replied with a diplomatic answer in the calmest way. "Well sir, I think equality is good for everyone." He paused to see the reaction of the ministers, but no one said anything so he continued, "if wealth is redistributed it reduces poverty and makes life better for the rich, because if there are no needy people in the society there will be less crime." He stopped again, this time to look at Barbara for encouragement, then he continued. "Besides, people will be better educated. If that happens, there will be more societal cohesion."

After he was done speaking, the man looked at him strangely then he broke into a hysterical laughter. When he stopped laughing, he remarked dryly.

"Fantasy, my friend, fantasy."

By now Kofi was genuinely ashamed at the way that his colleagues were touting their privileged positions and ill-gotten gains. He hurried through his meal and left the table. That evening was the last of their tour to the two Provinces. Now they awaited the final leg the next day, so he decided to retire to bed early. Besides, he was not comfortable with the nature of the conversation that was going on at dinner. The following morning, when Barbara came to the rendezvous place, only Kofi was there, ready and waiting. The rest of the group were late in coming out and that really incensed her. She was in a feisty mood and came out with guns blazing.

He had never seen her in such a mood before and was really surprised. However, her behavior was warranted; the group knew how tight their schedule was, therefore any lateness would delay their busy schedule and spoil the efficiency of the tour.

As it turned out, the lateness delayed their departure by almost two hours. Finally, everybody was assembled and the tour was ready to resume. The Provincial police came and joined the escort from the capital to lead them out of the city. After the team left the city, the escorting police drove to the rear of the convoy and waited for all the cars in the fleet to pass. Their job done, they turned around and returned to their base. Now they were left with their original escort from the capital to continue their journey.

They drove through main roads and some feeder roads. The drive through the countryside was the most fascinating. Parts of the roads were asphalted. However, in places the asphalt was breaking up leaving a lot of potholes in the road. As they drove on, the asphalt gave way to dusty roads. The dust formed a cluster of spiraling smoke behind them. They passed several school children walking from one village to another. A puzzled Kofi wondered why so many children were walking to school from one village to another. Probably their village was not big enough to have a school of its own. This was a sight all too rampant in *Abibiman*. Many children have to leave home early to avoid the heat and also to arrive just in time before their lessons start. It was not a pretty sight, but it was the reality. He was glad he had dedicated his life to serving the good people of this nation. In the meantime, the motorcade continued to their last and most important stop.

CHAPTER 22

A DURBAR FIT FOR A KING AND PRESIDENT

The last phase of the tour seemed the most important to the ruling party. It was also the most flamboyant. They journeyed all morning driving through urban areas and villages. They drove on paved roads and on unpaved roads. They drove through grassland and through patches of forest. Whenever they got to a village, children and adults alike lined the streets to wave at their convoy. All day they drove until at about six o'clock they arrived at *Ohenekrom*. When they got to the outskirts of the city, they were joined by additional police. Some were in trucks; others were in smaller cars and on motorbikes. The drive through town was therefore heralded by a heavy police escort. All this time they were sounding their sirens and forcing other cars to pull over. It was a real sight to see. This was the first time Kofi had experienced being in such a convoy and he wished it went on and on. They went through several environs of the city of *Ohenekrom* before pulling into the forecourt of a large hotel. It was the biggest hotel in the city.

After the convoy stopped, the police escort circled it several times and cordoned off the perimeter before giving the all-clear signal for them to disembark. Those police who were in open trucks were toting their guns as a show of force they could marshal against any intruder. Then they whisked the President away, escorted by a contingent of heavily armed police. Barbara asked the rest of the team to meet with the Chief of staff in the break room of the hotel for their assignments for the next day. After the chief gave them their schedule, they dispersed to their hotel rooms to be ready for another day.

This stop was the stronghold of the Freedom Convention Party so every member of the team knew what was expected of them the next day. The room assigned to Kofi was spacious overlooking a big river that runs through the city. In the distance, a bridge crossed the river. There was no vehicular movement on the bridge as the road traversing it had been closed to traffic. Throughout the night several policemen and women camped around the hotel. Besides the police, several people from *Ohenekrom* were hanging out in the vicinity of the hotel. They drummed and danced well into the night. When Kofi got to his room, he was tired and worn out, but he could not go to bed without calling Rebecca. They had grown close lately. They stayed on the phone for a while.

"Kofi you should be going to bed now because there is a long day ahead of you. Remember, you are in *Ohenekrom*."

"What about *Ohenekrom*?"

"They like to do things big; you will find out tomorrow."

"Okay."

"Good night."

She said not wanting to delay him. She hung up without waiting for his response. After the call with Rebecca, Kofi was feeling too tired he decided to go to bed without taking a shower. He slept more soundly than he had ever done since he returned to *Abibiman*. It was definitely the exhaustion from the long journey. The next day after breakfast they headed to the grounds of the rally. By eight in the morning, they had gathered at the durbar grounds together with some party faithful from *Ohenekrom* and its surrounding villages. Kofi and Adams sat close to the front seat behind where the President would sit. An hour after they were seated, a long line of police escort drove in leading the vehicle of the President and first lady. The president, in an elaborate ceremony, inspected a guard of honor and then took his seat. After he was seated, Kofi noticed several empty seats were remaining. He was curious because wherever they had been on this tour every seat had been occupied after the president had been seated.

"Why are there several seats empty?" he leaned over to Adams and asked.

"They're for the King, and his chiefs," Adams replied nonchalantly.

"Shouldn't they be seated before the President?"

"According to the tradition of the people, the king, the overlord of this land, is the last to take his seat in any gathering."

Kofi was aware the occasion was going to be graced by a durbar of the King and his chiefs, but he never expected the euphoria and the grandiose ceremony it was assuming. There was a hush over the crowd and a man with his cloth tied to his waist started beating a set of talking drums that was standing to the side of the durbar ground.

"That's to announce the entry of the subchiefs and the king," Adams murmured to Kofi.

Suddenly the drumming stopped and the first of the chiefs entered the grounds with his entourage. He was preceded by two men beating drums and two women dancing to their rhythm. Amongst his entourage of attendants and court officials following him, Kofi saw two men carrying stools, one person had a bronze sword and another a long staff. He had a big, embroidered umbrella hoisted over him by a stoutly built man who had also tied his cloth at the waist. The chief wore a long necklace reaching down to his navel. He also wore armbands, bracelets, and anklets, and a big shiny wooden sandal. The next chief was similarly adorned in his finest regalia. He also had an entourage of attendants and court officials following him and two people carrying stools.

Several other chiefs followed in a similar manner. They were all decorated in assorted beautiful traditional cloths and adorned with necklaces, armbands, bracelets, finger rings, and anklets. The umbrellas hoisted over them were each distinctively different. Some of the chiefs had big umbrellas while others had even bigger ones. The last chief to enter the arena had gold headgear, necklaces, armbands, bracelets, finger rings, anklets, and gold-studded sandals. His umbrella was so huge it would be better described as an awning and needed two men to hoist it. The bracelets and armbands seemed to weigh him down, so as he slowly walked into the durbar ground, he was flanked by two attendants, who each held an arm to support him. He had a bigger entourage of attendants and court officials who followed him, with two of them carrying stools. Kofi had never witnessed anything compared to the unfolding spectacle. He was dumbfounded.

"Why is there so much pomp and pageantry being displayed?" He asked bemused.

"The objects being carried by the servants of the chiefs, serves as symbols of the tribe, and the stools show the seats of power each chief sit on," Adams explained patiently.

"What about the umbrellas, why are some bigger than others?"

"The size of umbrella shows the position of the chief within the tribe. You saw how the last chief had the largest, he is the one that steps in if the king were to be missing in battle," he explained.

As the chiefs passed, their entourage was heralded by court musicians of drummers, and horn blowers singing the praises of their chief. They paraded the grounds for several minutes dancing to the drums with the accompanying music before taking their seats. After the chiefs and sub-chiefs had taken their seats, a court crier came to announce the arrival of the king of the land. The assembly fell silent. The court crier started reciting the accolades of the king:

There is no one like the king
The king walks slowly
The king is a god
There is no one like the king
The king is a god
There is no one like the king
The king's words are law
Give way, give way
The overlord is coming
Give way, give way
You can't step in his way

As soon as the court crier finished reciting the king's praises, a large procession of drummers, horn blowers, and musicians entered. They were playing music and extolling the praises of the king. They were accompanied by traditional dancers who were dancing to their music. The entire group went around the grounds for two cycles before it congregated in the center of the campgrounds. All eyes were set on them. From the center, they started playing and dancing towards the exits. Everybody thought their performance was over, but it had just begun. From where they were, they started reentering the arena. Their procession, this time, slower than when they first arrived.

As they reentered, the king's entourage followed, carrying him in a palanquin. His adornment was beyond magnificent, making those of the chiefs who had come before him almost pale into insignificance. The king was carrying an heirloom in his hands and regally dancing to the tune of the music in his palanquin. Behind his procession was a large entourage carrying an array of regalia, and heirlooms signifying his power and relevance.

"These items you see with the king were valuables left by the ancestors. It is likely they made most of them and the rest, they captured from their opponents in war time," Adams whispered to Kofi.

After this pageantry, the king was lowered down and slowly led to his stool which was prestigiously placed next to the President. Now that the king was seated, it was time for the meeting to begin. A fetish priest of the king came forward and offered prayers through the pouring of libation to the ancestors to protect their tribal kingdom and the president of the nation. There were various performances by school children, the boy scouts and some non-governmental organizations. After those performances, the traditional leaders gave speeches praising the President and his team first for visiting but also for the many development programs initiated on behalf of the people. From a political point of view the visit was a success.

The President gave a lengthy promise-laden speech. It had been a fanfare-accompanied and ceremony-filled day. The group left the durbar tired but fulfilled; they had witnessed a dazzling spectacle like no other. The proceedings ended in a reverse manner, the king was the first to leave, carried away in his palanquin, followed by the chiefs and sub-chiefs. Soon after, the President and some cabinet ministers were whisked away by helicopter to the airport to be transported by plane back to the capital. As for the rest of the group, they stayed behind to complete their journey by car the next day. The following day, the long journey back to *Sikakrom* began.

CHAPTER 23

CLUBBING MAKES FOR
A HANGOVER

The team returned to *Sikakrom* late in the night. The whole group were driven to the presidential palace. The president who had flown in the day before wanted to meet up with them before everyone dispersed back to their homes. The meeting lasted for only thirty minutes, after which Barbara assigned drivers to take team members to their respective homes.

"I am so happy for your contributions, you made the president and the party proud," she said.

"We are always ready to follow your leadership," they responded.

They sang the national anthem jubilantly and headed out to their assigned rides. It was a good trip, but now the hard work of putting notes together and coming out with viable plans for their ministries was just beginning. Being without her on the trip, Kofi was eager to see Rebecca. He wondered if she had missed him as much as he had missed her. First thing the next morning, he headed for her apartment. When he arrived, she was sitting under a tree in front of her place, and a male companion sat next to her. His heart skipped a beat and he started to breathe heavily. She noticed the change on his face; his eyes had narrowed, and his eyelids were fluttering. He was obviously in a faraway land with a thousand-yard stare. She pulled him aside and asked;

"Why the long face Kofi?"

"What do you mean?"

"Kofi, don't I know you? You don't seem happy to see me."

"Who's that young man with you?"

Rebecca broke down and laughed hysterically. "Oh Kofi, is that why you look so cross? He's, my brother. Who did you think it was?"

He started to smile; "I'm sorry Rebecca," he apologized, "I didn't know what was going on."

"Come on, let me introduce you to him."

She held on to his hand and pulled him along. When they got to his brother, she wrapped her hands around him and smile, before introducing him.

"This is Mr. Kofi Hope, my fiancé," she announced.

He smiled at her brother, relief flooding his face. Now the sudden flash of stress and anger that was burning him up moments before, evaporated. All the while Rebecca was also looking at him in admiration. Her brother was very happy to see him. Their family had always wondered about Rebecca because she had never brought any man home, so they were beginning to worry about her. He stretched forth his hands for a handshake with Kofi.

"My name is Peter Odom, Rebecca's big brother."

The two exchanged smiles as they shook hands.

"I've heard so much about you, Mr. Hope."

"Please call me Kofi, he replied, I hope everything you heard was positive."

"Obviously, you wouldn't expect my sister here to malign you, would you?"

He looked at Rebecca who was retreating behind the partition separating her sleeping area from the living room.

"No, of course not."

"So, what do you think of her?" He was speaking in a hushed tone now so Rebecca who had receded behind the curtain dividing her room would not hear.

"I must tell you sometimes her unique and irresistible beauty unknowingly seduces me," Kofi confessed garnering an uproarious laughter from Peter.

"What were you two saying about me?" Rebecca asked emerging from the partitioned area.

"We weren't talking about you," Peter replied as the two men exchanged a knowing look.

Kofi could see that Rebecca was genuinely glad to see him. As he chatted with her brother, she sat there looking at them interestingly. She was sitting at the edge of her chair with her upper body and torso leaning more forward and seeming absorbed in the ongoing conversation between them. Kofi had planned to take her somewhere to get some breakfast, but he now decided it best to leave so they could have time to discuss any family business he came for. However, when he made that suggestion, Rebecca objected vehemently.

"You must have breakfast with us before you leave Kofi," she said emphatically.

"Yes Mr. Hope, you must stay. How else will I get to know my future brother-in-law?" Her brother added his voice.

He could not refuse, so he waited for Rebecca to prepare breakfast for the three of them. There was so much food they could not eat everything. After breakfast they sat down and chatted for a while. It was well into the afternoon when he left. Rebecca saw him off a couple of blocks away from her apartment and promised to come and see him as soon as his brother had left. Not long after returning home, Adams called. He wanted to go to a nightclub to ease some of the pressure and stress of the tour. Kofi agreed with his suggestions, so they set a time to go. Adams arrived on time.

This was not the first time they had gone out. They had met in the past several times to go out to a night club or bar. At first when Adams had suggested the idea, Kofi had been hesitant but since he did not have many friends, he acceded to his request and went out with him. On this occasion, he had not decided to go out until Adams called. It was a weekend night, and he didn't have anything planned, so it was a good time to go out and have fun. Adams had arrived in a taxi but had let it go because he wasn't sure if Kofi was ready. He had a young boy who always came to help him. Fortunately, he had come by this evening, so he volunteered to go into the main street to get a taxi for them. While they were waiting for the taxi, Maggie called on the phone.

"What are you up to Kofi?" She inquired.

"I'm going to a club with Adams."

"Do you mind if I tag along?"

He looked at Adams who seemingly was sending him a conflicting message. His eyes were saying it was okay, but he was also jabbing his fingers downwards. He was left to make his own decision.

"Not at all, it will be a pleasure to have you come along," he replied finally. It was however a decision he would regret later in the night. After he hung up, Adams turned to him.

"Kofi, why will you invite Maggie and not Rebecca?" Adams asked.

"Why?" he looked comically at Adams, "I can't go out with another person because I love Rebecca?"

Adams saw that he was becoming defensive, but he advised him to only go out with other girls if Rebecca was with him. It was an opinion Kofi rejected, because he had no ulterior motive in going out with Maggie. Beside he knew Maggie had always been nice to him since he started working at the presidential office. As they were conversing, their taxi came. Since he didn't know where Maggie lived, he called her to get directions which he passed on to the taxi driver. She was beautifully dressed and had a particularly bouncy feeling about her. It appeared that she was not content to be just another drone, so she wore vibrant clothes. At his first outing with Adams, there were no incidents. So, he was hoping for the same tonight particularly with a girl present. At the beginning of the night Maggie was sober and behaved civilly. However, as the night wore on and after a few drinks she became increasingly raucous and exuberant.

Kofi was not a heavy drinker and only had a few bottles. Adams and Maggie however, continued drinking. The evening was descending into an alcoholic binge. Adams remained the more sober of the two, but Maggie became unreasonably loud, and was asking everyone to get up and dance. Anytime a song started to play, she would get up and dance. Since she was intoxicated, she was almost falling over as she danced but she would not listen to the pleadings of his companions not to make an exhibition of herself. When the music finally stopped playing, she became very quiet and angry because no one would dance with her. Then she attempted to sit down but sat on the edge of the chair and tumbled over. Adams and Kofi tried to help her get up, but she became loud and uncooperative.

"Leave me alone," she shouted so loudly everybody at the club looked at them.

When she saw people looking at her, she seemed to have recognized her surroundings and it briefly appeared to sober her up. After she managed to get up, she broke into a sob and cried without any provocation. The whole thing was strange to Kofi because he had never really gone out with a girl, let alone experienced such drunken behavior. Adams was no help by now because he had kept on drinking and was encouraging her to do the same. As the night wore on, he feared Maggie would let down her guard, and not only blend with the crowd but also allow herself to be taken advantage of by some of the party goers. Besides, Adams was also becoming drunk, so he told them they had to leave.

At first, they resisted, so he threatened to leave them behind. Only then did they agree to go with him. Getting a taxi was not easy but he eventually managed to find one. Since his companions were both drunk, he made sure to drop them each at home before he was also dropped off last. When he finally got home, he resolved to never go out with that pair again. In the morning, he was awakened by a phone call from Maggie. When he found her name on the caller ID, he went back to sleep. She continued to call until he finally picked up.

"I am very sorry Kofi, for yesterday," she apologized.

"If you say so."

"Oh Kofi, you don't seem to believe me, do you?"

"I have nothing against you Maggie."

"Sure?"

"Sure."

"Don't worry Kofi, I will make it up to you," she said and hung up.

It was only when she hung up, could he return to sleep. His head was thumping but he had sleep to catch up on.

CHAPTER 24

A COMPROMISING SITUATION

Kofi woke up with a hangover from the night before. Though he had not drunk as much as his companions, he was still feeling the effects. He had not consumed alcohol since his last night out with Adams months before, so the few bottles he drank impacted him greatly. He hovered between staying in bed a little longer or getting up and doing something around his flat. In the end, he settled for the first option and slept in for a while longer. As he lay in bed he thought about his relationship with Rebecca. They had only known each other for a relatively short time but he already felt strongly that she was the woman for him. He needed to take the necessary steps to make her his wife. He remembered a friend who had got married while he was in America. All they needed to do was to get somebody to officiate the ceremony. They didn't even inform their parents beforehand.

On the other hand, in *Abibiman* both sets of parents had to be involved. He was sure that the amount he would have to pay as dowry price would be substantial, but he was not worried about that. He remembered the saying among his people that a good bead pays for itself; paying a dowry for a beautiful and well-behaved lady like Rebecca would be worth every bit of it. As he laid in bed and contemplated those issues he drifted back to sleep. He was only awakened in the late afternoon when Rebecca called. Her brother had left, and she wanted to come over. Shortly after Rebecca hung up, the phone rang again. It was Maggie also asking to come over.

However, since Rebecca was coming over, he told her not to come. He wanted to spend some quality time together with Rebecca after their short period of separation because of the trip he took with the presidential team. He thought the matter was closed with Maggie. He unlocked his main gate so that Rebecca could come in when she arrived. He then went to the bathroom to take a shower. Just when he went into the bathroom, he heard Maggie shouting.

"Kofi, Kofi, Kofi."

He heard her alright, but he did not respond. He could hear her footsteps coming closer towards his bathroom before she retreated. He continued with his shower. Meanwhile, when she realized Kofi was in the bathroom, Maggie went into his bedroom and undressed. A few minutes later, when he came from the bathroom to his bedroom, she was lying on his bed wearing just a bra and panties. Since he only had his towel wrapped around his waist, he turned around and rushed to the living room hoping to get away from her. While he entered the living room, Rebecca was also opening his front door to come inside. At that instant, Maggie also runs from the bedroom to the living room half naked. Rebecca, her mouth widely opened, looked grimly at Kofi and then at Maggie; perplexity was written all over her face. Her dream of one day getting happily married was withering right in front of her eyes.

Kofi was equally shocked by Maggie's behavior; he couldn't find any words that would convince Rebecca, so he just stood there and looked at her shamefaced. After a few minutes, she seemed to have understood what was going on, she dashed out of his flat. Though he chased after her, he could not reach her before she left the flat. However, since he still only had a towel wrapped around his waist, he had to return to the house. Rebecca got out of his flat to find the taxi still waiting and she jump right back into it. By the time he put on something and raced after her, her taxi had already driven off. When he returned to his flat, Maggie was still there in the exact way he left her. She was just standing there straight-faced; she really didn't care if Rebecca left him.

"Oh, you are back," she said.

He stood there with an enigmatic quirk of the lips but said nothing.

"Don't worry about Rebecca," she said.

He looked at her, anger tearing through his veins, "will you just shut up and clear out?" He told her.

She did not move; she just stood there and shrugged her shoulders. That seemed to have angered him more. He gathered her clothing and pushed her out of his flat. Now he understood her idea of making up for her mess. She had every intention to drive a wedge between him and Rebecca. He should have been more careful. As she stood outside Kofi's flat, Maggie wondered what sort of person he was. She had tangled with even the President and prevailed. She remembered how she had seduced him, and he had taken her into his bed. Fortunately, that old fool John Biney had discovered them and had pleaded with her to keep the affair a secret. It was then that he promoted her from a lowly clerk in his office to be assistant to Barbara, the presidential spokesperson.

Kofi returned to his flat and sat down in thought. He contemplated the damage. What were the people at the office going to think of him when this came out? First, he had got arrested, and now he was cheating on the girl he truly loved.

"Well, I will cross the bridge when that time comes, for now I must think about how to explain this to Rebecca and get her back," he thought to himself.

He picked up his phone to call her, but she did not pick up. He continued calling her the umpteenth time before he gave up. He thought about contacting Adams or Kisito to discuss his predicament with them. Should a man go to his friends with any and every one of his problems? No way he was going to do that; this was a problem he had to solve on his own. Meanwhile, when Rebecca left his flat, she got back into the same taxi she had arrived in. On her way back she wept so much the taxi driver was disheartened.

"Is there anything I can do to help miss? The taxi driver asked concerned.

"No," she said and broke down sobbing loudly.

"Why are you crying then, miss?"

Rebecca was in no mood to talk, and she did not answer him. Instead, she continued her sobbing. Her dream of getting married to the perfect man had come crashing down right before her eyes. She was thankful when the taxi pulled up in front of her apartment. She didn't like telling strangers her problems, so she was glad she was out of the taxi. Immediately she entered her apartment, she slumped into a couch and wept as hard as she could. All the while her phone was ringing, but she decided not to pick it up because it was Kofi. Later her friend Ashley called, and she answered, but her tearful mumble made her incoherent. Realizing something must be wrong Ashley stopped what she was doing and took a taxi to Rebecca's apartment. When she arrived, Rebecca was still slumped on her couch, looking depressingly hopeless. Her legs were shaking uncontrollably, and her knees were knocking against each other.

"Whatever is wrong Rebecca?"

"It's Kofi," she said tearfully.

"What about Kofi?"

"I found him in a compromising position with one of our colleagues at work, the one I said has experience with men." After she said this, she resumed sobbing hysterically.

Ashley waited a little while then started rubbing her back to calm her down. Afterwards, she went into her refrigerator and took out a bottle of water, poured some into a glass, and gave to her.

"Please drink this," she pleaded.

Rebecca took the water and drank. "Thank you, Ashley," she managed to say in between her sobs.

"Please stop crying and tell me everything that happened."

Rebecca told the story of how she found Kofi and Maggie when she went to visit him at his house. While she was telling her story, Ashley sat still and listened attentively, her head in her palm.

"Do you think they were having sex?"

She asked when Rebecca finished her story. With tears streaming down her face, Rebecca looked sullenly at her and nodded. Ashley sat still for a while. She had her head in her palms for what seemed like eternity.

"Okay, he says he loves you, you come to his house, and he is having fun with another girl, why wouldn't he attempt to put on something before coming to see you?"

"I don't know. Probably to spite me?"

"You told me you slept with him on the same bed all night when you were at his parents?"

"Yes."

"Did he at any time of the night try to take advantage of you?"

"Oh, no," she blurted out.

"So why do you think now he will want to sleep with another girl?"

"I don't know."

Ashley thought that probably Maggie wanted to give an appearance of indecency on the part of Kofi to tarnish his reputation, but she had no way of convincing her friend. Though she was the same age as Rebecca, she was already married and thus seemed to understand men a little better. She was not going to extenuate the situation for her friend by supporting her latest theory about her boyfriend. She was going to give the poor guy a hearing. She stayed with her for a while, then she returned home. After Ashley left, Rebecca started to think through some of the arguments she was making. When they had shared a bed, Kofi was never naked at any time. However, in the case of Maggie, the two of them were almost naked. Why is that just an appearance? She was not convinced. At any rate, she was not going to go back on her word, she concluded that it was finished between her and Kofi.

Kofi on his part had his issues to grapple with. After both Rebecca and Maggie left, he could not bring himself to do anything. For a while, he paced back and forth in his living room not knowing what to do. Sometime later, he decided to call Rebecca again but this time her phone was turned off. After several minutes of trying to reach out to her in vain, he got into his Jeep and drove to her place. He knocked hard at her door a million times. Initially, there was no answer. Then he heard Rebecca come to the door.

"Who's there?"

"It's me."

You don't have a name?"

"It's me, Kofi."

"Please go away, I don't want to see you."

"Rebecca, please open the door, at least you should hear me out."

"No, I don't want to hear anything. Please go back home."

"Becky dear, please open the door."

Rebecca stopped for a second. She contemplated whether to open the door, then decided against it.

"No Kofi, go back home, I don't want to see you."

He stopped knocking but instead of going back home he sat down behind her door. He was hoping that she might change her mind and open the door. After an hour she still did not come out to check, so he knocked again.

"Who is it this time?"

"It's still Kofi."

"Please go home, I don't want to see you, what don't you understand about that?"

He walked away from her apartment dejectedly, with his hands in his pockets and with his shoulders slumped. The short distance from her apartment to his truck seemed like an eternity; he felt misunderstood and lonely, but he was also angry with Maggie for getting him into a big jam and possibly crushing his dream of a happy marriage.

CHAPTER 25

UNEXPECTED VISITORS

After returning from Rebecca's apartment, Kofi kept to himself. His head was spinning, and he was beaten. He did not go out again until Monday to return to work. He hoped the new working week would bring a solution to his predicament. When he arrived, Ellen was in her office as usual. They exchanged greetings and he went to his office to begin work. As he walked towards his office, Ellen saw there was a change in his demeanor, but she couldn't put her finger on what it was. Usually, he would stop at her office for a little chat before he went on to his office. Whatever it was she decided not to meddle in his affairs. As for Kofi, he was wrapping up the network system he was building for the administration, so he went straight to work.

When Lisa came in, he told her not to let anyone in because he was extremely busy and didn't want to be disturbed. Nevertheless, he would have given everything to see Rebecca. Later in the day, he sent Lisa to Rebecca to come and see him. Rebecca wanted to be polite so she told Lisa she would be there to see him, but she never showed up. At lunchtime, he went to her table, but she got up and walked away when she saw him approaching. Maggie also came in later and tried to join him at his table, but he told her to find her table. She then went to Rebecca's table. She was only halfway through her food, but she got up and left the cafeteria. There was a grim look of remorse about Maggie but neither Kofi nor Rebecca paid any heed to that. She just sat down at the table which Rebecca had just vacated and started eating. All this time Ellen who had just come to the cafeteria was watching what was going on. When she had her food, she went to Kofi's table.

"Mind, if I sit here with you?"

"Not at all."

Now Ellen became more unsettled. Lately, Kofi has been seen a lot with Rebecca, but suddenly she sits apart from him. And what about Maggie. She is always the happy person inviting herself to every gathering, now Kofi doesn't want to sit with her?

"Is everything okay with you today, Kofi?" Ellen asked confused about the drama she had witnessed.

"Yes, I'm perfectly fine thanks."

"Is there something you're not telling me?"

"Come on Ellen, when did I run to you with my problems?"

"Don't take offense, Kofi, I meant it in a good way."

They ate their food in silence. When he finished eating, he apologized to Ellen and left for his office. When he got there, there was a man sitting at Lisa's waiting for him.

"Have you been waiting long? He asked the stranger.

"Yes, but I have pleasantly been occupied by your secretary, even amused."

He was a neighbor of his auntie, and he knew him from the time when he stayed with her. They had only spoken a few times. Now he came to him because he needed his help.

"So, what brought you here today?"

"Well, you know, your niece just finished university and she is looking for a job."

Kofi hardly knew him, now his relative is his niece? He wondered. He knew if he gave him an outright no, he would go to his aunt to tell her how unhelpful he was. He was in a dilemma.

"Do you have her transcripts?"

"I didn't think they will be needed."

"Well since she has just graduated and has no work experience, they will need her transcripts to place her."

He thanked Kofi and got up to leave. But Kofi knew he had not seen the last of him. In this country you are employed not on merit but on who you know. He was willing to help but only if the girl did well enough to perform at whatever job she procured.

"I will suggest you go and get her transcripts so that we could figure out the next step," Kofi suggested as an afterthought, trying not to complicate issues.

That evening when he got home, he found his auntie Belinda, her husband Mark Prosper and their daughter Abena were waiting outside his door. They did not know if he would be going somewhere after coming home so they had come early.

"Wow Mister and Missus, and Abena, what a pleasant surprise," Kofi exclaimed when he saw them.

"Sorry for barging in on you," Mr. Prosper explained smiling broadly, "but we felt bad not coming to see where you live after you left."

"Not at all, you're always welcome here. And where is Kojo?"

"He had gone out to play football when we were leaving the house."

Abena, her eyes wide opened, ran from the living room to the adjoining kitchen. "Wow uncle, this place is beautiful. How many rooms do you have?" She asked excitedly.

"It has three rooms, with a toilet, bath, and kitchen," Kofi explained.

"You have a toilet in the house?"

She had never seen a house with indoor plumbing before. So, the whole thing was fascinating to her. Kofi showed them around the flat. First his bedroom, the guest room, and then the washroom. It was the washroom that captivated little Abena the most.

"Do you have a place to store your food, Kofi? I brought you some yam," Auntie Belinda asked.

He led the way to the kitchen and showed her where to put the yam, with Abena following them.

"Do you cook on this?" Abena asked, pointing to the stove in the kitchen. She had not seen an electric or gas stove before, because at home they cook with charcoal stoves.

"Yes."

"Do you want me to cook your dinner, Kofi?" Auntie Belinda enquired.

"Yes, what about you cook for all of us?"

She hesitated and looked at her husband sitting in the living room for encouragement, but he was not looking her way.

"Mami please," Abena pleaded.

Kofi showed her where everything was and how to work the stove. Then he went to the living room to rejoin Mr. Prosper.

"You have a nice place Kofi," the older man said.

"I agree," Kofi replied.

"Now tell me, Kofi. How is work going for you?"

"Work is fine."

"That's good."

"Yes, but sometimes I get troubled about the way my work colleagues behave."

"What do you mean?"

"The way they collect bribes and don't seem to care about the people."

"That's no secret to the ordinary people on the streets of *Sikakrom* or any part of *Abibiman* for that matter."

"Is that so?"

"We've heard time and again from the people running the country that they want to help us poor people but in reality, they are interested in their own wellbeing and that of their immediate families."

"Really? I didn't know the people are aware of the corruption in higher places. But why do they vote for them then?"

"You know, in this country people vote for their tribesmen. Hence, whether they are good or not, whether they are reputable is not the question."

"Is that the only reason?"

"No, there are other reasons, but that's the main one."

"So, Mr. Prosper you don't think there are politicians who care for the needs of the people?" Kofi didn't want to appear that he was supporting his way of thinking.

"When they appear to care, they are only taking advantage of the people's generosity," Mark Prosper replied.

"Is that right?"

Kofi asked feigning ignorance. Mark Prosper then stood up and went to the window closest to where he was sitting. He moved the blinds aside and looked outside. Kofi got up also and moved closer to him as he stood there by the window. Not much was going on outside, but Mark Prosper was still standing there and looking. Without turning to look at Kofi he spoke.

"You know Kofi, our political leaders are a bunch of phonies, the people's sorrows only serve as tunes for their ears."

He turned from the window and stood there in a pensive mood with a faraway look in his eyes. Kofi returned to his seat now but continued to focus his attention on the older man who was still reflecting. He returned to his seat and continued.

"They often claim to be working for the people by harping on the glorious melodies of dying for them, taking their pains, and working hard to make life easy for them . . ." he stopped, curled his lips and whistled the tune of a song before completing his sentence, "but in reality, the people's griefs are the songs for their parties and the stories for their pastime."

Kofi was astounded, by the way his elderly visitor, couched his opinion in such prosaic philosophical terms. His language was a little unnerving, but it was the most accurate description of the politicians of *Abibiman*. His was a view from afar, nevertheless, it resonated well with what he had been experiencing. Since working at the presidency, he had gained firsthand knowledge about the pervasiveness of corruption in this country, but he had never thought of the people knowing all the deals that go on in higher places. He recognized that as up-and-coming leaders, it was a challenge for the youth who are the future leaders of this country to sit up and do the right thing. As he sat there listening to his adopted uncle, he was silently making a resolution to himself; he vowed to work harder to rid corruption from every stratum of society. Mark Prosper now switched the conversation to personal matters.

"On a more serious note, Kofi, now that you have your own place, have you thought about marriage?"

"Yes, but I haven't found the right woman," he replied.

"Belinda told me you went to your parents' village with a woman."

"That's true. She is a girl from work who wanted to go with me to the village. Nothing serious."

"Well, if a girl will follow you to your parents, she is probably interested in you," he said.

By this time Auntie Belinda had finished preparing the meal. They all sat down to enjoy dinner. During dinnertime, Kofi brought up the subject of the neighbor who was looking for a job for her daughter.

"Now tell me, Auntie, this neighbor who is three apartments from yours came to me looking for a job for his daughter."

"Oh, you are talking about Kwame. Her daughter, so we're told, is a very smart girl."

"How do you know this Auntie Belinda?"

"Everyone in the neighborhood knows. They say she came on top of her class."

"So why isn't she continuing her education?"

"Kofi, if there is any help you can give them, please do. They are very poor."

When dinner was over, Abena was asked by her mother to wash the dishes and clean the dirty kitchen. They stayed for a while after dinner until late in the night. By that time of the night getting transport back was not going to be easy so Kofi gave them a ride home. Before they left him, he told them to inform the neighbor to bring her daughter to him the next day.

CHAPTER 26

LICENSING AND DOING
THE RIGHT THING

The Freedom Convention Party had been in opposition for a long time until the elections two years previously. In their years in opposition, their activities were mainly financed by the prominent members of the party. In *Abibiman*, political parties do not normally get donations. Their only means of raising support was through membership fees. However, when they were in opposition not many people applied for membership. In this country, most people want to be aligned with the ruling party so that crumbs would fall into their laps. The years in opposition had taught the leadership to maximize their chances of preserving their chances of ruling again. This, they said can only be done if they were able to strengthen the financial base of the party. In this bid they have resorted to some radical approaches. These included the promotion of cronyism and patronage, deceptive accounting, and illegal solicitations. This desire to perpetuate their rule had taken the act of patronage to another level. Through that program, reputable businesses and individuals paid large sums of money to authorities so that they could gain contracts; tax holidays; and access to duty-free regimes for their imports. Beyond that, the leaders did improper accounting by taking a percentage out of any foreign loans they contracted.

Moreover, they illegally solicited funds by requiring prospective investors to make direct payments to the party and not to the state. They seemed to have lost sight of the fact that what would return them to power was the improvement the people would see in infrastructural development and their ability to put food on their tables. These had been the guiding principles of Kofi since his appointment. He had sought to close any loopholes so that government expenditure would not run out of control. No more were investors paying extra for licenses; importers getting free passes on imports; or ministers getting percentages from foreign loans. Kofi had been the breath of fresh air the country needed. He had kicked against anything that smacked of corruption and was getting on people's nerves.

He and Joseph Baiden oversaw approving prospective investment licenses. In his quest to eliminate corruption he had not been taking the additional fee the party has put on investors. He had usually signed off the licenses without demanding the extra payments and had informed Baiden to do same. Therefore, when Lisa brought a prospective investor who had already been to Joseph Baiden, he did not ask for the additional fee. The would-be investor told Kofi that he was applying for a license to start a business in *Sikakrom* and had been coming to see Mr. Baiden but today he was not in and the clerks directed him to come and see Kofi.

"Good afternoon, sir."

As he spoke, he a somewhat detached look in his eyes.

"Good afternoon, please sit down."

The man sat down and handed his documents to Kofi. He looked at his documents and realized that he had fulfilled all the requirements. As he was going to his payment the fellow said regretfully.

"Sir, I still could not raise the thirty thousand dollars, but I assure you I will bring it when the business commences."

The man explained while handing his paperwork to Kofi, a frown etched on his face. Kofi was sure he had informed Mr. Baiden that requiring those extra fees was illegal. He signed all his papers and asked him to take to the clerks. He got down on his knees and thanked Kofi profusely. His expression was now relaxed and free of the frown lines that were there earlier.

"Why are you kneeling down?"

"In appreciation for granting my license."

"Come on, you didn't need to do that. After all you are helping to bring jobs to the nation."

The man started to pick up his approved documents so he could go to the cashiers. At this time, his hands were shaking. Kofi looked at him in astonishment.

"Why was he trembling and rushing to pick up his stuff, so that in the process he was dropping more items?"

He was not sure why he was shaking all over, nor why he seemed in such a great hurry. As the fellow left, Kofi decided that he would take up the matter with Joseph Baiden when he returned to the office. When the clerk took the investor's documents and the receipts, she saw that one item was missing.

"Where is your yellow receipt?"

"The officer who signed my documents said everything was in order."

"Really?"

The clerk did not say anything further. He signed off on his documents and gave him his license. When the man got his license, he was so elated he ran back to Kofi's office. His eyes were sparkling as he took an envelope from his pocket and smiled broadly before handing it to Kofi.

"In here is five thousand dollars."

"What is that for?"

"For helping me, sir?"

"You will do no such thing!" Kofi scolded him sternly.

Reluctantly he took the envelope, muttered something unintelligible and left his office. Meanwhile, the clerk who issued the license thought something was amiss. He went to Nicholas Hamma's office.

"Good afternoon Honorable, sir."

"Good afternoon young man. What can I do for you?"

"Mr. Hope just signed off on a license for an investor."

"Okay?"

"Well, I know they ask for additional money beside the normal fee."

"Yes."

"This time there was none."

Hamma told him not to worry because he would see Mr. Hope about the issue. After the young investor had left, Kofi stood up and gazed out of his window. The clouds were gathering so it was probably going to rain very soon. His desire was that if it should rain, it should not be a storm. He went back to his seat and sat down. Lisa knocked at his door and entered. She was followed by a young woman. Kofi recognized her as the lady who offered him a stash of dollars when he first started working at the presidency. He remembered that the first time she had sat down uninvited. This time she hesitated and waited for his invitation to sit. As she did so she looked nervous with her shoulders tightly drawn in and she appeared to be almost in tears.

He turned his attention to Lisa and told her she and his driver could go home. When he returned his attention to the young woman, her head was tilted, and she seemed to be in thought. Looking at her, he wondered why her confidence seemed to have deserted her. This person sitting before him was a far cry from that overconfident woman who came to him some time ago. Now she looked somewhat pathetic; her chin was quivering, and she was licking her lips nervously.

"Good afternoon, sir."

"What can I help you with, Ma'am?"

"I need your signature on a form so that I could go and clear my goods from the harbor."

"Can I see the form?"

"This is the form sir; all it needs is your signature."

"I see, but it says here you have to pay a certain amount."

"But sir, your office controls those payments so your signature is good to guarantee the clearance. This is what Mr. Hamma used to do for me before you came."

Now Kofi understood why the woman wanted to bribe him when he first took the position.

"I am sorry Ma'am but signing this for you would be causing financial loss to the State."

The woman got up and left, but a few minutes later he came back with Nicholas Hamma who stood in the entryway and spoke to Kofi.

"Mr. Hope, this lady is a big donor to our party, so we always help her out," he explained.

"Honorable Hamma, you better leave my office, otherwise I will report both you and the lady to the police for bribery and accessory to bribery."

"But Mr. Hope. . . ."

"Honorable Hamma, I hope you heard me the first time?"

The two left silently. Hamma could no longer do anything to help the lady because he was no longer the person in charge. As they left Kofi's office, their footsteps pitter-pattered the hallway and the rains also started, pitter-patter; pitter-patter, then its intensity increased clanging and clattering the roof. Back in his office, Hamma sat silently and so did the young woman. There was nothing they could do now.

"Please go and see Lucy the women's organizer of the FCP, he cannot refuse her," he said.

As the woman left, he slouched in his chair rage throbbing in him like a heartbeat. Every big occasion is heralded by the waving of a flag. He was humiliated and he was not going to take it lightly. That upstart Hope had disrespected him by turning both him and the lady away.

"I am going to show him not to disrespect his elders," he whispered to himself.

By the time Kofi left the office to go home, the rain had the force with which to wreak havoc; it had increased tremendously in intensity. He feared driving in the rainstorm but was more scared of the hail that was clattering the ground as if it had been poured there by a big excavator hanging somewhere in the heavens. He drove slowly watching out for other vehicles around him. He knew he was a careful driver, but he was not sure about those around him. All through the night, thunder boomed and rumbled on, the accompanying lighting ignited the skies repeatedly, and the rain hammered against the window. Later in the night, Kofi lay peacefully in bed like a child whose mother was singing a lullaby to send him to sleep. He was not the least worried about unfolding events. The meddling of Hamma was the least of his troubles. He knew he was on the right course. Hamma or no Hamma, there was no need to worry unduly, because the situation would resolve itself eventually.

CHAPTER 27

RUFFLING FEATHERS AT THE STAFF MEETING

Kofi had longed to be closer to the people so that he could see what they see and feel how they feel. Perhaps by so doing, he could share in their experience. Occasionally, he liked to sample everyday street life, eat from the roadside *chop bars*, the people eat from, ride the *Trotros* they ride and experience the rejections they are subjected to, the pain and aches they endure. One way of doing this was to leave the luxury of his chauffeur-driven car or personal vehicle and take public transport. For that reason, today, he left his truck at home and took public transport. He boarded a *Trotro* that plied the streets of *Sikakrom* daily. When the driver's mate noticed he was well dressed, he asked him to be one of two passengers to share the front seat with the driver. On the way, they came to a police barrier.

The police were stopping drivers and taking money from them. When it came the turn of the *Trotro* he was riding in, the driver took a twenty *Sika* note, added his license, and gave it to one of the policemen. The officer took the money, returned the license, and waved the driver on without inspecting anything in the *Trotro* as they were pretending to be doing. Once they left the barrier the passenger next to him made a remark symptomatic of attitudes in *Abibiman*.

"That policeman is good."

"What makes him good?" Kofi asked puzzled.

"Well unlike other policemen, who will take money from you and still hold you, he will let you go when he collects the money."

Kofi was astounded with his bizarre explanation. As their *Trotro* meandered in and out of traffic, he questioned the passenger's logic. He was appalled because many people in *Abibiman* failed to see bribery and corruption for what it was—as a crime. They accepted and glorified it as a fact of everyday life, which did nothing to help stamp it out of society.

"What a bleak picture we paint about our country. What kind of country is this where people openly condone and connive with wrongdoers," he thought to himself.

Some ten minutes after the police checkpoint incident, the driver announced that he had come to his last stop. As it turned out, Kofi had boarded the wrong vehicle, now he had to get on another one that would take him to his workplace. Due to that mistake, though he had left home very early, he reached the office at the same time as everybody else. Ellen came out of her office just when he got there.

"Hello Kofi, you're later than usual today."

"Yes, I used the public transport and got on the wrong *Trotro*."

"Why didn't you let your driver pick you up?"

"I usually drive to work myself."

"So, where's your truck? Is it broken down?"

"Oh, no, I just wanted to sample travel by *Trotro*."

"Oh, Kofi! What has come over you?" Ellen chuckled.

As he left her to enter his office, she began to chortle, then it turned into a belly laugh. She had never seen a person like Kofi Hope in all her time as a Presidential staffer. He enjoyed all the privileges of the senior staffers, but he seemed reluctant to use them. The day was moving fast. An often-postponed staff meeting finally took place. The chief was late coming to the meeting. It was well over an hour after everyone had been seated when they thought the meeting was going to be called off that he entered. He strode over to his seat majestically and stood there, his eyes sweeping enquiringly over the group. If they were expecting an apology, they got none. His intimidating looks were a challenge to anyone who would question his lateness. He cleared his throat and set the ball rolling. He began by congratulating all the staff for the work they had been doing. He then outlined his plans for the next quarter and sketched what he expected from each member of staff. When he was done speaking, he asked for contributions from the team.

Most of those present had suggestions to give. Some were positive, others less so. The suggestions kept rolling in. Kofi was thrilled with what he was hearing. Every staff member seemed energized and alert for the day's business and not afraid to speak up. He suggested that the top officials should constantly connect with people in their constituencies so that they would know what was happening on the ground. The next item on the agenda was the financial report. Kofi had a lot of questions on his mind, and he intended to seek clarification for all of them. He gave a comprehensive financial report that left many squirming in their seats. He emphasized certain expenditures on government outlay that seemed erroneous. These included telephone calls to private numbers; the use of government vehicles after working hours; and several items listed on the expenditure as miscellaneous.

As he continued his report, several sets of eyes were glaring at him. The chief-of-staff particularly had an unusually stern look. Nevertheless, he proceeded, determined to expose all the crimes staff members were committing. What infuriated the chief the most was his exhortation for members to be responsible in their use of government resources. The meeting ended with the chief announcing an impending rally of the party in a nearby city the following day. He appealed to every staff member to make it a priority to attend what was not going to be a protracted tour, but only a day trip. To save time he said that all the staff would be transported to and from the rally grounds by helicopter. After the meeting, Adams pulled Kofi aside.

"That was some deep revelation you gave there."

"Yes, that's right."

"Kofi, do you want some advice? From one insider to another insider?"

"What is it, John?" He asked confused.

"I know one secret you don't."

"And what's that?"

"You see, many in the administration believe that they need to make all the money while in government so that when the time comes for them to go, they will have some reserved for their needs."

"Is that so?" Kofi responded in mock surprise.

"They care less what the general populace thinks or what effect it will have on them."

"Okay?"

"If they perceive you're in the way, being too nosey, blowing the whistle, and being a snitch, they will run over you. It doesn't matter what you do, they will get back at you and push you out of the way."

"Thanks for your warning, John, but I would rather quit than stay mute and condone the wrongdoings of the staff."

"I'm just telling you that you will make enemies, so don't say I didn't warn you Kofi."

On that note, Adams left him to go to his office.

"I appreciate you," Kofi called after him as he left.

While he was speaking with Adams, honorable John Baiden was waiting to speak to him. After Adams left, he came to him.

"Can I speak to you in your office, Mr. Hope?"

"Yes, of course, I wanted to see you too."

As they walked towards his office, the older man asked. "How are you doing on the job, Mr. Hope?"

"I'm doing well, but every day I realize there is more work to do."

"Well, you don't have to do everything yourself. When you feel overwhelmed, assign some jobs to your subordinates. Remember your age notwithstanding you are a senior around here."

"Thank you."

As they entered his office, Kofi knew that there was more to John Baiden's visit than that small talk, so he braced himself for a possible long speech. He pulled a chair away from Kofi's desk and tug at his trousers before sitting down. He then stroked his chin and put on a serious face.

"You see, Mr. Hope," he began, "*Abibiman* is not like the developed countries where somebody goes into politics just for the love of it."

"OK?"

"Here, when you get into politics, it's to prepare for your future. Now you are young and energetic, but you are not always going to be young."

"OK, and so?"

"One of the things we have decided as a party is to have every party executive a player."

"What's that?"

"Every job you hold within government, you have to find a way to earn extra money and pay a percentage of it to the party."

"Ehh?"

"Our role as people in charge of licensing is to collect certain amounts and pay a percentage to the party."

"I think I've told you before that, that is not money we should be collecting?"

"Why?"

"Because we cannot account for it. Besides, it is plain extortion. It's a burden which stops jobs going to the people."

"Well, those extra monies we collect are not state money so we cannot be stealing from the state coffers."

"What about the investor, couldn't they have rolled that money over into their business?" Kofi asked indignantly.

"Well, what do you care about that, if they're not ready to start a business, they shouldn't come forward then."

"Hmm"

"Well, Mr. Hope, if you don't need the money remember, the party will expect you to bring something. I'm talking to you as an elder and a friend. Good day."

With that, Honorable John Baiden got up and left his office. Kofi sat alone, reflecting on this encounter. He thought about the plight of the people. He could now understand why there was so much poverty among them. Notwithstanding all the rich deposits of gold, diamond, manganese, bauxite, mineral oil, and numerous other mineral resources in the country, it was still considered poor. Was it any wonder, when you have people called honorable looking after your affairs who are anything but honorable? Wouldn't the people have been better off if they had as elected representatives self-confessed robbers and thieves to rule over them instead of these robbers who masqueraded as saints? There was no end to his worries, but it was fruitless to just sit there and brood about it. He packed and headed to his truck. As he was driving home many thoughts flooded his mind. In this country it seemed perfectly normal for ministers to 'borrow' their departmental funds for personal profit.

It was nothing out of the ordinary for appointments of high-ranking civil servants to be made based on patronage rather than merit. Seemingly, there was an official whose main preoccupation was the distribution of patronage to government supporters and their cronies. The government often tried hard to show the people they were working for them. The vast sums of money they borrowed for developmental projects were shared among government operatives. A fraction of those funds was used for projects around the country. No wonder projects remained unfinished after the budgets were siphoned off elsewhere. Those projects were used for avoidance, meant to create distraction. To throw dust into the eyes of the people. They were designed to give the impression that their leaders were working hard for them. But Kofi knew that most people never considered that their adorable leaders were pillaging the loans they have contracted on their behalf for hotel expenses, entertainment, and educational funds for their wards in London, New York, and Toronto. He comforted himself that worrying about these were not important. What was needed was action and he was already embarked on a course of action.

CHAPTER 28

A RALLY AND A REBUFF

At the office, everyone was working feverishly for the rally scheduled for later in the day. As people who doubled as government workers and party functionaries, they had to perform both roles to the letter. Before they left Barbara told them to continue to make the sacrifices they were making because the elections were imminent. She admonished them to try to be of good behavior to reflect positively on the party and President. Many of the girls from the party who work at the office, including Rebecca, Lisa, Ellen, and Maggie were present. Before joining the President's motorcade, Barbara told Lisa to get some boys to bring water to the entourage. Lisa walked away with a gracefulness that belied her timorous personality. Kofi had not seen her that way before and was pleasantly surprised. The rally itself went well. Ellen was sitting next to him.

As for Rebecca, she made a point of sitting as far away as possible. Occasionally Ellen would make some remarks in his ears. On one occasion Kofi sneaked a look at Rebecca, she was looking at them stoically but averted her gaze to avoid eye contact. Hamma was also there sitting among some group of party officials. He seemed to be in deep conversation with one of them. At one point, Kofi noticed him shooting a sideways glance at him, before turning his attention back to his companion. The rally itself was a success with a few glitches. The President spoke with an eloquence only he was known for. Kofi should have been happy because of the things the President spoke about, but instead, he was genuinely bored and depressed by his speech. He could not hide his disgust any longer. Even as the President spoke, one could sense a tense atmosphere. There were several *macho* men planted all around the grounds. A heckler rose from the crowd and shouted,

"Mr. President what are you doing about the arrest of those journalists who spoke up about corruption in your administration?"

Another also shouted;

"Mr. President why do we have only past government officials on trial?" The *macho* men who were planted in the crowd rose up and shouted at the men to sit down. A hush fell on the crowd when they saw the bodybuilders amongst them, and the president continued with his speech.

Storm clouds were gathering fast by the time the rally was ending. When it ended, Barbara told the team they would not be going back home because of the bad weather so she had secured hotel accommodation for all of them. When they got to the car park, a bus was waiting to take them to the hotel. Kofi sat with Ellen in the third row of the bus. Rebecca sat a row in front of them, oblivious to what was going on with them. When they got out of the bus, Kofi and Ellen walked side by side to the hotel. Maggie followed a distance away and Rebecca was by herself in front of them. She reached reception and was assigned her room before Kofi. When he saw her heading to her room, he left Ellen and went after her. Ellen saw him go but said nothing.

"Rebecca!" Kofi called after her.

"What?" She turned towards him but did not make eye contact as she tersely scowled in his direction.

"Please, can I talk to you?"

"Talk about what, Mr. Fixer," raising her voice, "You think you can fix every problem in the world with just a wave of your hand, don't you?"

He reached out to take her hands, but she wiggled them free from his grip. The once affable Rebecca was now a lioness. He was left speechless; he could stand other people saying mean things about him but not Rebecca. She had surely taken the feud with him to another level and there was no way she was going to forgive him. As tears streamed down his face, he turned around so she would not see his dismay, but she caught a glimpse of it anyway. She stood there stunned because she was not expecting that reaction. Moreover, she instantly noticed that he was not taking care of himself as she knew him. He needed a haircut. At least Ellen should have told him that.

"Oh, well it's none of my business now." She sighed to herself and walked away.

She was resolved not to show any sign of weakness in front of him. She could not pity a man who could do what Kofi Hope did to her. Probably because she had been able to sit down and weep after the incident involving Maggie, she was now much stronger emotionally and able to deal with it. Not so much Kofi. He was showing more signs of strain every day. As he watched Rebecca walk away, his heart sank. He stood there deflated and weak. After a while, he went into a nearby washroom to wash his face and then rejoined Ellen who was taken aback by his disconsolate appearance.

"What's the matter Kofi?" Ellen asked, her eyes widening, "you look a bit down."

He didn't answer, he just kept quiet. He was simply trying to put on a brave face, tough guy posture, but Ellen could see through the façade. There was no doubt that he was looking despondent like a man rejected. She knew he was hurting but she didn't know how best to help him. She wished he would open up to her so she could offer any help possible. Meanwhile, Rebecca was wondering why Kofi still wanted to reach out to her again. She had given him up since the day he caught him red-handed with Maggie. However, his approach tonight and tearful response to her rebuff, showed he must still care. Maybe he still loved her, but was she willing to be hurt again by cozying up to him? Surely, it was better she kept to things as they were. She had overcome a heartbreak, why should she risk getting hurt again? Kofi Hope was not worth going through all that pain again. She would chart her own course. Dinner was going to be served in about an hour's time so they had to go inside and get ready. Ellen had already collected her key as well as Kofi's and was waiting for him. When he returned, the look on his face was disheartening.

"Come and have a drink Kofi," Ellen said, her brows pulled together, "You look like you could do with one."

He stared at Ellen blankly. He did not feel like drinking but Ellen was only trying to be nice to him, so he needn't say anything mean.

"I appreciate that Ellen, but we will be late for dinner if we don't go to our rooms and get ready."

She agreed, so they walked together to their assigned rooms. He wanted to take a shower before going for dinner, but he had wasted enough time in the lobby, so he decided to do it later. He walked down to the dining room. Maggie and Barbara were at the same table, but Rebecca was sitting with a different group. Ellen was still not down so he selected a table close to where Rebecca was sitting with some co-workers from her office. He wanted to eavesdrop on their conversation. They were talking animatedly about different subjects. When he sat down, she was speaking about some experiences she had when she travelled with a friend. As she spoke, she had a touch of a smile on her face and her eyes were sparkling. She was telling them that she had a lot of fun but had no idea when next she could go on a similar trip. Kofi knew she was referring to their trip to his village, but he dared not interject himself into their conversation and get disgraced.

He simply sat there reminiscing about their trip to the village, and the fun they had together. How he wished they could rewind the clock to that time. He would give up everything to have that experience again. To see Rebecca at her adorable self again instead of this muted individual sitting at a table away from him, but miles away in spirit. As he was sitting there lost in thought, Ellen entered. She walked to where he was sitting and joined him at the table. There were still two empty chairs sitting by the table where Rebecca and her colleagues were. Ellen suggested they join that group. Without waiting to hear what he would say, she took their plates and joined them. He had no choice but to follow her lead. When they sat there Rebecca stopped speaking. Ellen attempted several times to get Kofi and Rebecca to speak, but she just kept mute.

Rebecca ate her food quickly and excused herself. Kofi watched her as she walked away to return to her room. He decided there was no way the gulf between them could be bridged because she was entrenched in her opposition to him. The next day, the helicopter flew them straight back to the office. Kofi was busy at work in his office when Lisa announced a visitor. He told her to allow the person in and then went back to work. He was a young man, cleanly shaven, tall, and lanky with bulging biceps and chest. He looked like somebody who had just returned from overseas.

"Please have a seat."

As he sat down, he lowered his eyebrows and with his chin lifted he looked anxiously at him.

"How can I be of help today?"

"My friend Paul directed me to come and see you."

"Who's Paul?"

"A guy you helped to get the license to start a filling station."

"Yes, I remember, but why did he suggest that you see me?"

"When he was here, he went to another officer but he was not in so they directed him to come and see you. He gave you rave reviews."

"I see." He remembered the incident involving the man who had gone to see Baiden before coming to see him.

"Oh yeah, I remember now. And what are you applying for?"

"The same, sir."

"So where are you based, and where is your source of income coming from?"

"Sir, I drive a taxicab in Chicago, Illinois."

"Oh, Chicago! I've spent some time in Lisle and Bolingbroke both in the Chicago area."

"In fact, I live in Bolingbroke. There are a lot of people from *Abibiman* who live there."

Kofi gave him the necessary forms to fill out. This young man's situation was surely going to throw a challenge to him. Here was a young man coming back to his homeland to invest. How could he extort any monies from him? He imagined the many sleepless nights he might have spent driving a taxi around the city of Chicago with all the risks involved. As somebody who had been there and done that, there was no way he was going to bring himself to levy any monies on him for the sake of a political party. By now the man had finished filling the forms so he stamped it and asked him to go to the cashier and pay the requisite fee. When he came back with his payment voucher, he endorsed it and asked him to go with the forms to collect his license. He left beaming. After the man left, he sat there and contemplated his action. Baiden had made it clear to him that the extra money was for the party.

"Well, the party should find its own money to organize their campaigns," he consoled himself.

CHAPTER 29

ZERO FROM LIBYA

It had been a busy day for Kofi. Every time the staff went out for field work, the return to the office was inundated with heightened activity. But soon enough the working day was over; he gathered his stuff and headed home. Fortunately, Ellen was the only one he saw on his way out. The other girls had already gone home. As he drove away, buried in thought, he wondered how this drama was going to end. Here he was in the middle of a dangerous and turbulent situation yet still remained completely calm and imperturbable. Who would have thought a year or two ago that he had those qualities? His calmness was even surprising himself.

But now thrown into the center of the action he had suddenly acquired this poise. He steeled himself and resolved that no matter what lengths he had to go he would stand up for the values his grandmother taught him, to stand up for the weak and vulnerable in society. To stand for the right course of action. He knew that if he failed to do the right thing, those who lavished him with praise today, would inundate him with criticism until he was humiliated to the bone. The same place where profligacy of praise abound, would see a dearth of applause. He would be deserted, left to himself to ponder his mortification. When he got home, he found something to eat and jumped into bed. He had been hanging out with Ellen at work, but it was not the same as it had been with Rebecca. Occasionally, Ellen called him but whenever he was alone, he never called her. The hole left by Rebecca was too deep for anybody to fill. He was contemplating this dilemma when he drifted into sleep.

When he woke up early in the morning at the usual time, the world was just waking up. He put on his tracksuit and went on his usual morning walk. There was a man ahead of him walking briskly, as if he was running away from somebody or something. The man glanced back over his shoulder. As he did so their eyes met. Burly built, around five feet nine inches and a wearied looking face. There was something familiar about him. He had a mark similar to the man who was about to be lynched when he rescued him. Suddenly, without any warning the fellow ran and knelt at Kofi's feet.

"Tank you very mauch man," cried the man, bowing repeatedly, "na me be dead now if you no save me."

"Walk with me," Kofi suggested.

"I no get opportunity to tank you, man," the man muttered as they started to walk.

They saw a small restaurant on the corner of the street, so he suggested they go in there to talk. When they walked in there and sat down, all eyes turned towards them. Kofi ordered two cups of coffee. His companion grabbed his cup and, in an instant, emptied its contents. He realized he was tired and hungry, so he ordered some food also. The man gulped down the food too.

"We never really got the chance to meet," he said, extending his hands to the man, "my name is Kofi Hope."

"The name be Zero," the man replied in his street language.

"Is that your real name?" Kofi chuckled.

"No be my real name but be what everybody around dey call me," he replied.

"Are you from *Sikakrom*?"

"No, I don came here wey I return from Libya."

"Libya?"

Zero explained that some time ago he stole his uncle's money to go to Europe. Unfortunately, some bandits in Libya captured him together with his traveling companions in the Libyan desert and sold them as slaves. He worked under harsh conditions in Libya. Such was his situation he gave up hope of ever returning home. One day he got the opportunity to run away from his captors. When he returned home, his family rejected him not only for being a failure but also for being a thief. The rejection was too much to bear so he came to the capital. However, without education and resources, he had not found any work. His only means of survival was to steal here and there. But whilst it is not a life to be proud of, it was seemingly the only thing available to him. Kofi sat and listened silently as the man narrated the story of his life. So intriguing was the story that he had only nibbled at his food. Zero on the other hand had finished his and continued to look at Kofi's plate all the while as they chatted.

"It was good meeting again and getting to know you," Kofi said as he got up and shook hands with him.

Eyeing his half empty plate, Zero took it and hurriedly gulped down what was left. The way he took the food, and looking at his gaunt face, he was clearly famished. It made him think. Certainly, the slump in the global economy was felt mostly by people like Zero. The combination of economic collapse and regional, ethnic, and religious wars had greatly increased poverty for hundreds of millions of people like him. But while the big and emerging nations might recover, the poorest couldn't cope. That meant there was no end in sight for the woes of the Zeros of society.

Abibiman being a raw material exporter had been suffering from a downturn in its exports. There was a point when European orders stopped coming, and the country's farm workers simply sat idle. However, as a country dependent on raw material and farm produce, when exports go down and there are no foreign investment inflows everybody suffers. A large percentage of the people of this country were at the global periphery and for them there was no hope of a rebound for a long time. Perhaps for many people like Zero, it was already too late, or was it? Kofi looked at his watch; it was already thirty minutes after seven in the morning. He had better be going before he is late for work.

"Do you want me to drop you somewhere?" He asked Zero but the man hesitated. Therefore, he took it to mean no. He got his wallet to pay for the food and found one of his business cards and handed it to him.

"Goodbye friend." He said to Zero as he left the restaurant.

As they parted, Zero still sat there nibbling on the bones from his plate. All day his mind was on Zero. His situation was very precarious, but he did not know how he could specifically help him. When he got to the office, he was still worried for people like him. He wanted to see if there was any statistical evidence, with which he could plead their case. A thought occurred to him that he should see the government statistician, Kwame Asap. He had met the veteran civil servant when he went to say goodbye to Rebecca before his first presidential trip, so the two knew each other casually.

Mr. Asap's office was adjoined by a shared office space that was used by the three clerks who worked for him. It was in this office that Rebecca worked. She was the only one of the clerks with a bachelor's degree, so the two others reported to her. To get to Mr. Asap's office, you pass through the clerks' shared working space, and then his secretary before you get to him. When Kofi reached the shared space, the other two clerks who were there with Rebecca were smiling at him. In contrast, Rebecca sat there expressionless; she did not even have a ghost of a smile on her face. She looked away as Kofi asked them if their boss was in the office. One of the ladies responded politely; she got up and led him past Mr. Asap's secretary and directly to the man himself. Mr. Asap was a friendly, amicable fellow. He reached out and buried Kofi's right hand with both hands in a warm handshake.

"What brings the great Mr. Hope to my humble office this morning?"

Kofi was surely flattered by this amicable show of camaraderie from a man who had served his country for such a long time.

"To see you sir, about some questions that are disturbing me."

There was a big named plaque conspicuously placed on his table reading, 'Kwame Asap, government statistician'. He saw Kofi looking at it and smiled but he said nothing. When he sat down, Mr. Asap commended him for the program he had put in place that had made the job of everybody working for the president much easier. He encouraged him to continue with the reforms he was undertaking even if it meant facing opposition. Kofi thanked him for his appreciative support; he assured him that he would continue with the work he was doing to make the country better.

After the initial exchanges, Kofi told him the reason for his visit was to seek information on the country's micro-economic health. He replied that the country had made some strides, but there were still some lingering issues such as employment provision, child-parent relations and the delivery of good education and a host of other issues. He was delighted with Mr. Asap because though he was old, he treated him as a colleague worthy of his respect. As he got up to leave, he requested data on the statistical breakdown of the country's imports and exports for the previous years and on its micro economic indicators. Mr. Asap told him to get that information from Rebecca since she was the one who worked with them and held the database. Before they parted, he commended Kofi on the good work he was doing.

"Just a word of warning for you, Mr. Hope." He was now talking in a whisper, "I have a lot of enemies within the government because I always stand for what is right." He got up and placed a hand on Kofi's shoulder. "To see a young man like you at the forefront of the fight is refreshing but you must tread cautiously."

"Thanks for your advice and help." Kofi said appreciatively, as he got up to leave.

After speaking with the statistician, he was motivated to push for more resources to finance programs for children so that by the time they get to Zero's age, they would not be a burden on society. Now he should get the information he needed from Rebecca to really get going; so, he headed her way unsure how she would react. Rebecca saw him coming out of her boss's office, she presumed the cold reception she gave him would not motivate him to come to her before he left the department. Hence, she was surprised when she saw him heading her way. She didn't want to create any scene in front of the other clerks, so she sat down quietly and waited for him as he approached. When he got to her desk he stood and waited for her to invite him to sit but she sat there with a faraway look in her eyes.

"Miss Odom, Mr. Asap sent me to you." Kofi finally broke the silence as formally as he could. While she hesitated, he could see her lips quivering.

"Yes, of course," a half smile on her face, "what did you need to see me for, sir?"

"Microeconomic indicators," he hesitated before adding, "also import and export figures for the last two years."

She went to a cabinet standing behind her to fish out some papers. When she returned to her desk, she had a big file containing documents. She placed the papers on her desk and set out to search for those files containing the information he requested. She sorted through the documents, her lips pressed together, a half frown lingering on her face and her attention focused on the papers in front of her; never once did she lift her eyes to look at him. She then took some sheets from the pile and walked to a photocopier that stood nearby to copy them.

"Shouldn't you put this on the website I created for your department?" He asked her when she returned to her desk.

"We're still working on them." She replied without lifting her head; she was trying to avoid eye contact.

"Rebecca you are gorgeous," he whispered under his breath, "even when you don't smile."

She kept silent; at first, she had a tight-lipped smile on her face, then she lowered her gaze and looked at him sternly before handing the copies to him. He took the papers, thanked her, and walked out of her office. Rebecca was a wounded lover, who was as unwilling to let go of her grief and seek remedy as her pride stopped her making or accepting a gesture of reconciliation between them. There was no doubt her stance was complicating issues. As he walked away from her office, he knew that the gulf between him and Rebecca was widening by the day, and he felt powerless to do anything about it.

CHAPTER 30

A MOVIE DATE AND AWKWARD ENCOUNTER

It had been a year since Kofi started working at the office of the president. It was a good experience. In one year, he had achieved much. He had set up a network system where all the computers in the presidential and adjoining building could talk to one another. He had also set up a financial accounting system network for the whole administration. He had done all this with due diligence impressing on his colleagues the need for hard work to get the country out of the doldrums. He had always been punctual, coming to work on time and putting in maximum effort. However, his colleagues at work did not seem to be taking any cues from him because many of them were still apathetic at work and poor timekeepers, but he had not allowed their attitude to dampen his spirit. He had been working in the hope that others might eventually catch the mood and start showing some pride in their performance and work hard for the sake of their country. One of the things he had lately been working on was a brochure outlining steps necessary for mitigating poverty among the people. This required extra hours which he put in every day after his colleagues had gone home. On this day after the office closed Lisa saw him lingering around.

"Are you not going home now, Mr. Hope?"

"I'll stay a little longer and then leave."

"Sir, lately armed robberies have increased, so it's better to drive in the daylight."

As she spoke, she twiddled her thumbs and rubbed the tips of her fingers together. He looked at her and smiled.

"I'm a big boy and can take care of myself."

She gently brushed her temple and headed for the door. "If you say so, sir," she said.

Lisa was just like any girl worrying unnecessarily about him, he thought. He brushed off her concerns and buried himself in his work. He did not notice the night creeping up until he looked out and saw that it was pitch dark. He got up slowly, gathered his stuff and headed home. The night sky was bright, and he could see the stars in the horizon. He took the main road from the office. It was almost deserted as the evening rush hour was over and most workers had gone home. He sped on until he reached a road around the central market. Here there was a lot of vehicular as well as pedestrian traffic.

Soon he left the main road and took the side street leading to his flat. Just as he turned into that side street, three gun toting masked men, stopped him. One of them fired a warning shot into the air, another came to the driver's side and commanded him to get out of the car. Once out of the car, one of the masked men demanded he lay flat on his stomach. As he laid there the second man who gave the warning shot came and commanded him to sit up. When he sat up on the floor, he could see the man trembling. The fellow turned to his companions and shouted in a rough voice.

"Blackie, Jambo let him go."

"Weytin now?" They both asked in their street language, astonished at his sudden change of heart.

He took off his mask, it was Zero. "Na dis be massa Hope, na him be good man," he told his companions.

Kofi looked at Zero; he was both surprised and speechless. He got up hurriedly and got back into his truck. He did not ask any questions, not from Zero or his companions. He simply drove away. Even before he left the scene there was heated debate going on between the men which soon turned into an uproar. The other two were scolding Zero for not only letting him off the hook but also for revealing his identity. He got home really shaken but also thankful. Thankful that Zero had stood up for him just as he had done for him. However, he hoped the event would teach Zero that he could be hurting good people with his lawless way of life. He had already had his dinner at work, so he quickly showered and jumped into bed. Sleep, however, was long in coming.

As he lay in bed, he worried for Zero and others like him. How could those people get something out of the dire economic situation the country found itself in? Every day his colleagues had been boasting of the achievements of the government. Whether the so-called achievement was true or not, one thing he knew was that the people were not reaping the fruits of their labor. To further complicate issues, the government had joined up with the IMF to force harsh austerity measures on the people. Though the world body had only intended for it to stabilize the currency and reduce inflation, which would ultimately work for the good of the people, the measures' severity had produced the opposite effect. Nevertheless, amid all the economic hardships the politicians, particularly those in the ruling party, had amassed wealth on the back of the peoples' sweat.

"If they want to plunder the wealth of the nation, why don't they create more wealth so that there will be more to steal?" Kofi thought out loud.

It was evident that the aimless pursuit of austerity without an end goal had gotten to the people. Is it any wonder that people like Zero and his friends would stand on the street at night to terrorize innocent citizens? He did not remember how long he had been pondering about the plight of the people before he drifted into sleep. The next day, as he was going to work the newspaper boys were standing by the side of the street as usual selling their merchandise. One newspaper headline caught his eye. He gestured to one of the boys for a copy. The headline article was about an impending strike by the masses of the FCP. The newspaper claimed that the looming industrial action was initiated by the rank and file of the party. It further alleged that even party members who were getting crumbs from the party bigwigs were beginning to feel the pain inflicted on them by their patrons.

Kofi had sought to calm anxious protesters in the past, but now, as he read about this latest unrest, he wished they would really take it up and protest indefinitely if that was what it would take to awaken these greedy leaders to the plight of the people. He did not see the justification why people here would go for days without a good meal as some do. This was in a country rich in natural resources, where the land was fertile and manpower plentiful. This would not have been painful if it were mere hyperbole. But this was the reality of the situation this country had found itself in. His mind went back to Zero and his fellow highway robbers. How could a decent man take up arms to terrorize his people if he had a way of making a living for himself? He was sure only violence would awaken these people who were raping this country. There was a seismic wave that was going to blow through the fabric of the nation.

When it was time for mass uprising, it would be like releasing a cork from a bottle, as if some latent energy had suddenly been released. And once released there would be no putting that energy back. He wondered if the politicians were not aware of trouble brewing. That they had overstayed their honeymoon. He was glad that the masses of this country had suddenly come to life. Though no one knew how this would end, he wanted them to rise up and put their leaders on notice. As Kofi contemplated the situation, he felt so embarrassed by the actions of his party members he wanted to run home and hide under his sheets. Suddenly he felt a strong aversion for those potbellied politicians whose only aim for entering politics was to amass wealth on the back of those poor working people. For days he had been arriving early and working hard but he didn't look very happy. At the close of the day, he was in his office when Ellen approached.

"Hello Kofi, are you doing okay?"

"Yes Ellen, why are you asking?"

"I noticed you've not been yourself lately. Is something the matter with you?"

"No, I'm fine thanks. Just busy."

"Kofi, when you first came, you were friends with Rebecca and Maggie also, but these days I don't see you with either of them."

"And what about that?"

"I just want you to be happy."

"Well, everything's good."

"I agree, but tonight I want to go out with you to watch a movie, if that's okay with you?"

He got up and strolled to the water fountain standing in the lobby to get some water and she followed him there.

"Yeah?" She seemed to be pleading.

"What movie do you intend to go to?"

"*Love brewed in an African pot.*"

"Oh, by Kwaw Ansah? That's an old movie."

"No, this is a remake, and it's having its premiere today."

Initially, he wanted to refuse. He had been seen often with Ellen lately and did not want to scupper any chance he had of getting Rebecca back. But he accepted the invitation anyway because he was feeling lonely. At about seven in the evening, Ellen arrived at his house in a taxi. She was looking splendid as if the moon's delicate light had just turned the world aflame with silver. Her comely stem-thin figure with her curvilinear waist was more prominent tonight because of the dress she was wearing. The most surprising thing was that she had a saffron tint to her facial complexion. Ellen was certainly beautiful, he thought, but his heart was still set on Rebecca; for no matter how hard he tried, he could not push her out of his mind. As he stared at Ellen, her crescent-shaped eyebrows inclined slightly, and her eyelashes blinked slowly. He knew he had been found out, so he murmured,

"You got me."

Ellen only bored an acknowledging look on her face, as if to tell him it was alright to admire her beauty. He admitted to himself, that he had never seen Ellen so beautiful before, but he did not want to cause any ripples, so he kept quiet. They found seats at the theatre but since the movie had not yet started, he decided to visit the gents. As he headed to the washroom, he thought he saw somebody that looked like Rebecca. When he came closer, he noticed her scrolled ears and elegant nose. You could never miss her. It was her alright and she was with a female companion; it was her friend Ashley who Kofi had not met yet. In the moonlight, she looked like an angel with her constellation bright brown eyes. She appeared not to have seen him, though they took seats a few rows from them. Whenever he got the chance, he would steal furtive glances her way.

After the movie when he left the theatre with Ellen, he saw Rebecca and Ashley in the foyer engaged in conversation. They said hello to them, and she replied grumpily. Kofi extended his hand to introduce himself to Rebecca's friend but before he could, Rebecca pulled her away. Left humiliated, he reached out to Ellen's hands and led her away outside to look for a taxi. When he glanced around, he saw Rebecca and her friend heading off and they were walking in the opposite direction. As she walked down the road Rebecca's shapely figure moved rhythmically as if walking to the rhythm of a song.

"Ahem!" Ellen cleared her throat to get his attention. She was surprised that, although Rebecca had humiliated him, his eyes were still following her. She wondered whether she was not attractive enough to him.

He returned his attention to Ellen, realizing she was watching him all the while as his admiring gaze had been following Rebecca. "I'm sorry, I got distracted." He apologized knowing Ellen had probably read his thoughts.

Though deep in self-examination, Ellen did not say anything. "Shouldn't we walk a little bit away from the crowd to find a taxi?" She suggested.

A large crowd had gathered, and everyone was trying to find a ride home. As they walked further down the road, a taxi pulled up for them and they got in. In the ride home, Kofi was silently thinking about what his next steps regarding marriage should be. Ellen noticed that he was very quiet and wanted to have a conversation, but his mind was elsewhere, and this wasn't the right time. Meanwhile, as they walked away from the theater, Ashley asked Rebecca who the handsome man was who had wanted to introduce himself.

"That was Mr. Kofi Hope," she replied.

"Rebecca, surely you're not going to leave such a handsome man for your friend?"

"Not all that glitters is gold," Rebecca replied tersely.

"Besides, you were very rude to him. Why wouldn't you let him introduce himself to me?"

"I'm sorry Ashley."

"I'm not the one you should apologize to, you know that."

Ashley did not bring up the topic again. Her only concern was the way Rebecca pulled her away. It seemed clear to her that she was making herself an enemy of a person she still loved, though she was in denial. Two years ago, Kofi had never thought about the subject of marriage. Now there were at least two women, vying for his attention and both were stunning. Rebecca and Ellen were both charming women. Maggie would probably have been a good candidate for him also. She was attractive, fun to be with, and a good people person. Nevertheless, the fact that she could force herself on him raised some red flags. Besides, they had not been on friendly terms since the day of the incident. Since Rebecca wouldn't speak to him, that left him with Ellen. Though pretty, she would not have been his first choice. He thought she was a workaholic, who would not have time for him if they were to get married. Rebecca though was still in his heart. She was modest, self-assured, empathetic, and calm under pressure as she showed on their visit to the village. He wondered whether he should wait for Rebecca to come around or just settle for Ellen. Soon the taxi stopped in front of Ellen's apartment.

"Hey Ellen, it was great being with you tonight," Kofi announced as he led Ellen to her apartment.

"The pleasure was all mine Kofi." She accepted his appreciative comments.

As she walked away, Ellen's mind went to the night. Kofi had been very congenial until he saw Rebecca. Could it be he still loved her, but something was keeping them apart? As much as she wanted Kofi for herself, she didn't want to be seen as coming between them. Perhaps she should stay back a little. After Kofi was sure Ellen was inside, he returned to the waiting taxi.

"That's a very pretty woman." The taxi driver remarked when he returned.

"Don't you think you should keep your opinion to yourself?" Kofi told the driver, annoyed.

"My apologies man."

He did not want to offend his passenger to risk losing his tip. The ride home to his flat was uneventful and without conversation. Kofi went to bed thinking about the girls. Earlier in the evening he had begun to make up his mind on Ellen. Now he was not so sure. After a long rationalization, he concluded that there was nothing to be afraid of in asking Ellen to marry him. However, he wanted to find time to talk to Rebecca, if she would listen, before he asked Ellen to marry him. His mind resolved, he slept soundly, thereafter.

CHAPTER 31

AN INSIDE JOB

Ever since Kofi had returned from jail, Nicholas Hamma had pretended to be on friendly terms with him. Sometimes he would approach him and make a remark hoping to have him say something. It however seemed the young man was surprised at the seemingly sudden change and was treading cautiously. When a clerk came to him about Kofi not taking an additional payment for the licenses he issued, he saw that as a trigger. Despite not knowing how to get the necessary information, that really didn't matter because he had a plan; he would bring up the matter sometime with the appropriate authority. What better way to get information than from the horses own mouth he reasoned. At lunchtime, he saw Kofi getting his food, so he walked up to him and started to make conversation.

"How busy are you with licenses these days? Are applications for new licenses increasing or declining?" He inquired casually.

Kofi was surprised at the question. "Why will this man come up with such a question at this time?" he thought to himself, "he must be trying to be slick."

He looked at him with a grin and replied that he did not have the records. The question was only a ploy to nail him, and he saw right into it. Hamma's only reason was to know if he was taking the additional fee imposed by the party to give out licenses, but he inventively refused to comment. When Hamma left the cafeteria, he met Lucy in the hallway.

"Good to see you Lu," he said.

"What are you up to, Honorable?"

"Was on my way to talk to the chief."

"What is it regarding?"

"How to implicate a person of our mutual interest."

"I was on my way to see Barbara but she's not in. Do you want me to go with you?"

"Good idea, but why don't you come in when I am already there so you can collaborate my story."

"You are a genius Honorable. I will be there then."

He was aware that he was not going to get what he needed from Barbara. Hence, he had waited for this opportunity when Barbara was out of the office to approach the chief. He went in with the pretense that he wanted to make a complaint to Barbara, but she was out of the office.

"What was your concern Honorable?" The chief asked him after he explained the situation concerning Barbara.

"I have observed that Kofi Hope is working against the party."

"And why is that?"

"He speaks against party functionaries all the time."

"Are you sure Honorable?"

"Yes, I've heard him time and again say that the politicians in this country all came from poor backgrounds," he stopped to read the expression on the chief's face before continuing. "He says these same politicians when voted into office, behave like they don't know anything about poverty."

Just then Lucy popped her head into the chief's office. "Sorry chief I didn't know you and Honorable Hamma were in a discussion.

"It's alright Lucy, the Honorable just brought a complaint, he will be gone soon."

Lucy pretended she was going to wait outside. "I'll come in when he's done, chief."

"Madam Lucy, I was telling the chief about how Mr. Hope has been stifling the activities of the party." Hamma announced seemingly to keep Lucy from staying outside.

She walked right into the office. "Yes chief, I've experienced it from him myself," Lucy volunteered.

"Chief, like I was saying, he says that many benefits from the sweat of the people through accessing higher education financed by them, but once they return from their overseas studies and enter higher offices, they feel entitled to receive the benefits of their offices which is denied the ordinary citizen." Hamma, unyielding, persisted with his accusation.

The chief looked from Hamma to Lucy. "Did he really say that?"

"Chief I think he can say more than that," Lucy chipped in. "For me what is more damning is the way he refuses to help any benefactor of the party."

As Hamma started to speak again, Lucy kept quiet and just listened.

"There was more sir, you know I haven't assessed those benefits so I could have kept quiet, but I did not like the way he was trying to malign people like you who received those benefits."

"What else did he say?" The chief asked.

"He said because of their newly acquired status; those who get those benefits lose touch with the dire situation of the ordinary citizen."

"I don't know if he really said those but isn't he right though. Some of us politicians sometimes do that as we saw with the previous administration."

Hamma continued to drive his point home. "The other day, at the meeting he brought up the idea that political operatives should be exposed to a direct experience and immersion in the circumstances of the citizenry so that they would feel the people's pain."

"So, when and where did he say these?"

"I think when he was conversing with some people the other day."

"Well Honorable Hamma, these are not serious issues. You cannot indict a man based on conversation he had with somebody. Besides, every person is entitled to their opinions."

Lucy was peeved at the way the chief was reacting to Hamma's accusations, but she kept quiet feigning disinterest. As for Hamma, his forehead scrunched up with concentration trying to decipher what the chief was implying. To say he was disappointed would be an understatement. He thought he could easily convince the chief to act against this upstart, but he was not making any progress. He was not going to let sleeping dogs lie though.

"There is another issue sir." Gesturing for the chief to lean in, he whispered, "I've heard that he doesn't accept gifts."

"That's admirable. Good for him," replied the chief.

Now Hamma was taken aback by the chief's reaction, so he exclaimed loudly. "Doesn't that seem questionable to you sir? I mean he's putting those of us who do in a bad light."

"No, it does not. Perhaps you should learn a thing or two."

Both Hamma and Lucy were getting more and more frustrated and even more so to shrug off the chief's comment. Now he thought about hitting a home run. "Sir, he doesn't even take the additional monies the party have asked all commissioners to put on licenses to be partly donated to party coffers."

"Do you have records of that?"

"I don't sir, but I intend to get them."

"Okay this conversation ends here. Do not make false accusations without reason. Come to me when you have your supporting evidence."

The chief dismissed Hamma and turned his attention to Lucy who was sitting silently with her head buried in her palms.

"Chief, I believe Honorable Hamma was raising a legitimate concern." She observed in order not to lose the impact they wanted to make with the older man.

The chief did not reply but he reasoned that they may be right; the young man may cause trouble for all of them. He remembered what he told the President when they visited him at his office and his revelation at the staff meeting. Eventually he might make it impossible for them to breathe.

"Lucy, do you think Mr. Hamma was right? Was he not being too hard on the young man?"

"Oh, chief you don't know how headstrong that man is."

"Is he?"

"Whenever I ask him anything, he never give me straight answers. Sometimes, he simply ignores me."

"You, Lucy?"

"Yes, even the iron lady."

They both laughed before the chief resumed a serious demeanor. It was probably time to act but he must leave it to Hamma to make a proper case against him then he could act, he concluded. When he left the chief's office, Hamma became more confused, but knowing Lucy was still there he knew she was going to work her magic on the old man. For his part, he had to find the evidence that the chief needed to implicate Kofi. Thus, he went to the head of the clerks to see if he could get the accounts receivable on new investments.

"Mr. Hope has put all the information on the net," he said.

"Splendid," he snapped his fingers as he exclaimed triumphantly, "at least someone around is useful."

Soon after, however, his euphoria turned into lamentation. When he checked the information, it showed the number of licenses issued and the fees collected. There was no indication of any additional payments. He went back to the chief clerk with his findings.

"Well, the additional payment does not go into government fund."

"And why is that?"

"It goes into a special fund created by the party hierarchy."

"Oh, I see, but how does it work?"

"The issuing officer receives thirty percent of the fund which is in U.S. Dollars and the rest is paid into the special fund."

"How do you keep account for these payments?"

"The investor is issued with a yellow receipt which is different from the receipt he or she gets for the regular licensing fees."

"Hmm . . . interesting, do you have the records for these transactions?"

"No, you will have to see Miss Bosan."

Hamma was crestfallen. If Ellen is the one who handles those records, there was no way she would give them to him. Now he had an uphill task, he reflected. If he were to ask her, she might tell Kofi and jeopardize his masterplan. He would find a way no matter what, he convinced himself as he left the accounts office. He initiated a new plan to sneak in when nobody was there: in other words, during the night. Getting something from Ellen's office was harder than Hamma had initially thought. It was like going through the eye of a needle since she was usually the first and the last at the office. It meant he had to find another way. From that day, he would return to the office and wait around to see if he could find a way inside. Once he was inside, he could get into any office. On the third day of his plan, he finally got lucky. The cleaning crew came earlier than usual, and the security guards opened the door to let them in. He watched behind a pole as they took their first round of cleaning equipment inside.

The guard left his post, and the door was left ajar. Slowly, he tiptoed inside hoping not to make any noise. As he finally entered, he saw the cleaners coming back so he ducked around a corner. When they went out this time, he was able to sneak back in. Usually when they are cleaning, the cleaners open all the doors of the offices so that they could vacuum everything together. So, he waited until they opened the doors then he sneaked into Ellen's office. When he entered Ellen's office, he went straight towards her cabinets. One by one he searched inside each cabinet and file, and there were several files. He was going to give up until he saw a glimpse of what looked like a red file tucked away by itself at the corner of one of the cabinets. When he opened it, he found the documents he was looking for. Those documents were all signed by Joseph Baiden, implying that Kofi Hope had not been collecting the incentive money. Quickly he made copies, tucked them under his office door, and waited for a way to get out. It was now mission accomplished.

Now it was time to find a way around the security guards who were back at their post. He noticed that the cleaners had a big garbage bin that they put in all the garbage they collected. There were already several bags of garbage inside, so he climbed inside instead of risking getting caught. Once inside, he buried himself in the garbage. Soon the cleaners came and wheeled the container out of the building. When they had removed it from the building, one of the cleaners left it with his companion and went back inside to get the rest of their cleaning gear. Whilst he was gone, the other one wheeled it to a big dumpster sitting behind the building away from the watchful eyes of the security guards.

"Wow, how come I've not noticed how heavy these are?"

The cleaner said to himself as he tried to dump the garbage into the dumpster. This task was usually carried out by one person. Tonight, despite his best efforts he was unable to do it. He left the container to go back inside to find his companion to give him a hand. The other cleaner followed his friend in disbelief.

"Unbelievable, you're so weak, you can't even lift up a light garbage can," he complained.

When they got to the dumpster, he asked his friend to step aside so that he could lift the garbage into the dumpster. As he lifted it, it was not as heavy as his companion had complained of; Hamma had successfully sneaked away. He angrily emptied the garbage into the dumpster.

CHAPTER 32

MAGGIE'S CONFESSION

It was a beautiful night. A night when the breeze from the sea had cooled down temperatures taking the place of the sweltering heat of the afternoon. The sun had been menacing during the day, now a full moon was portentous and visible. It lit up the sky like a luscious round ball, mellow and radiant. It was a night for striking friendships and making lasting memories. A good night for meeting with people and striking deals. It was a night for lovers. Unless you were Nicholas Hamma. He had sneaked into his office building to dig for dirt on Kofi, his assumed nemesis. He had achieved incremental success; he had what he needed and had successfully found a way of escape from his hunting grounds by way of the cleaners' garbage container. Now the fellow has brought the container to the big dumpster. How is he going to get out of the container without being noticed? Would those people understand whatever explanation he gave them if they were to find him? Will he not be apprehended and handed over to the security guards who will call the police on him?

He was in a quagmire. Had he taken things too far? But he could not wait any longer to see that fellow Hope growing in fame and stature. He had to do whatever was within his power to make sure that didn't happen, hence his present predicament. There was a stroke of luck. Only one of the cleaners was trying to lift the container full of bags of garbage into the big dumpster. It was too heavy for him, so he went to call for his companion's help. Hamma realized that was his chance to escape. He climbed up, out of the pile of bags of trash, but he did not have time to complete his getaway before they returned. With the cleaners' back, he was still in danger of being seen, so he ducked behind a nearby tree. In his hiding place, he could see the second cleaner easily lift the garbage container by himself and accuse his companion of laziness. He just smiled to himself that his ingenuity had landed one of them in trouble and caused an altercation. He had no care or concern over what happened between them.

Despite a full moon, they didn't see him hiding in the shadows and never suspected anything. He had parked his car away from the office so that he would never relate to any vulgar incident discovered in the morning. When the cleaners left, he climbed the barbed wire fence surrounding the office and tumbled into the bush below. He thought he heard some noises nearby, so he laid down in the bush for a while. Then he saw what looked like three masked people moving down the road. A little while later, he could neither see nor hear them, so he started to walk to the road towards his car. Hardly had he moved than he saw the three people with their faces covered moving cautiously away from him, probably towards their target. He watched on as their footsteps echoed eerily into the distance, his knees knocking against each other. Luckily for him, the three went in a different direction from where his car was parked. Nevertheless, since he didn't want to run into them again, he decided to take a shortcut to his car by walking through the adjacent bush.

The bush was spooky and quiet as if no human life lived nearby. He trod cautiously picking his way through the scrub trying to avoid stepping on branches, all the while making sideways glances and frequently pausing to listen, before moving on. He couldn't wait to leave behind the eerie moonlit bush and get back to his car, where he could see what was going on around him. Soon he emerged from the bush, relief written on his face. He ran to his car, got in, checking in his mirrors and looking all around to make sure he had not been seen, before driving off. He got home without further alarms. The first but crucial step of his mission was accomplished; he slept like a baby with no worries in the world.

The next day was busy as usual in the office. It was a full house day. Everybody was at post and doing their work. If anybody had paid close attention to him today, they would have noticed something fishy about him. He was acting strangely even by his own standards. Not only did he go to the cafeteria early, but he also went to the table where Ellen and Kofi were sitting having lunch together. Normally, he would not speak to them. But today he said hello to them and tried to make conversation. They were focused on their dialogue and did not pay much attention to him. When he went for his food, he chose a table close to the couple so he could listen in on what they were saying. Rebecca also came to the cafeteria but not while Kofi was there. These days she would make sure either she went early enough to avoid him or wait for him to leave before she ate. Today she waited until he saw Kofi and Ellen leaving the cafeteria.

Hamma was still seated when Rebecca entered. He had noticed how she often ate alone these days so he decided to go to her table after she had sat down to try and be nice to her. Rebecca was always wary of Hamma. She knew he didn't like Kofi and was only trying to get some information from her. While she and Kofi were not on speaking terms, she did not hate him and would never betray him to Hamma. So, although Hamma had tried on several occasions to get some information about Kofi from her, she had never fallen for the bait of his superficial pleasantries. Today was no different. He came over and tried to make conversation, but she ignored him. She had also not been on speaking terms with Maggie since the day she found her in Kofi's apartment. Today, however, after Hamma left, she was sitting by herself when Maggie came to her table looking grim and sad. As soon as Rebecca saw her, she turned away.

"I know you hate me for what I did to you," Maggie looking sullen and meek begged, "but please hear me out."

Rebecca took a sideways glance at her and blurted out. "Okay make it quick, what do you want from me?"

"I'm just pleading with you to accept Kofi back."

"I don't wanna hear anything concerning him, okay? I'm through with him anyway."

Maggie bowed her head, and her chin was trembling. She felt too ashamed to even look Rebecca in the eye. "Please listen to me, Kofi doesn't love me; it is you he loves."

Those words, the sincerity and humility with which Maggie was speaking spoke into Rebecca's heart. For the first time, she felt her resentment subsiding. Now she sat up straight and began to pay more attention to her.

"How do you know that?" She finally asked her.

Her companion looked subdued and had this empty stare as she spoke.

"Well, he has stopped talking to me since the day you saw me at his flat. Whenever he sees me, I can see that hatred in his eyes. It is more than I can continue to bear."

"Yeah?"

"Yes, he never slept with me. I had a hunch you would visit him after he returned from that presidential trip." She stopped and swallowed hard, "I wanted to push you away from him that was why I went there to try to seduce him."

"Eh?" Rebecca's jaws were gaping now, and she was blinking quickly.

"When I got there," she continued, "I found he was in the bathroom taking a shower. So, I sneaked inside his bedroom to wait for him."

"Are you sure he wasn't taking a shower to smell nice for you?"

"No, it's nothing like that. I had not even spoken to him. He didn't even know I was there."

"Okay, he went to take a shower then what?"

"When he came out, I was lying semi-naked on his bed."

"What was his reaction when he saw you?"

"He was shocked. He ran to the living room to avoid looking at me." There was an agonized look on her face as she spoke. "That was when I knew he wasn't interested in me. I've never been so humiliated in my life."

She broke down and started sobbing softly. Rebecca just sat there looking at her. She bore a quizzical look on her face but did not want to interrupt her or do anything to alleviate her pain.

Maggie continued her speech. This time she was speaking with a lot of emotion. "To throw yourself at a man who doesn't want you is shameful."

As she was speaking, tears were trickling down her face. She clumsily wiped the tears from her cheeks with the back of her hands. Then she sat up straight determined to see through her mission. "I cannot be so callous as to deprive you of your lover. And please, can you ask him to forgive me? I feel haunted anytime I see him."

Rebecca just sat there numbly as Maggie made her tearful confession. Now the full weight of her actions dawned on her. She had treated the only person she ever loved with outright disdain, accusing him of something he hadn't done and for a situation in which he was entirely innocent. She felt so guilty particularly because of the way she took the whole issue. It was obvious that she had been the unfaithful one: shunning a lover in his time of need.

"At least I should have given him the benefit of the doubt." She was speaking to herself at this time more than to Maggie. "I never even gave him a chance to explain his side of the story".

But was there something she could do? She hoped she was not too late for him already, because of how much time he had been spending lately with Ellen. Maggie had been standing all the while as they were talking. Rebecca looked at her closely and saw how miserable she looked. Now she realized she could not continue to hold a grudge against her.

"I love your sincerity Maggie, and I've forgiven you. I just wish you could have told me all this sooner, but I understand. I know Kofi will forgive you too. And now if you will excuse me."

It was only then that Maggie walked away. There was nothing more to be said. Rebecca watched her leaving, her shoulders drooping. It was not the buoyant, smiling Maggie she remembered. She had never really cared to look at her after the incident with Kofi. However, as she watched her leave today, she realized what a burden that incident must have been to her. She could no longer hold anything against her. She would let her know that as soon as she met with Kofi. She left the cafeteria in a hurry to go and look for him. She had almost reached Lisa's desk when she realized that she would have to look for an appropriate time to speak to him. She couldn't just interrupt him anyhow, considering how long they had been apart. A wrong or badly timed move could exacerbate the divide. Besides, she had been downright rude to him lately.

Meanwhile, for Hamma, the day ended very well in his opinion. He had sniffed around the cafeteria to get any news if Ellen's office had been searched by anyone. As it happened, no one suspected anything. Now he had all the documents he needed to prove Hope was letting the party down. If the chief still didn't believe him, he had made duplicate copies and he knew where to get the originals from Ellen himself if necessary. He had also received a letter from John Acres, one of the party's chief financiers; all this was good evidence he could use in his favor. He called Lucy and reported his findings. At the other end, he could hear jubilation in her voice. However, the reception from his wife when he told her was different.

"That fellow Hope thinks he is smart, but I am smarter." He spoke in a self-congratulatory manner.

"What are you up to this time, Nick?" His wife asked concern shown in her voice.

He was in an ebullient mood and dismissive of his wife's pessimism. "Don't worry about me honey, we will see who is still sitting when the music stops playing."

CHAPTER 33

A SIGNIFICANT DREAM

Rebecca returned home from work a relieved person. She felt like a huge weight had been lifted off her shoulders; Maggie had no hold on Kofi. He was all hers. Then a cloud of doubt floated across her mind, what if Ellen had already stolen his heart from her? Worst still, her own actions might have pushed him away. Several times he had called her on the phone, and she had refused to talk to him. She had done her best to ignore him and stay out of his way. She had been rude to him when she could. What made her think he was still waiting for her? She remembered the day at the rally when he left Ellen to speak to her, and she had rejected him, just like she did on the day at the theatre. She also remembered the day at the office, when her lover was there and other people instead of her were being nice to him.

She was having this nagging feeling that perhaps her actions might have done more harm to their relationship than Maggie did. With bated breath she inhaled deeply and exhaled slowly. She had to hope all was not lost. Nevertheless, she was beginning to loathe herself. Perhaps now there was nothing to be salvaged after all her uncooperative reactions to him. She was so confused she needed time to think. Still, she also needed someone to talk to. There was a couple who lived in her building who seemed to have this perfect marriage. She decided to go to talk to them to find out what made them unique. As she got to their door, she heard them involved in a heated exchange. The woman was accusing the man of being insensitive to her needs. The man on the other hand was condemning her of being ungrateful. He was listing all the things he had done for her which she never appreciated. She stood there for about ten minutes. For all that time the couple continued to trade accusations.

Perhaps there were no perfect unions out there. How could this couple she had always held in the highest regard be behaving as two children who wanted to upstage the other in the blame game? She and Kofi had never stood toe to toe like that. But who knows, they might do worse than that. She turned around and went back to her apartment. The couple's exchanges were an eye opener, but it did nothing to help her own situation. Ashley, her friend had always been helpful in such situations, so she put a call through to her. When Ashley answered she detected that her friend sounded unsettled.

"Are you okay dear you sound confused?"

"You're right about that."

"Okay, I was planning to come to see how you're doing, so what about I come to your house now?"

"Oh, would you?" Rebecca replied sounding relieved.

It took Ashley about an hour to reach Rebecca's apartment. She found she had prepared dinner, so they sat down to eat. Afterwards, Rebecca told her about Maggie's confession.

"The co-worker that I thought was involved with Kofi came to me today."

"Why do you say, 'you thought was involved', was it not true after all?"

"Well, she came to me to confess her wrongdoing."

"She did?"

"Yes, she staged the whole incident to get me to leave Kofi for her."

"That's wonderful, now you can go back to your Prince charming."

"Is it that simple?"

"What's the hard part now?"

"Well, I was rude to him; I wouldn't pick his phone calls and wouldn't talk to him. You saw how I treated him that day at the cinema," she paused to look at Ashley's reaction then she continued. "There's more, one day he came to get some information from me at the office and I was cold as ice."

Ashley just looked at her and smiled. She was not one to pass judgment just like that. She smiled at Rebecca and spoke calmly.

"Girlfriend, I thought you called to apologize to him after that incident at the theatre?"

"No, I didn't, me and my prideful heart. Anyway, there's another problem."

"Another problem? What else now?"

"There's another girl at the office Kofi is friends with now."

"You mean, the one we saw him with at the theatre?"

Rebecca nodded. She did not have the strength for words anymore.

"Oh no! Does it look like they're intimate?" Ashley asked, a strained frown displayed on her face.

"I think they're going together now." Rebecca acknowledged.

"Girl, you're going to fight for your man. Aren't you?"

"If I could. But how am I going to do this?"

"Go to him and apologize. Tell him you love him, and you want to get back together again."

"Oh Ashley, women in *Abibiman* don't do that."

"Women, who's talking about women? Girl, just think about yourself."

"Ashley, I wish I could be as bold as you."

"Besides, Kofi is an American Burger, isn't he? He will understand. I heard from the grapevine that in America, women as well as men can propose."

"Who spoke about proposing? All I want is to get back into his good books and perhaps give myself another chance with him."

She was now reminiscing about her time with him on the village trip. She recalled his reaction to the soldier ants, it was hilarious; his adoring looks at the lakeside. How he made her feel good on that trip. Meanwhile, Ashley knew she was dreaming about something because there was this faraway look in her eyes. She was not one to interrupt a good dream. She just stared at her as she seemed swallowed up in fairytale land.

"Why don't you invite him on a date?" Ashley said finally.

"A date, Ashley, isn't that the same as proposing?"

"Kofi would not be a stranger to that, trust me, he will understand."

"Okay Ash, I'll give it a try," Rebecca concurred timidly.

She paused to consider Ashley's suggestions. Kofi would see an optimistic person in her if she was able to take the initiative and ask him out. Before they had the altercation, he was the one person she could always talk to freely. He was so affable and encouraging, she didn't think he would have changed overnight to be a mean person who would reject the advances of a woman he once loved. Ashley stayed for a long time but at last she had to return home.

"Girlfriend I have to go home now. I left my baby in the care of my husband. Not that she will cry, but I have to give him some time off also after working all day."

She stood up, rubbing her eyes and yawning at the same time. After she saw off Ashley she returned home and reclined on her sofa. From what she was seeing from Ashley, marriage might be a good thing after all. Though they were of the same age, she seemed to have matured a lot since she got married. Well, at twenty-five, she also needed a man. Beside Kofi, no other man had ever touched her heart. The price of love was high, and the risk involved in it could be equally high. If he were to reject her, what would be left of her sense of self-worth? But isn't the eventual prize higher than any possible humiliation? Could she live by herself if she never gave him another chance?

Kofi was the one person she would want to spend the rest of her life with; a man who was tenacious and rarely gave up, even when the odds were against him. Nothing got in his way when he set a goal; he would complete whatever task given him no matter what it entailed. That night she dreamt that she and Kofi were married. Many people came to their wedding ceremony. He was benevolent on that day, extolling her beauty. Afterwards, they boarded a plane to go on their honeymoon. They flew into a big airport. Far bigger than the one at *Sikakrom*. Her sweetheart had rented a car when they arrived and they had driven on an expressway, one she had never seen before. They had driven for well over a hundred and twenty miles into a small town. There was this big lake with a waterfall. It was nothing she had ever seen in her life. There was so much to see, they had first walked around the place arm-in-arm and serenaded each other's company. Kofi had his arms wrapped around her waist all the time as they strolled around the town viewing the lake.

There were many people taking boat rides on the lake. There were two sides to the lake. They got into a big boat also. Her love was standing close by her. Everyone on their boat was given a red coat to keep them from getting wet from the water splashing against the boat as they sailed along. On the other side of the lake, she could see another group of people. They were also riding a different boat and they had yellow coats. The whole sight was captivating. The dream went on and on. Finally, she woke up, and she was in her own bed. However, she was not disappointed. It had been a significant dream; a sign from God that their union was made in heaven, and nothing was going to scupper it. Before she drifted back to sleep, she knew what she was going to do in the morning. She was going to invite her sweetheart on a date.

CHAPTER 34

MORE HOSTILITY AT WORK

K ofi was not only grappling with relationship problems. He was also contending with the attitude of workers in *Abibiman*; an attitude marked by lack of interest, apathy and a "something for nothing" mentality. Even a cursory glance portrayed the indifference people showed to their jobs, though it was what put food on the table for them. Most workers, he had observed, were more concerned about the extra monies they could make through bribery and other corrupt activities. Being punctual at work, or providing good customer service, was the least of their worries. Thus, they could be downright rude and uncooperative at their workplaces. They often approached their jobs as if they were doing somebody favors. Their attitude, he perceived, did not bode well for economic improvement.

He was comforted though, that while many were still very poor, there seemed a glimmer of hope in the horizon. He could see a rise of a middle class of some sort. Back in the USA, he often heard stories of starvation and deprivation in African countries. Though he could not dismiss that story, being here he had seen that things were slowly but surely changing. Nevertheless, they could still be so much better if everyone got on board and moved the economy forward. That was his mission, and he was going to remain steadfast to it. He was now at the workplace, so he parked his vehicle and headed for his office. On entering the lobby, he saw Barbara, Ellen and Lucy, the women's organizer at the reception hall. He greeted them enthusiastically;

"Good morning, ladies."

"Good morning, Kofi." All except Lucy replied.

The exchange of greetings over, he headed toward his office. After taking a few steps away, he turned around and saw the women staring after him. Lucy was casting a scornful look in his direction and saying something to her companions. She seemed to be carrying a grudge against him, but he didn't know why. Besides, she had never really stood 'toe to toe' with him for a chat. She always clammed up anytime he tried to speak to her.

He was determined to stand up to people like Lucy who appeared to dislike his contribution to the government. Despite her best intentions, her intransigence and desire to sway the party bigwigs to do her bidding did not in any way endear her to him. A few minutes after he settled in, Lucy barged into his office, her eyes darting everywhere. She was followed by the young woman who had come to see him for a signature. He was surprised she came in without seeking permission from Lisa and was determined to put her in her place.

"Do you have an appointment today Mrs. Bukari?"

"I don't need an appointment to come and see you Mr. Hope."

"Okay."

"I hope you know I am the women's organizer, a very important office in this party."

"I beg your pardon, Mrs. Bukari, but this is not the party. This is the office of the elected President of the nation."

"Is there a difference?"

"Yes, this office is meant to serve all the people of this country and not just party members."

This was the last straw. Lucy had had enough; at last, she descended on him like a lioness awakened from her cage. "Let me tell you mister that was very demeaning. This government wouldn't be here except for the women." She pressed her lips together as she spoke, giving her words an added venom. Intermittently, she would squeeze her eyes open and shut. "In this day and age, you should know that women as well as men are capable of doing the same things."

"This is not about the women; it is about the principle of keeping party from the government and . . ."

Lucy interrupted him and continued with her diatribe. "Gone are the days when men assumed women are bereft of intelligence." As she spoke her nostrils were flaring.

Kofi was becoming uncomfortable with her approach so he said. "Can we approach this issue in another way?"

"Mr. Hope, or whatever you call yourself, those days when men thought women were simply good for, excuse my language, shaking their butts to attract men are long behind us."

As the exchanges were going on, her lady companion looked on with an agonized look of bewilderment in her eyes and beads of sweat on her face. Her amazement at the drama unfolding before her eyes was obvious. She had never seen anybody stand up to this women's organizer. However, she wondered what her approach would achieve with this man who appeared unmovable. She took her handkerchief to mop the sweat from her face and watched on silently at the two combatants. She was so downbeat Kofi might have struck a deal with her but the thought of giving any victory to Lucy galvanized him to stand his ground. Meanwhile, Lucy continued with her attack.

"In the days we are living in, women as well as men have well-paying jobs." She got up and looked menacingly at Kofi pointing her index finger at him as he spoke, "women can be equally educated as men. Sometimes they are even more educated and more capable."

Those accusations were not going to move him, in fact he remained unfazed because he knew her assessment was wrong. Unlike most African men, he had an overall favorable view of women, not because he was in America. He had always respected women and never saw them as simply good for sex. He saw most women as beautiful and equally talented. He appreciated those who were tenacious and good at their jobs, like Barbara or Ellen. He never made any prejudicial judgments, nor picked any bones especially where a woman was concerned. Never, had he had any reasons to fear that anybody would see him otherwise because the ladies at the office knew his stance on women issues. He took a second look at her, and her demeanor made him even more determined to put her in her proper place.

"You're trying to paint me into something I am not to achieve your nefarious goals?"

"Everything I have said about you is true."

"Okay, ask any of my women colleagues if you're right."

"I don't need clarification from anybody. You think I don't know you've bought all of them off?"

He saw that this conversation was going nowhere so he decided to change his approach.

"I will appreciate that if you want to give me a message you not only book an appointment with Lisa but behave civilly when you come in here."

"I will do no such thing." As she said this, she stuck her tongue at him.

"Now, whatever business you came here with today is over, so please leave my office now."

She rose and gave him an icy stare, her face distorted in a crooked grimace. "Go on ahead riding the light, and don't let the darkness overtake you," With these words, Lucy stormed out of his office with the young lady following in her wake, even a tight-lipped smile could not mask her shock.

Kofi knew with that kind of attitude Lucy could stir up trouble for him, but he was determined to do his work without any meddling to fulfill his mission. He was not going to become anybody's poodle including Lucy's. Sometime later, as he sat in his office, he was still unsettled by her outburst. He wanted somebody to speak to. Ellen had left the office on some errands. Rebecca would have readily listened, but she essentially had abandoned him. At lunchtime he took his food to a corner of the cafeteria and sat down alone to eat. As he was sitting there, Barbara came up and pulled up a chair to sit beside him.

"How are you Kofi?" She inquired, concerned shown in her voice.

"I'm fine."

When he started working at the presidency, he used to think Barbara was aggressively stubborn and feisty, but his view had changed with time. Instead, he saw her as a person who was guided by empathy and reason in her relations with her colleagues. Though there were those who had often maligned her because they had been at the receiving end of her wrath. He had never doubted her sincerity and care for her colleagues at work. He knew her time overseas had rubbed off on her relationships. Those who have not experienced that culture sometimes misunderstand people like her. Barbara was the caring sister he needed at this time, and she was not disappointing.

"I heard you got into a fight with Lucy."

"How did you hear that?"

Barbara smiled but did not answer his question, instead she continued to speak. "When I returned from London and started working for the administration, I had a lot of pushbacks."

"You did?"

She nodded slowly. "Particularly from the men who were domineering, and many times demeaned my work because I'm a woman."

"You have adapted well though. Everybody now respects you because you are too good at what you do."

"You think I'm good at my job?"

"Absolutely, you are very good at your job, you surely picked up the good work ethic of the English, didn't you?"

"Thank you, Kofi," she smiled wryly, "it is good to hear that especially coming from a person like you."

"Yes, I mean it, if you were a man, I would have branded you as tenacious. That's how good you are."

Barbara got up, smiled broadly at him. "These days some women in *Abibiman* are equally overbearing." She reminded him.

He just smiled at her but said nothing.

"Yes, I mean it, so you are right to stand your ground when dealing with them." She whispered before walking away.

When Barbara left, his mind switched back to Ellen and Rebecca. He was hoping that Rebecca would give him a second chance. Otherwise, he was going to marry Ellen because he was tired of waiting. He got up and went to the vending machine in the cafeteria to get some drinks. Rebecca was standing close by, but he didn't talk to her. However, when he got his drink and was going away, she called him. He turned round with a stony-faced expression. She saw the look on his face, but she did not comment on it.

"Would you like to go out with me for dinner?" She asked staring nervously at him.

He thought he had been hit by a block of concrete. "I beg your pardon, Miss Odom?"

She noticed the formal way in which he addressed her, but she was determined to get things right, so she brushed it aside. She was no longer nervous. "You heard me; I want us to go out tomorrow." She said firmly her mouth twisting into a friendly grin.

"Really?"

Now he thought things were getting so fascinating, Rebecca inviting him out. What could have happened? Wasn't it the same Rebecca who wouldn't even stop to listen to him?

"Seven o'clock tomorrow at the same restaurant we went to on our first date." He heard her say to him.

"Seven o'clock then." He replied, as if in a trance.

He was really astonished at the turn of events. What might have happened to her to be nice to him suddenly? This was a different Rebecca than the one he had been dealing with lately. Whatever it was, he hoped it was for the better. The following day at work he found it hard to concentrate. His mind kept wandering to his date with Rebecca. He was wondering how she dared to ask him out on a date. He kept to himself all day and avoided the cafeteria and the break room altogether. When the day was over, he stayed in his office to make sure everyone was gone before he made his way to his car. He could not tell how he got home or how he took a shower to get ready to meet the woman he still loved but who might be going for another man.

CHAPTER 35

LOVERS REUNION

Kofi did not have a crystal ball to see that a super day lay in store for him. He did not want to build up expectations, only to be disappointed, so he dumbed down his emotions and kept his expectations low for the day. It was only his second day on the job, he had met Rebecca, this angel who had swept him off his feet. However, fate had not been so kind as to allow him a free rite of passage to enjoy his prized jewel. The devil had entered Maggie just as he had entered Judas to betray his master. Maggie had worked hard to put a wedge between himself and the only woman he had ever fallen in love with. Now his Rebecca, whom he had lost was going to tell him she had finally nailed down Prince Charming. What was her motive? Perhaps she just wanted to admonish him and tell him to move on.

Perhaps she was only coming to apologize for ignoring his request to speak to her on that rally trip. She might plead with him to remain just friends and nothing more. Probably she just wanted to draw a line under the stand-off and move on with no hard feelings. To say he was a bundle of nerves was an understatement. At the appointed time, he jumped into his Jeep and drove towards the restaurant she had chosen. As he turned from the side street from his flat into the main road, there were a lot of people protesting. They were carrying placards accusing the government of selective justice. He wondered what had happened, so he turned his radio on. Just then it was announced that a verdict had been reached in the trial involving the ex-government operatives. They had all been found guilty and sentenced to various prison terms. The crowd had impeded traffic and now he faced an unwanted traffic jam.

As it was, he arrived at the restaurant late but Rebecca was not yet there. It occurred to him that she would have been caught up in the same traffic too. He had butterflies in his stomach as he sat there and waited. Luckily, she did not keep him waiting too long. He sat alone about ten minutes before he was relieved to see her arrive. She was immaculately dressed in a traditional African dress, and it had a certain creativeness about the way she wore it. She was also wearing truly exotic braided hair which was impeccably adorned with beads. Her whole appearance was asserting;

"I am a woman of substance."

As soon as he saw her, all his anxieties evaporated. This was a woman dressed for her man and nothing else. Walking up to his table, she did not wait for an invitation to sit down. She smiled broadly, took her seat opposite him and apologized for her tardiness.

"I'm sorry for being late."

"You're alright."

He signaled a waitress over and they ordered their food. As they waited the lady brought them something to drink. He looked at Rebecca sitting across from him. She was not as tense as the afternoon when she asked him out. Even as she sat there, she bore a coy smile on her face. He looked on with admiration and returned her smile with interest.

"Kofi, can we talk while we wait for the food." She asked finally her face tensing up.

"Sure." He answered delightedly. He didn't know what she was going to say, but now that they were sitting face to face, he was more relaxed.

"Maggie came to see me yesterday." She began.

"What did she want?"

"She came to apologize for putting a wedge between us."

"Aha?"

"She said she staged the scene so that I would give you up for her, but it seems her plan did not work."

Kofi sighed relief flooding his face.

"You know, Kofi, I feel so silly for not listening to you and instead put you through this ordeal."

As Rebecca apologized, Kofi just looked at her. There was nothing to hold back on, he forgave her right there.

"Now tell me Kofi, do you still have room in your heart for me?"

"Yes, you must know I love you, and only you, and I have always loved you even while you were ignoring me."

"But lately, I've always been seeing you with Ellen."

"She's a descent woman and I wouldn't have minded marrying her."

Rebecca's heart skipped a beat. "What do you mean Kofi?"

"I thought you were gone, so I was going to propose to her."

Rebecca kept quiet and just looked at him quizzically. "Really? Just like that?" She exclaimed. Her eyes widened and her mouth was left gaping. She just stared intensely at him.

"What did you expect me to do? I thought I'd lost the woman I loved because of some stupidity, so perhaps it just wasn't meant to be and I should move on," he clarified.

She reached out and grabbed his left palm with both of her hands but did not say anything to him. They sat in silence in that posture, they were only interrupted by the waitress who brought their food. Kofi stopped eating after a little while and stared at her.

"What?" She asked.

"What do you mean?"

"Why are you looking at me?"

"So, I shouldn't look at you?"

She was more relaxed now. As she ate, she continued to smile at him.

"How did you come up with the plan for a date?"

"Let's say I got some good advice."

"From who?"

"Ashley."

"Who's Ashley?"

"My friend, the one I was with on that night at the movies."

"I thought you didn't know it was me because you wouldn't let me introduce myself," he said sarcastically.

"Yes, I saw you with Ellen, and I knew it was you, but remember, we weren't on speaking terms?" She said flirtatiously.

"She must be a good friend, Ashley, I mean."

"Yes, she is."

By now they had finished their main course and were waiting for the desert. A familiar tune was playing:

Yɛ neɛ woho bɛtɔ wo
Mentie obiara asɛm
Yɛntie obiara asɛm

"Come on dance with me," she invited him.

"Shouldn't we wait for another song to dance?" He asked concerned it would be misconstrued if somebody knew what it stood for.

"That song is suitable."

"I don't want to be misunderstood."

"Don't be ridiculous. It's very appropriate. It means we will not care about whatever anybody says about our relationship."

"I hadn't thought about it that way," he said as he led her to the dance floor.

She danced with finesse but his movement was not so smooth. However, she did not seem to notice nor did she complain about her partner's dancing. When the song ended, they returned to their seats. They were both very happy now. Rebecca especially was speaking more animatedly. As she spoke, her lips coiled beautifully round appearing to conceal something.

"You are so beautiful Becky, and tonight you appear more gorgeous than ever." Kofi whispered. He was lost in thought about her beauty and admiration for her stylish dress sense.

Rebecca just gazed at him with those beautiful eyes but said nothing. He could not resist it any longer; he tacked a strand of her braided hair that was hanging on her forehead behind her ears. Then gently he pulled her closer and kissed her heart-shaped lips. They were soft and puffy and tasted strawberry sweet. Rebecca looked at him with the eyes of innocence radiating love, but did not kiss him back. He noticed she was feeling nervous, but he never asked why. She stayed still as he held her in his arms, then she withdrew and sat quietly looking intensely at the ground. A few minutes later she seemed to have overcome her initial nervousness and she lifted her eyes to look at him and spoke;

"Kofi every woman will like to be with you. You are the perfect gentleman. You are not only polite, you are also respectful, considerate and attentive to a woman's needs. I couldn't have asked for more, and I wouldn't want to lose you to any woman, not even Ellen."

He felt so happy that such a pretty woman will make such profession about him. He looked at her and wondered how in the world he had thought at one time that she was hiding behind her unique pulchritude to unknowingly seduce men. The Rebecca, sitting in front of him now looked so innocent. She was no such person who would use the appeal of her beauty to reach out to men to willingly oblige her bidding. Even now, she was sitting in front of him demanding nothing but love, though she was too shy to say it. Right, there he knew his mind was made up. She was going to be his wife. She was likely the one who would be a good mother to his future children. The sort of woman who can hold a household together with or without a man. He pulled her towards him. This time there was no resistance. She was willing to be kissed, and she kissed back.

"I love you very much Becky."

As he spoke, he drew her closer as if she was going to ran away from him.

"And I love you too, Kofi. You are my Prince Charming." She replied as they kissed passionately.

"Becky, dear, I love you and I want to live the rest of his life with you. will you love me in return?" He whispered into her ears.

"Yes! yes! yes! I do love you too. I have always loved you. Kofi Hope my prince," Rebecca blurted out.

As she was speaking, she was looking intently at him and nodding her heard vigorously. They held hands as they walked to his truck. Then they wrapped their hands around each other's waist half singing and half miming. They were mimicking the words of that song that had been stacked in his head.

Yɛ neɛ woho bɛtɔ wo
Yɛntie obiara asɛm

They were really into each other now, and their happiness knew no end.

"What are you going to tell Ellen?" Rebecca asked after her excitement died down.

"Well, I didn't tell her I loved her."

"But she might have seen it in your actions?"

"Don't worry honey, I have it covered."

He drove Rebecca to her apartment. For the first time, he got around and opened the door for her. She thanked him profusely and threw herself into his arms. As he held her in his arms, he lifted her chin gently so that their eyes were aligned and gazing at each other. All this while, she held tightly to him not wanting him to loosen his hold. At the same time her eyes were beckoning him to kiss her again. Taking the cue, Kofi wrapped his arms around her and drew her closer. This time she took the initiative and pressed her puffy, heart-shaped lips against his. As they engaged in a passionate kiss, the warmth from Kofi's body sent waves through Rebecca's chest. They stayed in this posture for what seemed like eternity. Neither wanted the other to leave. Finally, Kofi released his hold and Rebecca gracefully walked away, giggling into the darkness.

CHAPTER 36

A BEGINNER'S ROUND
OF GOLF

When Kofi had first started working as a presidential staffer, Nicholas Hammer thought he would be just a blip like most returnees turn out to be. They are usually at their crusading best when they return. Like Kofi, they arrived with lofty ideals but would soon get swallowed up by the system and adopted the norms of their peers. So, he dismissed Kofi's principled stand on the basis that it wouldn't last, presuming that he was going to come around and fall in line just as they all do eventually.

He had however, seriously misjudged and underestimated him. Here was someone whose character was impeccable. People had offered him bribes, even offered to do things for him, all of which he had refused. He was not lazy, rather, he was always in on time to do his work. There seemed nothing to implicate him of wrongdoing. All the workers could attest to his incorruptibility. Even Barbara of all people who seemingly 'hated men' was infatuated with him. Since he wouldn't be corrupted, the only thing he could do was to trump up charges against him. He had not been successful when he brought up the topic with the chief-of-staff. But he knew all was not lost, because he had asked him to bring supporting evidence to corroborate the accusations he was making.

Now that he had all the paperwork regarding the transactions where he failed to generate income for the party, he had a stronger case. But he still wasn't sure if that alone would convince the chief to fire him. Whatever it took he was up to it; and once he was done with him, he would not know what hit him. He surmised that what it would take to have all his plans materialized was to be able to convince the chief. He could do that by building friendship with him.

Lately, he had gone out of his way to serve him and to be his right-hand man. Furthermore, he had been devising more ways he could grow closer to him such as sitting with him in the break room; or repeatedly checking on him and inquiring about his health. Whenever they met, they would talk about different topics, even those that bored him to death. One afternoon, as they were sitting in the break room, a game of golf was playing on the television. The chief was showing keen interest, so it prompted him to ask a few questions.

"Chief, it seems you like this game."

"You don't know Nicholas; this is the gentleman's game."

"Yeah?"

"Yes, when you play this game, it shows that you've arrived."

Hamma was surprised at how the game energized him. He knew he had hit the nail right on its head. Probably he should go play a golf game with him to assure him he really cared.

"I haven't really taken to this game chief."

"Oh, you would love it, Nicholas."

"Chief, do you think I can learn it?"

"Oh, it's easy," he said laughing.

"I will have to go with you then so you can teach me how to play this beautiful game."

The conversation ended there, and Hamma forgot all about it in the meantime. Though golf was not new to *Abibiman*, it was not a popular game. Its main enthusiasts were the elite, the expatriates and the politicians. If there were a few players, there were even fewer courses available for the larger populace. The chief-of-staff, unlike Hamma, had been playing golf for a long time and had grown a passion for it. For that reason, he saw it as another avenue to get closer to him. Three days after their chat about playing golf, the chief brought it up again at their lunch break.

"Hey Nicholas, do you still want to go playing golf?"

"Oh yes chief, I am just waiting for you to invite me."

"Well, I'm playing this weekend, you want to join me?"

"Yes, but chief, don't you think I'm going to make a fool of myself?"

"Well Nicholas, take it that you are going on one of those your early morning walks, and then you learn a few rules and you are in the game."

"Okay then, count me in."

At the scheduled time Hamma got to the course before the chief. Since it was a members' only club, he waited for him outside the clubhouse. As was customary with the chief, he was late. When he arrived, they went into the clubhouse to get their carts.

"Glad you're here chief; I was getting nervy sitting out there by myself."

"Did anybody give you a hard time?"

"Not at all."

As they walked to the clubhouse, the chief saw that he was looking nervous.

"Hey Nicholas how do you feel now that you're here?"

"I think I'll be okay, chief."

"Yep, I know you'll be fine, all you need is to learn a few simple rules, and practice your swing."

He looked at the chief and smiled nervously but did not say anything.

"It's not that serious, Nicholas, not as if you are going to play in the PGA Championship or the Masters,"

"I hope everything will be alright."

"You'll be fine," he reassured him.

The chief came with his own clubs, but since Hamma was new to the game, he had to borrow some. "You didn't bring any clubs, did you?"

"Sorry chief, I didn't know I was supposed to bring my own clubs."

"No worries, club members are allowed to bring guests, so you can also borrow some clubs."

Now they were at the clubhouse, so the chief spoke to the attendant on duty.

"Hey John, can you get Honorable Hamma some clubs."

The fellow got up promptly and led Hamma to the room where the clubs were stored.

"Honorable, please make your selection," he told Hamma.

"How many clubs do I need John?"

"Fourteen."

"Why is it fourteen?"

"I don't know honorable, but those are the rules."

He stopped and looked up at the ceiling. "Rules, rules, rules, just like Hope. You cannot do this or that."

"Were you talking to me Honorable?"

"Tell me John, why should people be restrained from doing what they want?"

The attendant just looked at him, he didn't know what all the fuss was about in selecting clubs to play a game.

"Okay Honorable, I have to be out there to take care of other clients. Please shut the door behind you when you leave." With that he left leaving Hamma alone to select his clubs.

As he stood there, he forgot about the clubs he was selecting. Instead, his mind went back to Kofi on how he was trying to prevent people from getting extra money from their patrons. He was still deep in thought when the chief popped his head in the storage room.

"Still making your selection Nicholas?"

"Yes sir."

Hurriedly he completed making his selection. After, he started running after the chief who was headed for the carts. When he got to him, he thought his load was heavier, so he counted the clubs he brought.

"Looks like you have an extra club here," he said.

It was not his intention to make the wrong selection, but he had been irritated with the idea of being restricted and had subconsciously objected to it.

"Should I return it to the storage room?"

"Don't worry about it, just put it somewhere in the cart."

They headed for the course. He had seen golf courses several times, but it had never seemed so fascinating to him as it was today. There was the green part and some areas with sand dunes and a lake in the middle. The chief told him that the lake, the dunes and the forest area were intentionally created to serve as hazards during play as was the lengths of grass. On the putting green, the grass was short and smooth.

"Can you give me any reason for the different lengths of grass?" John Biney asked testing Hamma's golf knowledge.

"I've no idea chief."

"Well, on the greens, the grass is in part smooth and short to make it easier to putt into the hole."

"Interesting."

"Also, the grass length is varied to increase difficulty, or to allow for putting in the case of the green."

"The whole concept is fascinating chief," Hamma said as he reached out for a club, "now chief can you demonstrate how play begins?"

The chief took a club himself and stood at the teeing green and aimed his ball towards an area where a flagstick and hole were located.

"That area is called the putting green."

They started play and he was enjoying it. He began to think of himself as a pro. Now he could boast to his friends and family that his golf buddy was the chief-of-staff. As play went on, at one place the chief used mounds of sand to elevate the ball. At another place he used a container of sand for the same purpose. Yet at another place he used a piece of plastic to tee the ball. This was getting Hamma greatly confused.

"Why do we use different objects to control the ball?" He asked.

"Different objects as in the plastic peg, the container of sand and the mounds of sand?"

"Yes chief."

"They all serve the purpose of a tee or in layman's terms a peg to prevent the ball from moving before it is being hit."

"I see."

They went on to play until they had completed a full round of 9 holes. At which time Hamma was feeling pretty exhausted. "I'm glad the game is over chief," he said.

"Who said the game was over?"

"Oh, it's not over?"

"No, but we will take a break and then come back to finish play."

"Oh, chief, I thought the round was over."

"Yes, one round is over, but you see golf is normally played over 18 holes. This course has only 9 holes so we usually play it twice to get the required number."

Hamma had no choice but to go along with it. They went to the clubhouse to refresh themselves with some drinks.

"Hey chief I have the papers that showed that Hope is not collecting the party's money."

"Okay bring them to my office on Monday."

He smiled broadly, relieved that his plan was working perfectly. When they went back to play the fatigue was showing through for him. He hit a ball into a hazard area, and instead of attempting to make the next swing from the hazard or hit a new ball in an area across from the hazard; he decided to take his ball to a neutral area where it would be easier to hit. The chief noticed what he was trying to do. He walked up to him and put his arms around his shoulders.

"In golf whether you know how to play the game or not the fundamental rule you have to observe is fairness."

Hamma looked at him with a guilt-ridden face. "Why is that chief?" He asked confused about what he was saying.

"It means that you play the ball as it lies, or the course as you find it."

His mind turned to that assessment. Was he giving Hope a fair hearing? Was his insistence on getting him fired fair?

"Well, the game of life was different from that of golf; because no one seeks to play it fair. Life is the survival of the fittest; each one for himself and God for us all," he muttered to himself.

The chief turned around and asked, "I didn't hear what you said Nicholas."

"No chief, I wasn't talking to you."

After he said this, he resumed his preoccupied train of thought. He was not going to be dissuaded by golf and its apparent obsession with justice and rules of fair play. What was just in life was when you strived for something and attained it notwithstanding the obstacles you encountered. Now, this fellow Hope was an obstruction and he had to be moved out of the way.

"Let's get back to playing Nicholas," the chief admonished him seeing he was in dreamland.

As play resumed, Hamma had lost concentration he was tired and this led to him committing several penalties simply because he did not clearly understand the rules.

"Be careful with the number of penalties you commit because they will be counted towards your score as if you have given extra swings at the ball," the chief told him.

Casting a dejected figure, he bit his bottom lip as he sliced his ball into the woods nearby.

"You have extra strokes to play for playing your ball into an unplayable position," the chief told him.

By now his frustration was evident as he stood there pinching the bridge of his nose. "The game of golf is not a stroll in a park," he said.

The chief smile at him. "The best way to gain expertise is to come to the course often. Practice makes perfect."

"Okay chief."

"You can also watch video clips to learn about perfecting your swing, physical conditioning and mental visualization."

He pretended to be listening to the advice of the older man, but his mind was elsewhere. His desire was not to improve on the game, because it was only a means to attaining what he wanted in the short-term. Meanwhile, he knew in life there was no gain without sweat so he had to pretend things were going right for him. He took another swing of the ball; this time it landed perfectly on target.

"Yes," he stabbed in the air, "I got it at last."

"Bravo," the chief applauded, "now you're on your way to becoming a pro."

As they walked back to the clubhouse, he was deep in thought. Though he had that successful hit, he did not think golf was something for which he would find joy in; he was better off staying home after a hard day's work to watch a football game on TV. So, knowing his quest would be granted by the chief, he wouldn't need to live his life under the pretense of loving a game he loathed.

CHAPTER 37

THE DIE IS CAST

The day after his date with Rebecca, Kofi returned to work in high spirits. He was glad things were finally working out between them. That was his private life, but he had a business to do on behalf of the good people of his country, so he had to go to work and do his best for them. The parking lot was empty when he pulled in. That meant there was no one in at the time. He walked briskly towards the office mouthing the lyrics of a song. Ellen came out of her office when he heard him.

"Somebody is happy today," she said.

"I didn't think you were in yet."

"I decided to come in earlier than my usual time because I have some work to take care of before everybody comes."

He started to walk towards his office, but Ellen stopped him.

"Now tell me why you are in such high spirits."

"Nothing in particular."

"That didn't sound convincing," she said as she playfully squinted at him.

"I've something big coming up, but I'll tell you when the moment is right," he added as an afterthought.

He excused himself and went on to his office. Since Lisa was not yet in, it gave him the chance to start work before he got interrupted. He had some items to clear so he plunged straight to work on them. By the time Lisa came in, he was halfway through his scheduled work for the morning. Soon it was lunchtime, and he went to the cafeteria and bought lunch.

Both Ellen and Rebecca came in and they joined him at his table. Ellen was surprised Rebecca joined them on her own accord, but she did not ask for an explanation. She noticed that the couple were now cozying up to one another, so she decided not to come between them.

"I have to go now guys," she said as soon as she was done eating.

When she left, Rebecca turned to him. "When is the last time you had a haircut?"

He had not been to a barber for a long time. Perhaps Rebecca did not like the way he was looking. "Don't know, maybe six months or more," he replied.

"Well, I'm taking you to a barber after work."

"Can't we make it another time?"

"No."

At the close of work, he was sitting in his comfortable office chair with his legs on top of his desk, when she came in. "It's time to go Kofi," she said.

"Home?"

"Yes, but barber shop first."

He got up reluctantly and followed her.

"We should have made it another time, because I have work to do today."

"Consider cutting your hair part of your so-called work."

When they entered the barber shop, there were two barbers at work. One of them was well built and stocky whilst the other was taut with a firm body and strong muscles.

"Madam Rebecca," the stocky barber said when they got in, "I've not seen you for a long time.

"Yes, long time," she replied smiling, "I brought you a new customer. He hasn't found a regular barber yet since he returned from America."

"Welcome *Boga*," the stocky barber turned to address Kofi. "Please have no fears, Madam Rebecca knows I do a good job."

There were two other people who were waiting for their turn for a haircut. One of them was an old man with a white beard. The other was young and thin in an unattractive unhealthy way. The old man was sitting there leafing through a magazine. Whilst the younger thin man was combing his hair repeatedly. There were no chairs left so he got up and gave his chair to Rebecca, who passed it on to Kofi.

"No, you take it, Becky, women first they say, remember," he said.

The stocky barber turned to the taut one. "Get a chair from the office for the American *Boga*."

The taut barber stopped his trimming work and went inside to get a chair. Apparently, the stocky one was the master and he the apprentice.

"Thank you," Kofi said when he brought the chair and set it beside Rebecca.

"So, *Boga*, have you come to stay, or you will be going back," the stocky barber asked.

"I've come to stay," he replied.

The old man turned to him, "So you left a well-structured society for one so chaotic and classically disorganized?"

Kofi gave him an oblique glance before speaking. "Our country, unlike others on this continent has the potential similar to that of America because there are so many things that are common to both countries."

"The only thing common to both countries may be the Atlantic coast," the thin man said.

"Have you forgotten that both are richly endowed with mineral and human resources?" Kofi asked him.

"That's where the comparisons end," the old man cut in, "remember America is an industrialized behemoth and our country is . . ." he stuttered looking for a word to complete his sentence.

"A wimp?" Kofi supplied his missing word.

"Thank you," he pointed his index finger at him in a congratulatory gesture, "a W-I-M-P, that's the word, barely able to stand on its own two feet."

While the conversation went on, Rebecca had a small mirror in her hands which she was looking at to fix her makeup. All the while, the thin young man had his gaze focused on her. Whilst the old man was speaking the thin young man just stood there with his arms crossed over his chest beaming. When he was done speaking, he turned his attention from Rebecca to him,

"Headmaster today you are missing the classroom. What is a behemoth, and the other word, wimp?"

The old man turned to him with a smirk on his face. "Young people these days do not read," he said.

The apprentice barber paused his work and looked at the old man. "Headmaster, I agree with you, there is too much greediness around. Every citizen looks for their own welfare and cares little about their neighbor next door. . . ."

The stocky barber took off where the apprentice stopped: "The major actors controlling our economy only act as leeches who borrow in the name of the country and use it for their own needs," he concluded.

The thin man who was waiting for his haircut would not be left out; "If there are people who care about this country and the poor inhabitants, they are few and far between," he chirped in.

Rebecca looked from one man to the other, she found their conversation fascinating, but she didn't say anything. She simply returned to applying her makeup.

The old man turned to Kofi, "Young man, do you now believe there are glaring disparities between this country and America or the Western countries?" As he said this, he smacked his lips in satisfaction.

"I don't dispute any of the things you've said, but home sweet home. I don't think I can just abandon my country and go to live in another country forever," he said.

By now, the barbers had finished with the two clients, so they asked the old man and the young thin guy to come. The young man however ceded his turn to Kofi.

• • •

Kofi looked at the old cabinet sitting adjacent to his desk. He had been busy organizing business at his office, he had not been able to open it let alone check its contents. At last, he got up and strolled to it. When he opened it, he found a mirror attached to its door on the inside. He was transfixed to the mirror as he looked at his reflection. That haircut had surely transformed his looks. He ran his fingers over his eyelashes and then moved on to check the contents of the old cupboard. There were several files that seemed discarded as well as some old newspapers. He took one of the newspapers to see what was in it. One article particularly caught his eyes. It was from the inauguration day for the President. He was clad in a colorful traditional attire. It seemed so unique it was probably purposefully sown for the occasion.

The newspaper contained snippets of the President's inaugural speech. One particularly headline of the day screamed at him: THE PRESIDENT DECLARES ZERO TOLERANCE FOR CORRUPTION. He started to read, and it was full of lofty ideas about how he was going to protect the public purse. He had stated categorically that under his watch no minister was going to be above the law. That every one of his ministers, himself included, would be accountable to the people. He thought that was a powerful pronouncement. He found himself wrapped in a voiceless bewilderment, unable to find the words to properly express the feeling.

"How was it even possible for the President to make that claim? How could he watch his ministers loot the resources of the country with his tacit approval? How could that even be possible? How could he have so profoundly lost his way?"

He had so many unanswered questions. As he sat there, he was left musing and pondering over those pronouncements. "In this moment I must reckon, whether it was coincidence or fate, I have been thrown into the middle of this brewing storm," he told himself.

As he contemplated the situation, he was not sure how many people would stand with him in his fight against corruption. Nevertheless, he concluded that no matter what happened, he had embarked on a mission of no return. There could be no going back now. His mind went back to the mirror in the old cupboard. Perhaps it was put there for a day such as this. He looked into the mirror and started mouthing, mumbling out loud to his image.

"I must incentivize the people. I must get them to fight with me, to show a love for the country; to say no, to bribery, corruption, and graft of any kind. Even if I don't get them on my side; I must still fight on even if it leaves me standing alone."

There was a gentle knock on his door; it was Lisa. She came in to pick up a file he had readied for her. "The mirror says you are handsome, sir," Lisa said as she walked out of his office.

When she left, Kofi continued, "even if the ground upon which I stand cave in, I must hold fast to the tiniest straw I find, and fight on." His voice was getting louder and louder and crescendo through the room.

Lisa ran up to him, "Sir did you call me?"

"No Lisa, I did not call you." His mind was still on his predicament, and he continued speaking to himself, "I am the hope of this nation."

Lisa ran back to him, "Sir, were you calling me?"

"No Lisa I was not calling you."

She walked back slowly to her desk, "why was her boss talking to himself?"

Kofi was unmoved, he wanted to get everything off his chest, so he continued, "I am the called out one to fight the battles others abandoned, and to uphold the torch others extinguished. I will soldier on, and if I perish in the inferno that is obvious to light up, I do not care."

Now Lisa knew her boss was in dreamland, she sat down, a resigned shake of her head and a look on her face as she returned to her work. After that soliloquy he felt better. Now he was re-energized and reset to go back to work.

Nearby, at the office of the President an important meeting was going on. The chief of staff had sufficiently been convinced by Hamma at that golf game. Now armed with the findings he had revealed to him; he was making his case for the dismissal of Kofi. He thought the young man was a radical who must not be allowed near government. People like him have no worries so they would want to cut the source of support for others. He was not going to allow that to happen.

"What was it you wanted to talk to me about John?"

"About the young man Hope."

"Yeah Hope, he has done very well setting up that excellent system."

"Yes, I know what he has done, but he is bringing down the party."

"In what way?"

"He refuses to help the financiers for our party."

"What do you mean?"

"He has caused them to lose money because he will not help them clear their goods out of the port."

"How is that the young man's fault?"

"If they pay all the monies required at the ports, they cannot sell their goods at a profit."

"And what does that mean?"

"They cannot continue to contribute to the party."

"If others are paying those monies, why should they be exempted?"

"Well in the past we've given them those deals and they in turn contribute to the party. That's not all, we charge all investors an additional money which is donated to the party."

"But that's wrong. I'm glad there is somebody who has the balls to stop those corrupt practices."

"I beg your pardon, your excellency?"

"Please leave the young man alone."

"Mr. President, do you know how you got into office?"

"I don't care, the young man is doing an excellent job, and he stays."

"If he stays you know the party leadership will get to you. I can go to the press with your small escapade with that young staffer."

"Are you blackmailing me, Honorable Biney?"

"Let's see who will still be president in the morning."

The President knew how callous John Biney could be. He dared not step on his feet. He stood up, drew in a deep breath and exhaled slowly, then he put his fingers to his forehead and shook his head pacing back and forth. As for the chief, he stood there, pinched his lips together tightly, and waited for the President to make up his mind.

"Okay, you can fire him, but don't put any obstacles in his way to securing another job."

"It's settled, I will make sure he finds another job and soon."

On that note he left the president's office triumphant and contented. John Biney was an astute politician and very crafty. He never minded playing it dirty if it would get him what he wanted. Such had been his mantra since he got into politics, playing hardball with both foe and friend. He was the party's choice to become the chief of staff. The president had no hand in his choice. Unlike him, the President was a highly respected intellectual who was working with a pristine university in Scotland. He was both articulate and knowledgeable; a person whose friends could depend on him. It took a lot of convincing to get him to become the candidate of the FCP. He has brought a lot of honor to the presidency in *Abibiman* particularly among the diplomatic corps and with foreign governments.

Notwithstanding all the gravitas he carried both at home and abroad, within his party there were often shackles put on his activities by the power brokers, among them John Biney. After John Biney left, the President sat down and bemoaned his decision. This was one decision where he could have put his foot down, but his escapade with that young staffer had really manacled him. But how long could he continue to bow to the whims and caprice of a greedy politician? He should have settled that issue with his wife. As it is, he had allowed too much water to flow under the bridge so for now that secret should remain buried.

CHAPTER 38

FEELING THE PRESSURE

I t was a sun glinting day; a day when the sun cast sharp and dark
shadows, and made you squint when you stepped outside into its glare.
The bright day however meant little to Kofi. To him it might as well
be a dark gloomy day, because he had a lot of things on his mind. He was
deep in thought when he went to the cafeteria for his lunch break. At the
time Rebecca came in, he was sitting there; his eyebrows slightly raised, his
head pushed forward, with a faraway look in his eyes. She walked across the
room to where he was sitting and put her hands on his shoulder.

"Are you okay Kofi," concern shown in her voice, "you look a bit off-
color; are you feeling alright?"

"Yes, why?"

"You don't look happy."

"Me, not happy?"

"It's written all over you."

"Can I order you some food whilst we talked about this?"

"Oh yes, but I can't let you pay for my food."

She went to the counter, ordered her food and came to sit with him.
When she sat down, he answered her query in the most affectionate way.

"Well in answer to the questions you asked, it is nothing to do with you
Becky."

"Oh, there you go again," she was salivating the affection in his address,
"I like it when you call me Becky, but please tell me what's bothering you."

"Remember when I came to your office to get some information?"

"Yes, but I don't want to be reminded of that encounter. I was so mean to you."

"Well, I put up a brochure outlining steps that we can take to alleviate poverty for the people."

"Yes?"

"I returned home because I shared the vision of the President which he eloquently explicated when he came to my base in Denver, in the USA to campaign."

"What has that got to do with the brochure?"

"It's in line with that vision to help the country grow."

"Can you expand on that, please?"

"It explores ways we can tackle the entrenched corrupt practices in the system."

"I see."

"My attempts at tackling the problem have been met with ridicule, arrest and a campaign to destroy my good name." He stopped to look at her before he continued. "By presenting this to the president, my aim is to get others to fight this battle with me."

Rebecca knew he was so concerned about righting the wrongs of the big people but she was not sure if his work was going to have any impact on them. She also knew those people were nation wreckers who were bent on pillaging the resources of the country no matter what anybody did. She did not think he would be able to transform those apathetic people to change their ways and work for the progress of the country. Nevertheless, she needed to be wise in how she approached him on the subject knowing it was his desire to see those changes taking place.

"I believe the president has been fighting this war all along," she said.

"He might have been, but my brochure will rekindle his resolve should he feel like giving up."

"Oh yeah?"

"Not only that, it will make my voice heard louder by those working against the interest of the people and probably get them to change their minds."

She looked at him sullenly and was beginning to get worried not just for him but also for her future, because somehow their fates were intertwined.

"You're taking on one tough task, Kofi and I hope for the life of me that you succeed."

In some way, he agreed with her view, but he was convinced that somebody should stand up for the little people, and he was that person. However, he needed to be strong so that he could become the example to those who in the future would want to stand for the weak and vulnerable. Otherwise, any person with a great idea would be swallowed up by the corruption culture of the country because they have no one to look up to. As they sat there, each lost in their own thoughts, Ellen and some staffers also came to the cafeteria. They saw that the couple were engrossed in conversation, so they went to another table. Though they found their own table, they would occasionally look in the direction of the couple.

"Do you see how Ellen and her group keep looking at us?" He finally broke the silence.

"You don't need to worry about them Kofi. We're two adults, and we can do whatever we like."

When he returned to the office after lunch, he went back to work, but he couldn't help stopping occasionally to ponder the mess he found himself in. Soon the day was over, but he was slouched in his couch contemplating issues. He was only awakened to reality by a tug on his door.

It was Lisa. "It's time to go home now sir," she said.

By now the two had been working together closely, not as boss and secretary but as colleagues. Not only had Lisa been helping him in every way possible, she also personally cared about his welfare. She was always concerned when he spent too much time at work.

"I'll be going home soon so don't worry about me," he assured her.

She closed the door behind her and left. Soon after Rebecca popped her head in and urged him to go home. She reminded him she didn't want the situation that happened to him the other day. So, saying she went inside his office and started packing his stuff so he could go home. He got up and walked out with her.

"When do you think I should go and see your parents?" He asked her when they started to pull out of the parking lot.

"Three days ago, I thought I had lost you to Ellen. I was so jealous when I saw you with her all the time."

Kofi turned to look at her. She looked solemn and thoughtful, and he could see a unique display of maturity in her behavior. She was now her old thoughtful and considerate self.

"So, why were you keeping away from me?"

"I can't believe I misunderstood the situation with Maggie and nearly broke your heart. But please forgive me."

She seemed to have ignored his question, but he understood. If Maggie's behavior had not affected her the way it did, then probably she was not in love with him; because when you love somebody their misstep can surely affect you.

"I hope you have truly forgiven me as you said before."

"What is there to forgive Kofi, is this going to be the last time we will have misunderstandings?"

"I know, it was a tough situation."

"No, but that should not have happened if I was not consumed by an irrational jealousy."

"Eh! Talking about Maggie, I haven't seen her today."

"She called in sick."

They were so absorbed in conversation they didn't realize they had reached Rebecca's. He switched off the engine and led her to her apartment. When he returned to his car, he drove off singing happily to himself. He was wondering whether to drive to Maggie's place to see her since she was sick. He intended on telling her she was forgiven. He contemplated it for a while but decided against it. Any such move, he reasoned, should be done in the presence of Rebecca. What if she tries to seduce him again? It was not a risk he was willing to take, so he drove home.

Kisito was waiting at his gate when he got home.

"How are you, old pal?"

"Splendid as usual."

"What made me deserve your august presence?"

"Doesn't a man check on their buddy when they haven't seen them for a while?"

"Well, come on in."

As they do in this part of the world, when he was seated, Kofi gave him water. He gulped down the water, he was probably very thirsty.

"Do you want another cup?"

"Please, if you would."

He fetched him another cup of water. This time he drank it a little slower.

"Aaaahh," he exhaled in delight, his eyes blinking rapidly, "he who gives water gives life, water is life."

As he was drinking his second cup of water, Kofi's eyes enquiringly swept over him. He hadn't changed a bit in all the years he had known him; gentle and caring. He was like a brother to him. You would think in the age of the mobile phone, he would give you a heads up when he is visiting. That, however, was not the Kisito he knew. Presently he turned and addressed him.

"Well what mission brought you here tonight, old pal?"

"I've not seen you for a while, so I wanted to see how you were doing."

"Nice of you to think about me."

He invited him to go to the kitchen with him. Hurriedly he cooked dinner for two, glad that somebody was there to keep him company. At dinner he was quiet, contemplating the situation at work, but also anticipating the return of Rebecca into his life. The conversation around dinner centered around the element of bribery and corruption that permeated throughout *Abibiman* society. Kofi brought up the topic and lamented how it was depriving the people what was due them. Kisito listened sympathetically, as he lamented the deplorable state of affairs in the country. When he was done speaking, Kisito went into one of his philosophical diatribes.

"When others are singing, you cannot simply stand aloof. You either sing along or keep quiet and listen. . . ." He stopped and looked at Kofi, his eyes squinting, probably to get a closer look at him. Then he proceeded, "you can't talk while the singing is going on. You'll be taken for one of two things, a lunatic or a disruptor."

Kisito had those innocuous bland sayings. However, sometimes he might be speaking the plain truth cloaked in irony and satire but his way of expressing it sometimes obscured the obvious. It epitomized the mindset of most people in *Abibiman*. They never saw anything wrong with hush money and bribery. Most believed that if it opened doors for anyone looking to move up in society, then it was legitimate. The ends justified the means in other words. Therefore, he was not so much surprised by his good friend's stance. As he was contemplating the situation Kisito continued speaking.

"It's children who whimper in the face of a storm, adults know its destructive force, so they take shelter before it strikes."

It appeared as if Kisito was taking a sly dig at him, but he meant no harm. "Remember, you cannot stand in the way of a storm, it will not just sweep you away, it will wipe you out and your memory will be no more," he concluded solemnly.

They had a long chat then it was time for him to leave.

"See you later," Kisito said as he rose to leave, "you sure you're going to be okay by yourself?"

Kofi knew he was looking for an excuse to crash on his couch, but he couldn't take him away from his family, so he did not entertain any suggestions for him to stay.

"Sure, I will," he replied.

As soon as Kisito left, he jumped into bed; it had been a long day.

CHAPTER 39

WHAT GOES AROUND

K ofi woke up with a start. It was Monday morning. Another day and another week. He could not tell when he fell asleep the night before, but when he woke up, he felt sore and fatigued. He had struggled all night to sleep. He had been tossing and turning, his sleep shallow and fitful. He was feeling stressed and burnt out. Throughout the night he had been awakened in contemplation of his role in the unfolding saga. He had counted the ceiling tiles of his bedroom over and over. He had run several scenarios in his head and had done anything he thought possible to remedy the situation he found around him.

At the beginning of the previous week, he had two main issues he was grappling with. There was the issue of Rebecca. Now that was settled, he had his lover back. He was shortly going to perform the marital rites. He only needed to inform his parents, and Rebecca her parents. He did not foresee any problems from either family. He was not put off by the issue of dowry. He still had some of the money he saved when he was in America, so it would be money well spent. Therefore, the marriage issue was as well done and dusted.

The second issue related to the situation at work and all the pushback he was getting from some of the leaders. Some of them had been pressuring him to rewrite the programs he had set up. He had not heard anything directly from the President concerning that. It was the chief who told him some ministers disliked those programs because it left no wiggle room. He knew what they meant: his program had made it difficult for them to dip their long hands into government funds. He was not willing to compromise on removing any of the checks and balances he had put into the program.

Unfortunately, none of the solutions he was coming up with seemed to offer him any comfort. He had considered how to bring to the attention of the President the pressure the chief and others were putting on him because of their corrupt activities. He considered asking another person to accompany him to talk to the President, but who could he trust? Somehow, he knew he had a mission to inform the President to sit up and take notice if he wanted to help the people as he had always advocated. Nimbly, he got out of bed and walked to the window. He stood there with his hands akimbo, and his head lifted up as if he was looking into the heavens. He then pulled aside his window blinds to look outside.

There was a dreary and lifeless feeling about the day. The sky was heavy with dark clouds. It had collected a substantial amount of moisture. Surely rain should be in the forecast. There was a lot of frantic movement. Everyone out there seemed to be running to some place even this early in the morning. Probably everybody was preparing for an imminent rainfall, even a storm. He checked his phone for any news for the day and his refrigerator to see if he could find something to fix breakfast. Just then his phone rang; it was Rebecca. She sounded exuberant and excited at the other end, so though feeling down, he managed to garner the strength to reply in the same upbeat tone. He was thinking about her welfare and didn't want to get her depressed like he was.

"I was just calling to see how you're doing."

"I'm doing great. Do you need a ride to work?"

"No, I cannot keep you waiting because I know you always go to work early."

"But it's a Monday, remember, transportation will be difficult."

When she hung up, he checked his watch; it was only six o'clock. He took a quick shower but did not eat breakfast; what better excuse to have her fix something for the two of them. He arrived at Rebecca's to find she was ready and waiting for him. She had breakfast prepared for two and it was sitting on her dining table. They ate hurriedly and got on the road. Traffic was unusually heavy today; therefore, he left the main roads for some side streets. He had been back in *Abibiman* for two years and had been driving everyday so he thought he knew the roads very well. But alas, his road knowledge was not enough. When he left the main road, he followed some side streets which he really didn't know. He came to a location where the road divided into two. He randomly chose one of the roads, but it went into a dead end.

He returned to the junction where he took the wrong turn. This time he took the route he left behind. That road led them on and on and through a familiar neighborhood. There were several people standing on the side of the road looking for transportation to go to their various destinations. Traffic had come to a stop now, so he took the opportunity to look at his surroundings. Among the people standing on the roadside, there was a heavy-set woman, a man and a boy who were separated from the rest of the crowd. The woman and the man were standing whilst the boy was sitting on a stone nearby. The man was shifting his weight from one foot to the other and the woman was desperately pacing back and forth. As for the young boy he was sitting on the stone with his heard in his palms.

As they got closer, the woman stopped pacing and flagged them frantically. He looked at Rebecca for clues to his next action. She was nodding her head, so that was the sign they should consider those people, so he pulled over. The man got to them first then the woman followed dragging the boy along. As they got closer, he recognized them. The man was Yakubu, the little boy was Suleimana, and the woman was the same one who poured dirty water all over him. His impulse was to drive off, but Rebecca stopped him. When they got to the truck the woman spoke panting heavily.

"Papa! papa! Please, my son is very sick can you give us a ride to the hospital?"

Yakubu recognized him and he exclaimed. "*Naagode Allah*, Mr. Hope, is that you?"

"Do you know him?" The woman asked Yakubu.

"This is the man who gave Suleimana the football," he replied.

The woman opened her mouth widely and covered it with her right palm, recognition dawning on her. It was the same man she poured the stinking water on. By this time, he had parked and was going to help get Suleimana into the truck. The woman kneeled on the roadside before him, her hands open and lined up one on top of the other. Then she crawled on her knees and held on to his right foot pleading for mercy. He reached out and helped pull her up.

"Get up, you will hurt your knees," he said.

"Papa, don't worry about an old fool," the woman replied.

Yakubu also tried to explain to Kofi what prompted him to betray him to Nicholas Hamma, but Kofi raised his hands in protest.

"All is fine Yakubu, let us not open any old wounds," he remonstrated.

All this time Rebecca was watching what was going on but she did not say anything. To say she was surprised would be an understatement. She was astounded and nonplussed. When the surprised guests settled in the truck, Kofi drove them to a nearby hospital. After they dropped them and were driving away, he looked into his rearview mirror. The woman was still stunned; she watched them drive away with her mouth wide open.

"Where do you know them Kofi, and why was the woman asking for your forgiveness?"

"It's a long story Becky, one day I'll tell you everything."

Kofi glanced at his fuel gauge; that Good Samaritan act, coupled with the detour and traffic jam meant he was running low on gasoline. Usually, he filled his tank on the weekend this time he did not; so, there was a risk of running out of gas. By this time, he had already driven past several filling stations. Fortunately, at the next intersection there was a large filling station, so he pulled in there, parked by a pump, and waited for an attendant to fill his car up. Another familiar face approached his car. He was unrecognizable. He was almost done filling up his tank before he recognized him. It was Zero his friend. He exclaimed in amazement at the transformation. He was nicely dressed, and the weariness seemed to have left him. He looked happier than he had ever seen him.

"Is that you Zero, my friend?"

"Yes Sah, Massa Hope!"

"Look at you, you're all changed."

Zero obviously shared Kofi's joy for him. He stood there with his hands clasped behind his back and began telling his story.

"Na our last meeting, wey I see say I no be good so make I make change . . ."

He was talking about the armed robbery incident on the roadside when they stopped Kofi. That incident had opened his eyes to realize that people like Kofi cared for him. For that reason, he saw the need to act to salvaged something out of his messy life. That roadside episode had been an epiphany awakening to him, and a recognition that he needed to put his life together. He cleaned up and started looking for a job. The pay was not too much but now he didn't need to be afraid of anybody. All the while as Zero was speaking, he looked at him, his hands shoved into his front pockets, and his face beaming. At last, something good was coming out of his efforts. He took him to the passenger side of the Wrangler, where Rebecca was sitting.

"Come meet my woman Zero."

Zero clasped his hands behind his back and bowed slightly to Rebecca.

"Madam, na massa Hope saved my life, na him be good man."

Rebecca smiled at Zero, she was in total agreement with him. Kofi was indeed a good man, and he was her lucky catch. He drove on in silence from the filling station towards his office feeling rejuvenated. Earlier in the day when he left home, he had been in no mood to play music or listen to the news as he normally would. It was only after he picked up Rebecca that his mood started to improve. Now he was very happy; Rebecca was by his side; the mean woman had repented and Zero was a new man. The sight of Zero working was not only refreshing, but it was also a great moral victory for him.

The saying "what goes around comes around" had never seemed truer. Rebecca looked at him, all smiles. She realized he was very happy after seeing that man whoever he was. She didn't want to spoil the occasion. She would just act as a witness and allow him to savor his victory. She only had admiration and respect for this man beside her who had such a big heart. She took control of the radio in the truck. She didn't need to ask for permission; this was her man's truck. She set the radio at full blast to the station they usually listened to whenever they were together. It was playing that song that was stored in his heart:

Yɛ neɛ woho bɛtɔ wo
Yɛntie obiara asɛm

They sang along as the song played; they were prepared for the day. For the moment, he had no cares, his lover, Rebecca, was beside him and that was all that mattered.

CHAPTER 40

THE STORM BREAKS

The turn of events in the morning: the apology of the woman; and the sight of Zero all cleaned up and doing meaningful work; all filled Kofi with such joy. However, when they arrived at the office, and he parted with Rebecca, the dullness returned. He had still not figured out how to deal with all the problems confronting him at work. He was silent, but myriad thoughts were going through his mind. Probably a storm was about to hit, but he couldn't say definitively. He convinced himself that the storm would pass, he would speak to the president, and everything would be fixed. So, thinking, he hummed to himself as he walked the lobby to his office.

Though he was a little late due to that benevolent act, and the fact that he stopped to chat with Zero, several of the staff were still not in. The chief-of-staff's door was ajar, so he figured he was there. He also saw Ellen, leaving her office to go and get some coffee. He waved at her and walked on not intending to lose any more time this morning. Lisa was already there and working on some assignments he gave her the previous day. They exchanged greetings and he went into his office. Two hours later Lisa was done with her work, so she came in to show it to him. As they were talking the phone on her desk was ringing. It completed one cycle and resumed ringing again.

She turned around and said; "Sir, my phone is ringing."

Within a few minutes, she ran back and stood breathlessly before him. When she spoke, her voice was laced with concern.

"It was the chief, sir, and he wants you to stop whatever you are doing and come see him right away, sir."

"Is everything alright?"

"I don't know, but he insisted I ask you to see him immediately."

He got up heavily and headed to the office of the chief of staff. As he was entering the office, Nicholas Hamma was also leaving. He had a look of triumph and elation in his eyes. That made him a little nervous, knowing his nemesis may be happy on his account. Before he entered the chief's office, he looked over his shoulders, Nicholas Hamma was still there. He was smiling sheepishly and gestured by slashing his fingers across his throat. Kofi ignored him and brushed aside any feeling of impending doom from his mind. He crossed his fingers and boldly entered the chief's office, where he found him standing by a big cabinet in his office and shuffling through some papers.

"Sit down Hope and I will be with you in a minute." He instructed him in that deep intimidating voice of his, as he continued searching through his cabinet.

Kofi sat down and watched him, opening and closing different compartments inside his cabinet. Whatever he was looking for seemed important because he stayed there for a long time. Finally, for what seemed like eternity, he closed the cabinet and walked back to his seat and sat down, his eyes scanning his desk. Once he sat down, he took off his eyeglasses and cleaned them. Then he put them back on and continued to stare at his table. For an umpteenth time, he took off his eyeglasses and put them back on before finally taking them off and leaving them on the table. Now he was looking at Kofi, eyeball to eyeball as he began addressing him.

"I was going through the licenses issued to new companies. It happened that you have issued more licenses than Honorable Baiden."

"Yes?"

"We charge an additional fee of thirty, forty, or fifty thousand dollars to issue one license depending on the type of business. This money goes directly to support party business."

"Really?"

"Yes really, how do you think we get the money to finance all the campaigns?"

"But sir?"

"Shh," he raised his index finger to his lips, "don't even say anything."
Kofi just looked at him confused.

"You also caused the party to lose some big-time donors because you wouldn't help them clear their goods from the port."

He took a piece of paper from a file on his table and pushed it to him. "Take a look at this . . ."

It was a letter from John Acres saying he was not donating to the party for the year because he did not get any breaks. He remembered Acres, the fellow who had come to his office to offer him some money. However, he never came to him for favors. Probably he knew he wouldn't play ball. He felt proud in that instant that people knew he wouldn't condone any nefarious activities. So, despite the chief's accusations he knew whatever fate was in store for him, he would leave the outfit with his head held high. The chief then showed him another document. It was a list of donors for the last three years. It showed that there was a decline in donation for the last two years running.

"As you can see the party's account receivable has gone down two years running."

"I can see that."

"Do you know it's your fault?"

"In what way, sir?"

"You are a wise man Hope . . ."

The chief took out a white envelope from inside the side drawer of his desk and handed it to him. He didn't know what was in the envelope, but he wanted to keep his curiosity to himself. So, he started to walk away.

"Come on open the envelope."

"I will do it in my office."

"No, please open it now, I insist."

Slowly he opened it. It was a letter addressed to him from the chief. As he opened it to read, he stopped in surprise. It was a letter of his dismissal. He stood there confused and mortified. He looked on in disbelief and wondered why he would be dismissed. Who dismisses a worker without having first written him up? This would be sheer injustice if it was allowed to stand. Moreover, he did not think he was at fault for anything. Like any other person, he knew he was imperfect, however, in this case, he did not see where he fell short. Therefore, they did not have any recourse to fire him. Several thoughts raced through his mind; not that he couldn't find a job, no that was not the issue. He wanted to stay on because he was determined to finish what he started; to uproot the canker of corruption from this society. Hence, he was not going to go silently. There and then he made up his mind to appeal directly to the President. As if the chief read his thoughts, he said;

"The dismissal is final so you should not bother to go to the President."

"Does the President know about this?"

If Kofi's question was surprising, the answer he got from John Biney was even more shocking. The chief nodded his head before speaking;

"Nothing is hidden from the President," he affirmed.

Then slowly, it dawned on him that the President might have been in the corruption business with his cohorts all the time. He believed he had been naïve to have allowed his public pronouncements to fool him. Though he knew one day he was going to be dismissed if he kept on crusading like he had been doing, he had nonetheless not anticipated it coming at this time, but this surely was one of those moments when irony and coincidence brought a truth to a person out of nowhere; when he realized the world was not as he was living it. At that moment, it was as if the dimensional plane he stood on suddenly shifted, swinging, and moving under his feet, leaving him confused and unsettled. It was an overwhelming feeling because slowly he felt that the world around him had transformed. He was probably naïve to have accepted this position thinking he was in to help a president bent on rooting out corruption from the society. How could he have been so wrong?

He could sense a storm brewing, and though he was right in the middle of it, all he could do was to whimper, helplessly unable to prevent it. His thoughts were flowing rapidly now. Many more might come, he lamented, but the storm will rumble and boom until it overwhelmed them. Until their wills were tested and their resolve weakened. Until any remaining energy was drained and their power sapped. Until they were made to doubt their stance and felt worthless. He consoled himself that this country would rise from the ashes. It would not remain in the doldrums forever, one day a savior would arise who would put country first. His thoughts were that he should have seen the ominous signs.

However, how could he team up to pillage this country he loved with nefarious characters who cared less about the country and its welfare? How could he have changed from all the opinions he held; the countless articles he had written about how this country needed reform to get on a sound footing? How could he, how could he? It was much ado about nothing, it was simply a whimper in the storm, not an ordinary storm, but an unrelenting African storm. As he got up from the chair, he was sitting on, to leave the office the chief turned to address him.

"You're a good man Hope, I will help you find a new job; we will give you a good reference, it's just that this job is too big for you."

Kofi turned and looked at him, he did not need his help, he could find his own job when the time came. As he left the older man's office, only one thought occupied his mind. How could he break this unpleasant news to Rebecca? Was that going to be the end of their relationship? Slowly he packed his things from the office making sure he did not take anything that was not his. He called Lisa and wished her well. At this point they were both moved to tears. For the first and only time, the boss and secretary embraced; except now they were just friends. He took one more look through the window of what was his office a few minutes ago. The clouds had grown darker than they were in the morning.

When he passed by Hamma's office, he came out and gleefully asked what was happening. He just kept walking not offering him any answers; but as he passed, Hamma jumped up in elation stabbing in the air at the same time. He was happy that now things were pulling together for him. Others came out of their offices to stare as he left. He could feel the long gaze of Hamma and the others piercing through him as he kept walking. They all knew what was going on, but they pretended they knew nothing. In this office things going on were known to everybody. He was the only one who was always kept in the dark because they suspected that he was different. He continued walking. At first, he walked slowly, but as he turned the corner, he quickened his steps to avoid the staring eyes of Hamma and his jubilant colleagues. As he stepped out onto the balcony, he could see the clouds more clearly.

Suddenly the rains started to fall clattering the roof. The rainfall was sudden, as sudden as his dismissal. Both were ferocious, and destructive in their intent. The rains were not as destructive as the lightning storm preceding it. It rumbled and thundered, lighting flashing through the afternoon sky. Abruptly all seemed chaotic, just as his life and ambition had been thrown into confusion. On the balcony, out of sight from the prying eyes, he hesitated to wonder whether to go to Rebecca and tell her about the events of the morning, but he decided he didn't want to drag her down with him. Well, he didn't need to worry because from the opposite end of the balcony he saw Rebecca running in his direction. She was shouting his name. He couldn't bear to wait there and talk to her so he kept walking.

Rebecca kept calling his name. He shouted back just when he stepped outside into the pouring rain. He felt her footsteps behind him. He did not turn around as he shouted to her not to get herself wet, but she could not hear him over the clattering noise of the rain. The African storm had hit hard now, all his shouting had been in vain, and even now, as he shouted to Rebecca, it all sounded like a whimper in the pelting rainstorm. Rebecca reached out and cycled him in a hug, firmly holding on and refusing to let him go. The couple just stood there in the African storm embracing as one. Maybe his voice was no longer a whimper, after all, Rebecca knew the consequences of listening to a faint voice, but she was listening, and she was there with him in his moment of need in the storm.

ABOUT THE AUTHOR

Pastor and teacher **Akwasi Oppong Ofori** is an ordained minister of the Ghana Baptist Convention. Formerly the Lead Pastor at Solid Rock Baptist Church in Aurora, Colorado, he also served as the first chairperson of the North American Baptist Association of the Ghana Baptist Convention. He is the author of several non-fiction books, *Recovering Storytelling for Ghanaian Preaching, I Will Lift Up My Cup, Wonderfully Made, The Secrets of Superstars* and *Embrace the Challenge.* Originally trained as a teacher at the Wesley College of Education in Kumasi Ghana, he has a Diploma in Biblical Studies and a Bachelor of Theology (BTh) degrees from the Christian Service University College in Kumasi Ghana and the International Baptist Theological Seminary in Prague the Czech Republic respectively. Rev. Ofori also holds a Master of Divinity (M. Div.) from Denver Seminary in Colorado, USA, and a Master of theology (Th.M.) from the Toronto School of Theology of the University of Toronto Canada. Rev. Ofori is completed by his wife and two surviving children.

www.ingramcontent.com/pod-product-compliance
Lightning Source LLC
Chambersburg PA
CBHW020413110726
47899CB00006B/1973